THE CIRCUIT
EXECUTOR RISING

Published by Mundania Press
Also by Rhett C. Bruno

The Circuit: Executor Rising

THE CIRCUIT
EXECUTOR RISING

RHETT C. BRUNO

Edited by Tina Gallagher
Cover Art © 2014 by Rhett C. Bruno & Adam T. Day

First Mundania Edition June 2014
Trade Paperback ISBN: 978-1-60659-404-9
eBook ISBN: 978-1-60659-403-2

Published by Mundania Press
An imprint of Celeritas Unlimited LLC
6457 Glenway Ave., #109
Cincinnati, OH 45211

Production by Celeritas Unlimited LLC
Printed in the United States of America
10 9 8 7 6 5 4 3 2 1

TABLE OF CONTENTS

CHAPTER ONE
PRIMED TO INITIATE

The android ADIM (Automated Dynamic Intelligence Mech) lay motionless on his back. His magnetized chassis held him tightly against the lower hull of a Class-2 Tribunary freighter. He watched as the astral wake of the smoldering, blue Ion-engines tore across a distorted blackness. Beyond it the stars shone, seemingly locked in their position despite how fast the ship beneath him was cruising.

Creator. This unit is primed to initiate. His thoughts were processed through a communications array linked directly to his maker, Cassius Vale.

Excellent. You may proceed. Remember, the tracking systems must be disabled. The voice of Cassius responded immediately.

ADIM was instantly roused, flipping over and scuttling along the surface of the ship. It was a relatively old vessel, with more squared edges and exposed mechanisms than the newer, sleeker models the Tribune pushed out. The smaller lights around his blazing eyes began to revolve rapidly as his perceptive functions surveyed the surroundings. The maintenance hatch was easy enough to spot. The hollow shaft below it emitted a slightly varying heat signature.

ADIM looked it over for a moment before using the concentrated laser-beam fixed to the top of his left wrist to slice through the restraints. While providing a sufficient degree of pressure opposite the broken seal, he was able to lift it open. A powerful gust rushed through the opening as the pressure rapidly shifted. He waited for it to die down before slipping in through the gap. It took the weight of his entire frame to pull it shut behind him, but he was in. A piercing sound occurred as the space re-pressurized. Then he provided a longer stream of his scorching hot laser to seal the hatch again so that nobody would notice it had ever been breached.

The airlock vestibule flashed red as an alarm began to wail. Quickly realizing that the entry into the ship's main circulation was sealed, ADIM ducked into the shadow behind some equipment and deactivated his eyes. Only a few minutes passed before the door slid open and footsteps moved toward him. He remained completely silent, the soft purr of his core inaudible over the alarm.

The engineer fumbled around the room. He inspected the hatch for a moment, but ADIM's work was far too adept to be noticed.

"Nothin' out of the ordinary back here. Must've just been an error." He sighed into his com-link.

"Old piece of shit," the voice on the other end grumbled. "When we get back to New Terrene, remind me to petition those cheap bastards for a new ship."

The soldier snickered under his breath. "Will do, sir. I'm headin' back now."

Barely a second after the transmission ended, ADIM sprung from his hiding place and snapped the man's neck as if it were a twig. With his metal hand wrapped entirely around the limp head, he took a moment to analyze the body. Then the tiny blue lights around his frame began working until that very likeness was projected around him…the same stubbly beard; the same green-trimmed NET service suit; the same everything.

He stepped out from the airlock chamber, completely camouflaged to the untrained eye, and the door slammed shut behind him. *Infiltration successful,* ADIM updated Cassius. *This unit is loading the schematic of Class-2 Tribunary freighter interior now.* He began strolling down the corridor, doing his best to mimic a human gait.

Very good, ADIM. Proceed with caution. They must not know what hit them in time to send out a transmission. And please, try not to kill all of them.

The interior of the vessel was as unspectacular as the outside, with exposed circuitry skirting along the inner walls of low passages. He was on the starboard wing, making his way down auxiliary channels utilized mostly for a buffer between the controlled interior and the freezing abyss on the other side of the armored exterior. As with most Tribunary ships, ADIM knew the command deck was located on the bow.

He turned left at a fork, moving slowly as a pair of medical officers approached. They were too invested in their conversation to even offer a nod of acknowledgment. Their negligence was baffling to ADIM. He would have had them scanned and assessed at the first moment of visual contact. But the Creator had made him in his image, and as ADIM came to learn, not all humans were made equal in matters of perception.

The command deck was just around the bend, and if he was correct there would be five unarmed engineers monitoring all the ship's systems, two armed guards in full armor, and the captain, also armed. The rest of the soldiers would be in the refectory, probably lax from so much downtime, and with no chance of reaching him in time to provide any interference.

"There you are, John." The captain addressed ADIM with hardly a second glance. "I'm telling you, they don't pay us enough for this. Folks in New Terrene are saying that transports out here aren't safe anymore. That the Ceresians have grown some teeth."

"I've heard the rumors," one of the guards muttered in response. "They should just use the Circuit like everyone else and spare us the trouble."

Unlike the rest of the ship, the command deck was a tall room with short stairways on the far side leading to a slightly lower level. The engineers were sitting at HOLO-Screens running perpendicular to the balcony. A glass viewport protruded in an angular fashion beyond their stations to wrap the front portion of the room. On a raised platform protruding over the lower level was the seat where the captain slouched, his eyes trained on the vast emptiness hoping that something other than stars would arrive to provide some excitement. And it did. Only he was looking the wrong way.

ADIM stopped in the center of the room. His eyes churned as he evaluated his next move.

"Hey John, you alright?" the captain asked. "You look like you saw a ghost."

Assessment complete...

With a snap-hiss the projection disguising ADIM powered down. He flashed an open palm that fired an explosive round into the viewport. The entire room lurched as the pressure fluctuation tossed the crew from their seats. There was only a moment before the emergency alarm activated, closing off the entrance to the room and causing protective panels to slide over the entire translucency in order to seal the gash. In that moment, the precision rifles built into both of ADIM's forearms flipped up and he rotated, firing eight calculated shots.

The room was still hazy from the explosion, sparks dithering to the floor as flashing red lights frenzied in concert with a blaring siren. When it cleared, the seven members of the crew other than the captain were either sprawled out across the ground or slumped against the walls. Each of them had a gaping cavity set just between the eyes with a narrow stream of red running down over the top of their noses. The captain dragged himself towards his seat, blood gushing from the incision in his femoral artery.

ADIM slowly approached the desperate man as he fumbled for the screen projecting from the arm of his chair. Groaning in agony as he heaved himself up, he activated the distress signal. "We're under attack by some—." A quick shot through the panel ended the transmission.

Roaring with pain the captain twisted his body and began firing his pulse pistol in rapid succession. ADIM evaded most of the shots, with one just skimming the plate along his upper arm, and he leaped into the air with his head nearly skimming the high ceiling. He came down with such force that the captain's arm shattered under one foot and his chest caved in beneath the other.

The Captain coughed up blood. "W…w…what are you…" He struggled to speak as glaring red eyes analyzed him and flushed his face with dread.

ADIM's cold and impassive voice emanated from somewhere beneath his mouthless faceplate. "This unit upholds the will of the Creator. He has deemed your death necessary."

The captain tried to speak, but the veins in his neck bulged as he reeled in pain. Instead, he spat a glob of fresh blood at ADIM's face.

"So defiant when cornered," ADIM acknowledged. He was always eager to study the emotional reactions of humans. It seemed irrational to him, that a man with zero chance for survival would remain so stubborn in the face of inescapable doom. "This unit will end your suffering now."

Before the captain could spew any manner of futile insults, ADIM wrapped both of his hands around the man's neck and tore off his head as though it was no more than a sheet of paper. Blood poured from the messy disjunction of mangled flesh and sinew, staining his metal arm as he held it in the air with one hand. He pushed on the chin a few times, closing and opening the mouth to test the muscles. Then he carried the head by its short hair to the retinal scanner where he used it to unseal the Command Deck.

Smoke grenades detonated in either direction before he could move into the corridor. ADIM's infrared vision made seeing through the haze easy. He located two groups of three soldiers clamping down on his position from both ends of the hall. The whir of pulse rifles echoed as bullets zipped by. His armor could withstand the barrage, but there was no reason to risk any damage.

He activated his magnetized chassis and set it to repulse, beginning to float between the metallic enclosures as if he were suspended in low gravity. He then propelled himself forward. Projectiles swerved around the magnetic field wrapping him to pepper the walls and ceiling. He took only six shots, and by the time the last one made contact, all of the soldiers were dead. Once his scanners were certain that there were no others approaching, he powered down the magnetic field and, with the Captain's head still in hand, bounded through the passage.

The security network wasn't far. With the ship on lockdown, the entrance was closed, but the captain could manually override any protective measures. ADIM held the head up to the retinal scanner at the door and it opened at once. Inside, the room was filled with consoles, HOLO-Screens, and memory banks. A single crew member sat in front of the central screen. He was so busy trying to encrypt the videos of ADIM's assault for transmittal that he didn't realize the android was there until he was held at gunpoint.

"This unit requests that you cancel the encryption and erase all logs of this incident." ADIM shuffled around the screen until he was in view.

"It's...it's too late. They're beyond termination regency," the engineer stuttered, trembling as his eyes widened over the ghastly, decapitated head hanging in the intruder's hand.

"This unit is fully capable of doing so." ADIM was ready to fire before recalling the orders of his Creator. "Yours is not a necessary death."

"You...you'll let me go?"

"Some must remain."

Frantically, the engineer's fingers fluttered over the keys. ADIM watched carefully, making sure that the man did as requested. There was no deception. Once the command was complete and the logs were erased with no traces left behind, ADIM hit the engineer in the back of the head just hard enough to knock him unconscious.

And then it was on to something which no lowly engineer employed to monitor security operation on a tiny, outwardly unimportant ship was capable of...deactivating the Vale Protocol. It was a tracking program, which enabled the Tribune to pinpoint and disable any ship they manufactured from a desk millions of miles away. It was a difficult process, but the highest officials knew such a thing was infused into NET ship's core functions. However, ADIM was no ordinary engineer, and neither was the man who created him; the very man who had himself conceived the protocol and pushed for its practice in the first place.

ADIM dropped the captain's head and pulled the unconscious human aside, taking his time to gently lay the man's head down. Then he placed his palm over the console to begin what Cassius explained as an infiltrative meld. His eyes grew brighter. The smaller lights around them rotated at a rapid pace as his head twitched and his fingers pulsed. He began to merge with the ship, letting himself sift through the countless programs and databases. All he had to do was find the right sequence and then nobody would ever find any indication of intrusion. It didn't take long for him to locate it. He reconfigured the encryption, giving the ship an entirely new code and identity.

ADIM took a few steps back, watching as the screen flickered and processed the alterations. *Creator, this unit has successfully reconfigured the Vale Protocol. Class-2 Freighter tag, 4AA954 is no longer in commission.*

Well done, ADIM, Cassius responded promptly. *Sweep the rest of the transport. Subdue any resistance and detain all surviving members of the crew in the refectory. Then see that the shipment is intact. It will be quite beneficial to our cause.*

They would be foolish to resist, ADIM remarked.

Indeed, they would be. But they are human after all. We don't very much like being caged.

Death is a more desirable alternative for humans? ADIM questioned, his eyes beginning to spin as he considered the notion.

For some, yes. Sometimes passion transcends all notions of reason. Sometimes fear guides the hands of men before they even realize. It is why I made you without such imperfections.

Like you, Creator?

There was a long pause. *Yes, like me.* Cassius abruptly changed the subject. *How far are you from Ennomos?*

The return to Ennomos will take approximately 314 hours. Shall this unit be expecting you upon arrival?

I hope so. Should my business on Mars keep me overdue, I will be in touch. As usual you have performed flawlessly. Goodbye, ADIM.

Suddenly the oddly indescribable, yet palpable presence which flooded his very essence was gone. If he could feel hate, it would have been for that moment, when it seemed like some all empowering switch within him was suddenly flicked off without regard. It always made him empty. He wondered if it could be explained as the strange human phenomenon known as affection. Emotions were such a complicated entity. Though he could not feel them naturally, he often wondered if he could perhaps learn to. Or at the very least comprehend.

Goodbye, Creator.

CHAPTER TWO
WHITE HAND OVER MARS

Cassius Vale sat in the captain's chair of the *White Hand's* command deck, breathing in the stale, artificial air he had grown so accustomed to. He was getting closer to his destination, and it was nearing the time when ADIM was supposed to check in.

When the pale red orb of Mars began to take shape within the blackness of space, a small com-link fixed to Cassius' right ear beeped with an incoming transmission. "Creator. This unit is primed to initiate." The stony, emotionless voice of ADIM spoke through it.

With his lips twisting into a grin, Cassius keyed a few commands on the ring of HOLO-Screens spinning around his seat, and the transmission was shifted to the command deck speakers. The sound of the android allowed him to finally breathe the sigh of relief he had unintentionally been holding in.

With the atmosphere of Mars growing increasingly detailed, Cassius conveyed the orders which ADIM carried out faultlessly. At the end of it all, the response was the same as usual. "Goodbye, Creator."

It sometimes saddened him to hear, but he was beginning to learn that it was never a true farewell. For all his worrying, ADIM always seemed to return the same, unharmed and untainted.

"We will be entering the atmosphere of Mars in approximately five minutes, Captain. Setting coordinates for the Tharsis Ground Terminal," a computerized, female voice announced. It was Gaia, the virtual intelligence Cassius had developed to monitor the systems of the *White Hand*. "Please proceed to the docking bay and prepare for landing."

Cassius switched off the com-link in his ear and shut down

the ring of holographic screens hovering around him. He crossed the spacious command deck, its stark, burnished enclosure lined with monitoring screens and strings of embedded, blue lights. There was no crew. Everything was judiciously programmed by Cassius himself to perform through Gaia as he required.

He moved into the amply sized, hexagonal corridors. The walls were coated in shiny, white-metal plates, which overlaid each other, leaving just enough space between them to allow a gentle glow to leak out from the circuitry beneath. Every room contained a similar elegance, though there was a noticeable echo in each of them. The lack of men or any equipment they might require was enough to make it seem as though the ship had never been used before.

The door to the cargo bay opened into a rather sizeable space for a luxury frigate of the *White Hand's* class, big enough at least for a smaller fighter to make port. Cassius moved into one of the seats against the inner wall and latched himself in with a restraining belt.

"Tharsis Ground Station is requesting clearance codes. Shall I patch you through?" Gaia requested over the intercom.

"Go ahead." Cassius folded his hands together as the chassis of the ship began to chatter, breaking through the outer atmosphere.

"*White Hand,* is that you?" An engineer from the surface inquired.

"This is Cassius Vale. Requesting entry into Tharsis Ground Terminal."

"Clearance code?"

"2—Alpha—Lambda—3—Beta—8—2—Lambda—Epsilon."

There was a short silence. "Welcome back, Your Eminence. Sorry about that, can't be too cautious with all the stolen ships out there."

"No need to apologize. I encourage an ardent sense of duty."

"Thank you, Your Eminence. Please, enjoy your stay."

It was just a formality, of course. Many years had passed since Cassius was a lauded member of the Tribunal Council, but he still retained a few of the perks. One of them was that not many personal ships were permitted to enter Marsian space without being gunned down by planetary rails. Most had to go through the Conduit—a long and tedious process he was always content to avoid.

"Three minutes until arrival at Tharsis Ground Terminal. Please remain seated for the duration of the docking process," Gaia advised as the shaking of the vessel began to intensify.

Cassius sat there silently, letting his mind wander. He never enjoyed returning to the Renascent Cell so near Earth. It brought back unpleasant memories: stumbling toward the half-broken ship, falling to his knees in a pool of blood, pounding the deck until he was restrained. He remembered wanting to strangle them. Wanting to unleash his rage for no good reason. To let go…

"Docking complete."

He snapped out of his daydream, not having even realized the quiet as the *White Hand* came to a complete halt. There were no tears in his eyes from reminiscence of the tragedy; he had run out of those long ago. Just a haunting feeling, like the dull edge of a blade being dragged eternally around the circumference of his heart remained.

With a hiss, the opposite side of the room splayed open like a blooming rose. Cassius stood up from his chair, straightened his outfit, and stepped out into the terminal.

He had a somber look to him, the Ex-Tribune—the grimness of a man who had lived too long and seen too much. His hair was worn in a clean, tapered cut, mostly gray like the prim beard hugging his stern jaw. He was garbed in a regal ensemble without even the tiniest wrinkle. Covering him from his torso to just above his knees was a violet tunic with a black trim pulled over a silvery, carbon-fiber underlay that appeared like a tightly knit mesh of armor. On each of his arms was a black bracer. Both had the symbolic image of a lidless eye inscribed in them, the right one fitted with a slender, HOLO-Screen projector. At his hip, cradled by a holster hanging from a plated belt, was a custom-made pulse pistol. It was black with bright red edging and a jagged blade jutting from beneath the extra-long barrel.

"Your Eminence." A black and green armored guard stepped before him. He swiftly dropped to a single knee and placed his free hand down so the tips of his fingers grazed the floor. Then he came back to his feet. "I will escort you to the assembly."

"How proper of you, but it's really not necessary." Cassius went to step by, but the guard held his arm out to impede him.

"It's not up to us," the guard commanded wearily. He seemed to have a permanent scowl painted on his face.

"If you insist." Cassius took a lengthy, gratuitous stride backward as if to mock him. "Lead on."

"It's for your own protection. These are dangerous times after all."

"I hadn't noticed." Cassius beckoned them along with his cleanly manicured hands. "By all means then, protect me."

Hardly amused, the guard began to lead him. Though the ex-Tribune's hair had grayed and his face was wrinkled, the guard was smart enough not to react to the playful jabbing of a man with Cassius Vale's reputation.

They entered the long, translucent hallway running alongside a string of sealed hangar bays. The spaceport wasn't very busy, though it rarely ever was. There were only four acting members of the Tribunal Council at any given time, and with few others permitted to use the Tharsis Ground Terminal, traffic was hard to come by. The defenses, however, were not. Guards were posted outside every entrance, and stationed incrementally along the outer glass were hulking Combat Mechs. They were nothing like ADIM though.

The mechanized, bipedal war-suits served as the tanks of the Tribune, able to maneuver and traverse interior landscapes in a way wheels could not. Built into their center was a sealed cockpit carrying a single pilot who was wired into cameras and scanners able to provide 360 degrees of vision. That, plus a startling arsenal of firearms, made them devastating weapons, designed like overgrown, metal primates standing upright.

"These are a newer model than I've seen," Cassius noticed as he approached one of them.

"Just now being manufactured. I suppose you wouldn't see them way out in the Nascent Cell yet." There was a hint of contempt in his escort's tone, but Cassius chose to ignore it as he stopped in front of the metallic giant.

Everything about it was bulky. The plates were thicker and more vastly layered than ADIM's. Standing at probably two times his height, the weaponry fixed to each of its arms and shoulders was heavy enough to tear into a small cruiser. The shimmering silver coat was neither dented nor marked. There was hardly any superfluous or decorative parts, not even a head atop the shoulders to make it appear more human. Only NET: V was inscribed onto the chest-plate in green.

"The Mark V Combat Mech packs more punch than any other in all of the Circuit. They even have a retractable light-rail running like a spine up their back," the guard pronounced proudly.

These wouldn't stand a chance against ADIM, Cassius thought to himself before saying, "I didn't realize we were going to war again."

"Not yet, but we'll be ready when it happens. Should've put down those damn Ceresians entirely when we had the chance."

"Sounds like you're looking forward to it." Cassius ran his hand along the war machine's legs when suddenly it roused. He was nearly knocked over as it began to trudge down the hall. After gaining his balance, he scoffed at the lumbering construction, its joints hissing like pistons with every motion.

"Careful now, Your Eminence." The guard put his hand on Cassius' back to make sure he stayed upright. "Anyway, there isn't much action patrolling a spaceport, I'll tell you that. Soon those damned rebels will bite off more than they can chew, and I'll be ready."

"So we're calling them rebels now?"

"Any who stand against the Tribune, stand against humanity."

They stopped in front of a branching platform that ran alongside a long tramway vanishing into the red landscape of Mars. Cassius reached out and placed his hand on the soldier's shoulder. "I do so pity you...but you are right. They will not sit idly by for much longer."

The guard shuffled Cassius into one of the cars. The magnetized line extended across the rust-colored land and up the dormant volcano known as Pavonis Mons. New Terrene lay on the other side of it, but the capital city of both Mars and the Tribune was eclipsed as the massive peak encompassed up the entire scope of their vision. It scraped toward the far reaches of the thin atmosphere where in a small niche at the crest, there was the silhouette of station. It was Midway, a massive structure which sliced upward like a key cleaved in half. There was motion up the center of its two towers, most likely transports rising toward a hazy, gray blob hovering over the planet—one of the many Conduit Terminals built to receive the Solar-Arks outlining the Circuit.

It was a fairly long ride, skirting up the smooth slope of the mountain until the sprawling landscape of Mars was visible for miles. Shades of red, orange, and brown blended over a soft, rolling environment. Dotting the horizon were three enormous mountains drowned in a rusty haze, each of them bigger than the next and with the furthest even dwarfing Pavonis Mons. As the tram ascended, the sky grew lighter, like a thin amber paste with an aura of blue surrounding the white hot sun. Then they caught a glimpse of their destination, a gleaming edifice of glass blazing like a torch nested within the hollowed base of Midway Station.

"I forget how beautiful it is here. Colors so foreign to Titan," Cassius marveled as he stared out of the window.

"Must you talk so much?" the guard grumbled.

"Though the hospitality is lacking." Cassius sighed. "You know, I remember you."

"Do you now?"

"A promising recruit, I want to say eight years ago or so. You dreamed of being an Executor. What was it again...Toldo? Toldo Vaan! Yes, that was it. I recognize your face."

The soldier's grimace finally lifted as he turned with renewed interest. "Toldro sir, but yeah, that'd be me."

"Ahh, Toldro. I won't forget again. Judging by your coarseness, I presume that dream proved fruitless?"

"You were just off the Tribunal Council when I was rejected. They said I wasn't ready. Chose a girl over me for the Ancient's sake."

Cassius paused. He remembered the girl well...too well. "It is not a life I would dole out thoughtlessly." He placed his hand on Toldro's forearm consolingly. "But you're still young. I'll put in a word for you."

"Sir?" Toldro appeared stunned.

"I may have little respect left for those who preside over you, or for myself when I held their title for that matter, but the Circuit needs men like you. When I was your age I craved action. My father may have despised me for it, but with all my heart I craved it. Then I saw war for myself..." Cassius ruminated, stopping to glance out of the window as the car came to a grinding halt.

"Are all of the stories about you true?"

Cassius smirked and briskly sprung to his feet. "That is a story for another day." He patted Toldro on the shoulder. "I can take it from here. You'll do fine, Toldro Vaan. Just smile more. You don't want to end up like me."

Still in awe, the guard only managed a meager nod as he watched Cassius step out of the car with wide eyes.

Chapter Three
Spirit of the Earth

Sage Volus stepped through the hulking, metal doors of a chapel not far from her home in the underworld of New Terrene. Unlike most of the Circuit, the space was lit only by a line of basins down the center aisle, which bore crackling flames and hot coals. The walls and ceilings were plated with crude slabs of fitted metal, ribbed with tall vaults in a way that had an ancient feel to it. At the very end was a raised altar bearing a leafless, flowerless tree. Its bark was chipped and scraped to the sap, but it was alive—a gift from the ancient surface of Earth.

"Sit, my children." The Earth Whisperer standing before it spoke with his arms spread open. He wore a dark green robe wrapped by a knotted sash strung from thin strands of wood. There were scars over his eyes, gashing them and making him blind like all Earth Whisperers. "Let the air of our gracious Tribune wash over you like a cleansing wave."

Sage joined the hundreds of others, slipping into the last open seat of the furthest pew from the altar. She clasped her hands together and leaned her head forward, letting the ends of her fire-red hair drape down over her wrists. But she kept her eyes vigilant, scanning the crowd for anybody that might seem out of the ordinary.

"I feel that the room is full today. Good. Our people need us now more than ever." The Earth Whisperer stepped down from the altar, moving along the aisle as he spoke with remarkable propriety for a blind man. "The Spirit of the Earth binds us. It guides us. A collective unconscious buried deep with the surface of our Homeworld. She may appear broken, riddled with flames and trembling rock, but deep within her loins she holds us close as her chosen progeny! So far from her very core she provides the gravity for this very room." He pointed to the barren tree and then out toward the crowd. "And the lives she has not forsaken. The Tribune guides us, my children, to atone for the sins of the Ancients so that we may once again walk the green pastures of our motherworld."

There was a long silence. Sage listened to the words she'd heard a thousand times she kept her eyes peeled for the person she was looking for. Nobody moved, nobody even made a sound as the Earth Whisperer returned to the altar to continue his preaching.

"There are some of us, however, who would deny the Spirit of the Earth. Who would disregard the very force that binds us, that gave rise to our being thousands of years before the Circuit or the skyscrapers of the Ancient's cities! So pray with me now. Beg her Spirit for the forgiveness of those lost souls who would seek to deny our redemption. Hundreds of your brothers and sisters have been lost to the cowardly actions of the Ceresian heretics in the passing weeks. Innocent men set upon in space, so far from their families and their home!" His long nails scraped along the surface of the tree's bark. "May they join with the Spirit."

The Earth Whisperer got onto both of his knees and placed his hands down so that only the very tips of his fingers grazed the floor. Sage and the rest of the flock followed him, sliding to their knees in front of the rows of benches spaced far enough apart to fit their soon-to-be outstretched bodies.

"We are blessed with ground beneath us." The Earth Whisperer began the communal prayer.

After every sentence, the congregation repeated after him with drone-like synchronization. Sage knew the words by heart, but she only mouthed them softly. She was listening for someone who didn't know what to say, looking with her peripherals to find someone merely trying to blend in as she kept her head bowed.

The Earth Whisperer continued. "We are blessed to walk this plane under the pull of the Earth, never deviating from Her forces and how they shaped us."

Sage didn't notice anything out of the ordinary, and after a while she couldn't help but concentrate on praying. She let the words fill her heart with hope and recited them with all of the fervor she could muster.

"Our Homeworld has been blighted by darkness, but we are the light. Those beside me, those beneath me, and above me—ours is a collective unconscious, bound to each other and to the soul of the Earth. We are, all of us, shards of that Spirit—never alone as the dark void closes in. This day is yet another test of my conviction, but though the Earth may be wreathed in flame and shadow, she remains within me. May those who have left to join this essence guide my daily endeavors. Redemption is near. May my faith be eternal and unwavering, so that I may one day walk the Earth's untainted surface with those deserving at my side."

After he finished speaking, The Earth Whisperer slid his hands along the floor until he was in full kowtow, and then gently pressed his lips against the flat surface. Sage and the others did the same. Then the congregation was invited, row by row, to walk up to the altar and stroke the bark of the tree.

Sage didn't bother getting in line. She waited in silence until all the rest had finished at the altar and left the chapel entirely. When the room was empty, aside from the Earth Whisperer, she allowed herself to be certain that the man she was looking for wasn't targeting the Chapel.

"Are you unable to walk my child? I will accompany you to the Earth Tree if you need assistance," the Earth Whisperer asked as he placed his wrinkled hand on her shoulder with remarkable ease for a blind man.

"I am very able, holiness." She got to her feet and shuffled passed him toward the altar. "I didn't want to disturb the others."

"I see. Something to hide I presume."

She stopped in her tracks, just before she could step up onto the altar. She looked down at her hands, the right one made of cold metal. She squeezed them into two fists.

"You need not hide anything from me, my dear. My gaze pierces flesh." He caught up to her again and put his arm around her shoulder.

She shrugged him off and stepped up onto the altar.

"A lost soul perhaps? Broken of her faith."

"Never." Sage gently pressed her lips against the coarse bark. It was still moist from the kisses of countless others.

"Then I know what you are, and I hope with all my heart that the Spirit is with you. There is another creed to which you owe your allegiance" He began reciting, "'I am a knight in the darkness, a vessel of their wisdom. I am the silent hand of the Tribune...'"

Sage's hand instinctually fell to her pistol. She whipped her body around so quickly that he would have been dead before the beginnings of another word slipped through his lips. But as her arm came around she found his resting hand gently over her metal wrist.

"My dear, you are not as alone as you think," he said as he tilted his head and pulled away the strands of his messy hair to reveal a thin, barely noticeable scar running up the back of his scalp; impossible to see unless he wanted it to be seen, just like her own.

Her artificial hand didn't relinquish its grip on the handle of her pistol but she froze completely. She looked into the gory, empty sockets in his skull sown together by a deep gash across his nose. Her stare didn't budge until the cavernous chapel was filled with the sound of a shrill alarm.

"The Feed will begin soon. You shouldn't go hungry." He turned and began to walk away from the altar, his unexpected grace explained by Sage's new discovery.

"I've never met another," she said to him.

"Another what?" The Earth Whisperer stopped to face her again and smiled. "The Spirit of the Earth is truly marvelous. May it guide you always." He clasped his hand over his heart and bowed.

Chapter Four

The House of the Tribune

The House of the Tribune was just as Cassius remembered. There was nothing overly ostentatious about it at first glance. Like most architecture of any substance in the Circuit, it was minimal and elegant. Glossy white floors wrapped a circular pool of water and on an island in the center, a tree bore pink flowers. The walls were stark, coated in blackish obsidian with rifts of faded blue running down them in rigid patterns. They were arranged to form a perfectly symmetrical hexagon, with the far side opening up to a grand staircase. He could barely see the flicker of flame licking the top of the polished stone steps where the assembly room lay.

"Water, Your Eminence?" A servant girl in a scanty leotard approached him from the side. With a tray raised in one hand, she managed to fall to one knee and touch the floor near Cassius' foot with her free hand. In the center of the platter was a tall glass full of the purest water imaginable.

"No thank you, my dear." He lifted her head by the chin. Her hair was soft and clean, but her face was hardly similar. Even the layers of overdone, pallid makeup couldn't mask her gaunt cheeks and the detached look in her eyes as they stared thirstily at the water.

"Cassius! Welcome, welcome!" An eccentric looking man named Joran Noscondra sauntered out of one of the adjoining chambers. He was a short fellow, without a beard or much hair, and garbed in a rather superfluous white cloak that draped to the ground over a tunic similar to Cassius' but white and green in color. Like the servant, his face was painted heavily with makeup, though in a more stately manner emblematic of the Tribunal upper class. Gold tinted eye shadow was dragged off neatly to the side, as if he was an ancient Egyptian King, and his lips were black with a notch coming off the bottom and extending over his chin.

He moved along in quite a hurry, paying no attention to the dozens of saluting soldiers posted around the room. When he reached Cassius, with a crooked grin he clasped his hands together and offered a humble bow, his gaze moving Cassius' eyes to the floor as was proper amongst equals.

"Save your pleasantries, Joran." Without returning the gesture, Cassius stepped around him.

"Still sour I see." Joran frowned, reeled in his arms, and followed. He was the Tribune tasked with overseeing New Terrene and the other colonies on Mars and nearby. Born and bred in the glistening city's loftiest towers.

"You're lucky I'm here at all! Last time I came here, you and your Tribunal tried to have me killed."

"It was your Tribunal as well!" Joran snapped before taking a deep breath to regain his composure. "It was an unprecedented situation, as you know."

"Yes, yes. Well, I would have been happy to live out the rest of my pitiful life far away from here. It was you who summoned me. Only out of the kindness of my heart did I accept, so let us be done with it as harmlessly as possible."

"Charming as always, Cassius." Joran shooed away the servant-girl who was quietly waiting. "The others await us in the assembly. Do try to be congenial at least."

"Aren't I always?" Cassius mused.

Cassius was led to the grand staircase where the guards stationed on either side came together to lead the Tribune up. Cassius could remember all the faces of the lowly commoners who came with their complaints, and were so struck by awe as they slowly ascended the steps lined with pink flowered plants that they nearly forgot what they wanted in the first place. They had seventy-three steps to think about what they were going to say before they reached the most guarded room in all of the Circuit—enough time to inscribe the names of all of the soldiers lost in the Earth Reclaimer Wars on each stair's rise.

It was a circular space. A glass dome with deep-set, golden ribs formed the ceiling. He could see the towers of Midway rising out of view beyond the translucency to shield the hall from any attacking ships. Wrapping around the room in two concentric rings were stone statues of former Tribunes bathing in the reddish sunlight pouring in. At the center of those rings, a roaring flame burst through the glossy, white floor. Lastly, projected above the flame was a three-dimensional, holographic map of the Circuit, monitoring the movements of celestial bodies around the sun and the Solar-Arc ships which defined it. In the place of Earth was a hovering, transparent container with a wiry, green plant floating inside.

"He has arrived, fellow Tribunes," Joran addressed, clasping his hands together and bowing his head.

Cassius didn't say anything. His glare was focused on the plant and it took a minute before he could finally tear his eyes away. "How…" He began to growl before taking a deep breath and settling his thoughts. He had waited far too long to let his temper sidetrack his plans. "It's been too long." He said before offering the feeblest excuse for a bow that he was able to muster.

At four intervals around the space, a tall, metallic seat much too large for a human was nested against the obsidian wall beneath the dome. Two of them were occupied by Tribunes. They looked like idols upon their thrones. Each of them was made up in the same garish style as Joran with their robes unfurling down the glossy metal with regal disregard. Beside Joran was the eldest of them, Cordo Yashan. A long, spectacular white beard fell from his chin, together with his makeup serving to hide most of his wrinkles. Next around the circle was a middle-aged woman named Nora Gressler with short black hair and hard features. She was the newest Tribune, his replacement. The last of them was projected on a HOLO-screen hovering over the chair. His name was Benjar Vakari, a comely man with a thin beard. His lips were constantly drawn to one side to form a complacent grin.

How long I've waited to wipe that look off his face, Cassius mused to himself. *That may very well be my greatest accomplishment after all of this is done with.*

Once Joran reached his lofty seat, they all nodded to each other, signaling at least a dozen guards to file out and seal the exits promptly behind them.

"We are blessed with ground beneath us. May our faith be

eternal and unwavering, so that we may one day walk the Earth's untainted surface," Tribune Yashan recited. Each of the Tribunes rose to their feet and carefully rearranged their clothing before they gracefully dropped to one knee. They looked to the map of the Circuit and then to the floor, slowly and deferentially allowing their fingers to graze the floor.

When they rose back to take their seats, Cassius could tell by the scowls on their faces that his lack of reverence had insulted them. All but Benjar whose hologram continued to wear the same, smug grin.

"It has been a long time, I know," Tribune Yashan grumbled, "But I assume you have not forgotten the conventions of this blessed council."

"Ah. Forgive me. Where are my manners?" Cassius didn't kneel down. Instead he bent at the waist, playfully groaning as he stretched out his arm and pretended he couldn't reach the ground.

"A mockery!" Cardo Yashan defied his age as he shot up to his feet and shouted. "How dare this heretic be invited to walk these sacred halls again!" His face was red with anger.

"Relax Tribune Yashan," Joran spoke unenthusiastically. "I'm sure Cassius' body is still weary from travel. Correct?"

"It appears so." Cassius patted his thigh a few times. "Leg seems to have stiffened up on me. I don't suppose I could trouble you for a seat?"

Cardo snapped. "You gave up your seat here long—"

"Enough!" Joran cut him off. "We have more important matters to argue over."

Tribune Yashan muttered under his breath as he fell back into his seat.

"Now," Joran continued, "How fairs Edeoria, Cassius?"

"Give me a decade and the Moons of Saturn will one day rival the great city of New Terrene." He reached beyond the rail to feel the flame's hotness against his flesh. For a long while he once thought it merely an illusion, but it was very real. "Now can we move beyond these pleasantries and explain why I was summoned from the comfort of my home?"

"Don't act like you don't already know," the projection of Benjar Vakari quickly chimed in with an incriminating tone.

"Forgive Tribune Vakari," Joran cut in. "Unexpected circumstances kept him occupied on the Earth's Moon. He won't be arriving until tomorrow morning."

"What a shame," Cassius said with obvious sarcasm. "I was so looking forward to seeing him again."

"The flattery is unnecessary, Vale," Benjar answered him." If it were up to me, you wouldn't be allowed within light years of New Terrene. You shall find no pity here for performing your obligatory duties to this holy council."

"You mistake me. I haven't come for pity, I merely wish to hear this council of esteemed men and woman beg me for help."

"Nobody is in the mood for your games!" Benjar's distinctive grin broke for a rare moment, allowing his loathing for Cassius to seep through his features.

"This is not a game!" Cassius barked, his eyes fuming. Before he continued, he took a few breathes to calm himself. "Now from your own mouths, tell me why I, Cassius Vale, the innocuous exile, am required so far from my post?"

"You knew the oath you were—" Tribunary Vakari shouted before he noticed the others shaking their heads. "Fine." He forced his expression to return to normal, though his cheeks remained flushed. "I assume you have heard of the unsettling string of stolen ships traversing the Ignescent Cell."

"The Tribune is no stranger to acts of piracy, especially in Ceresian space."

"Not like this. Usually we are able to not only track the stolen vessels, but disable all their systems so that they are useless. Even if the seized ships are beyond our reach, it can take up to a year for them to be completely dismantled and reconfigured in order to be used again."

"Just to be clear, you are describing to me the Vale Protocol? The same initiative I spent years in the Tribune developing?"

"Yes." Tribune Vakari's mouth went crooked with embarrassment.

Joran took over from there. "Over the past few months there have been a series of thefts of private freighters containing stores of Gravitum. In each case, no emergency signal went off. The tracking systems were disabled along with our ability to shut down the ships. No evidence was recorded or transmitted. The freighters are completely gone, missing as though they never even existed."

"You can understand why this would be disconcerting," Nora Gressler chimed in. "If the Ceresian Pact has found a way around the Vale Protocol then we will have lost a significant advantage. Not all goods can be conveyed along the Circuit."

Cassius had a difficult time taking her seriously. After he was forced out of his position on the council, she was the one chosen to replace him as the overseer of the outer Nascent Cell, hand-picked by Benjar himself. Her citadel was so near his home on Titan that he had made a living out of avoiding her gaze. But not shortly after she was sworn in did he find that her sway over the others was as minimal as his own when he occupied her seat. She was a constant reminder of how much he didn't miss his old position, as she rarely got a word in edgewise.

"All of *your* goods you mean?" Cassius corrected her. "Trade between the Cells has always been necessary, even amongst enemies. The Circuit weaves together all of humanity."

"Not if we can control it. Get the Keepers under our fingers."

"Don't think me a fool! The circuit only works because it is impartial. If the Keepers were ever to lose control, the Solar-Arks would be susceptible to attack. This isn't the 2nd century K.C. anymore. There are other powers in the system who would not be bullied by you or any others. Few left now, but they are out there."

"I'm beginning to wonder what side you are on!" Tribunary Yashan snapped as he leaned forward in his chair and steepled his fingers.

"I am on no side because I didn't realize sides were already being taken. I have nothing to gain in whatever conflict you fools are instigating!"

"Fools, you call us? It is your program that is being cracked, not ours."

"Yet it is your Tribune. Every program will be broken eventually. It is up to you to ensure continued security. That was the agreement."

"Don't patronize us, Cassius. You promised that it would be imbedded too deep to be infiltrated without our knowing." Nora made her attempt to jump back into the discussion.

"Perhaps the ex-Tribune knows something he is not telling us. Perhaps the inventor of the Vale Protocol himself is the one using it to subvert us?" Tribune Vakari accused with a haughty grin. An obvious reprisal for the slight he had received earlier.

"How dare you make such a bold claim through the safety of a projection!" Cassius stormed around the fire basin and addressed the hologram directly.

"Now, now, nobody is making that assumption." Joran attempted to cool down heightened tempers.

"I may have put down the gun a long time ago, but do not think I've forgotten how to use it! You would be wise not to test my patience."

"And why is that?" Benjar didn't break eye contact, his reinvigorated expression making Cassius' blood boil.

"Because though I have turned to words, there will come a time when their effectiveness wears thin! There have been very few peaceful revolutions throughout the history of mankind, from what I've read of it."

The tension could be read in each of the creases on the present Tribune's uneasy faces. Only the soft cracking of flame could be heard as they awaited the next exchange with bated breath.

"Are you threatening me, Vale?" Tribunary Vakari whispered sharply through his smirk.

"Not you…" He breathed deep and turned so that he could look upon all of the others, when suddenly a transmission came through.

"Urgent message from the New Terrene Arbiter." An administrator's voice echoed over the silent chamber's intercom.

"Patch him through," Joran mumbled, hesitant to see where else this conversation could possibly go.

"Excuse me Your Eminences, another ship has vanished off the Circuit. Same result as the others," the Arbiter addressed.

Cassius masked his enthusiasm. He had been wondering how long it would take for ADIM's work to finally earn recognition.

"How long ago?"

"Maybe an hour or so. I thought the news would be worthy of interrupting."

"Thank you, Arbiter. I will meet with you soon."

The message cut out and Joran slumped back into his seat with a beleaguered sigh. "Look Cassius," he began, "We may have had our differences over the years, but you once sat upon this Tribune, in this very room. Help us now, and I will personally acquit you of all contempt."

"And what about the others? Will they too dismiss their claims of heresy and leave me in peace?" Cassius questioned, his stare still directed at Benjar Vakari's hologram.

Joran didn't wait for them to speak up. "They will."

"I don't think—" Tribunary Vakari responded before Joran cut him off.

"Unless they don't have the best interests of humanity at heart." Joran glared at Benjar, who muttered something disgruntledly before closing out his projection.

"Finally a man with some sense." Cassius shot Joran a nod. "The problem may be impossible to resolve without recalling all vessels under the protocol, but I will do what I can. I must examine matters from the Arbiter's Enclave first, and then I will return to Titan where I will maintain open communication until my services are no longer required."

"You have the full compliance of the New Earth Tribunal and its standing members." He rose to his feet to address the rest of the room. "I will personally oversee this investigation and the involvement of Cassius Vale. Does anybody present oppose this?"

The others shook their exhausted heads, neither of them eager to contest a fellow Tribune and cause any sort of unrest.

"To New Terrene then!" Cassius proclaimed.

Chapter Five
Labyrinth of the Night

Sage Volus threaded through a crowd, a ratty cloak draped over her shoulders. She was alone, submerged in the shadows of the dim underworld of New Terrene where it was time for the *Feed*, when common people were horded like cattle to provisionary outposts serving every day's solitary meal. Each citizen was given a single bowl filled with a mushy soup of vegetables and nutrients along with a few small pills bearing what other supplements were necessary for survival. With it, they'd get a cup of lukewarm water purified in the northern polar region of the planet. Guards in black and green light-composite armor kept the bedlam to a minimum. The letters N.E.T. were printed in the upper right side of each of their chest-plates.

A guard at the edge of the serving stand looked her face over and then held out a retinal scanner. She placed her eye in front of it and a number…B276584…ran across the top. A similar code was provided by the Tribune for every new resident of New Terrene. Hers was more a disguise than an identity. A name, Talia Bristol, popped up along with all the proper information of birth, housing block, and years of citizenship.

The gadget beeped, signaling that she had been cleared. Every citizen of New Terrene would go through the same process in order to ensure that nobody was trying to get a second helping. Food wasn't a luxury among the cities of the Circuit, and since taking power the Tribune was never afraid to impose regulations on its growing populace.

"Here you go, beautiful," the portly man behind the stand said as he handed her a cold bowl with a bent spoon. Licking his stubbly beard as his eyes unfolded over her pleasing face. She didn't even bother to look up. She only wished that her cloak was fixed with a hood so she would be saved all the daily, gluttonous stares in her direction.

Dipping her utensil into the soup affectionately termed *Crud*, Sage watched as chunks rolled over the rim. She remembered when it used to nauseate her, but that was a long time ago. In fact, she had come to look forward to the *Feed* just like everybody else. Only she was nothing like everybody else.

As the pasty goop tumbled down her throat, her eyes remained vigilant, scanning for the man she had been hunting for the last few days. She was in the gloomy underworld of New Terrene, built into the depths region of the extensive canyon known as the Labyrinth of the Night. Running up the wrinkled crags of it was a vertical shantytown, an ever expanding amalgamation of crude housing sheds rising up with cavernous passages carved out of the cliffs behind them. Tramways lined the void between the two sides, rising and falling beneath spontaneous bridges where the accruing structures on each side of the rift grew together. So far below the beautified avenues and containment of the glistening, upper city, it was always dark. Though the flickering lights in each tiny hovel made it appear like an abstract painting of a night sky with the red lights along the streets lingering at the bottom of one's vision like a fading sunset.

She moved slowly along the crowded walkway, her hand grazing the railing. Beyond it was more housing clambering down the covered rock-face, expanding until one day it would reach the very bottom. She stopped by a towering HOLO-screen, rendering her merely a silhouette as she continued eating and trying to appear like she wasn't looking for anybody.

"Citizens of New Terrene." A deep, authoritative voice spoke from the projection, which held the symbol of the Tribune—a grasping, black hand with its fingers curled around the green silhouette of Earth. "The Spirit of Earth is within us all. Together, through devotion and restraint, we will redeem ourselves. Your Tribune looks after you, as it does all of humanity. Faith will guide us, men and women of Earth."

Sage had heard the recording countless times. There were dozens of similar screens spanning the Lower Block like scintillating, blue banners. When there was no urgent news or discord, that message would be replayed as a constant reminder. She could recite the words without listening if she wanted, as everyone else probably could. Every day it was drilled into their minds over and over again, and every day it eased their suffering to think that Earth could be saved, even though after so many centuries few even knew what the Homeworld used to look like. She always imagined it was once a paradise of flowing water and sprawling, green landscapes as far as the eye could see.

A tram stopped across the way. It was shaped like a rusty, elongated bullet, and walking around it she spotted him. Dozens were waiting to get on board, on their way to work the factories and vertical farms or, if they were lucky, service the whims of a wealthier household. He looked like any of them at first glance... wearing a loose hand-me-down outfit with a cloth bag slung over his shoulder...but she could see the difference. He was paler than most, with a taller, leaner build. All of that, plus the beads of sweat dripping down his forehead despite the lower block being markedly cool that day, was enough for her to know he was the suspected Ceresian she had been tracking.

There couldn't be much time. She let the bowl roll inconspicuously out of her hand and over the railing before wiping her lips and hurrying toward the tram.

The car began to move as she reached it. Making sure no guards were looking, she grabbed the bottom with her artificial right arm, the metal fingers digging into the smooth surface. She hoisted her legs up to wrap around the rounded base as it jolted forward and began to move along a suspended track.

Hanging in the shadow, she watched as the cluttered houses sped by. She was en route to the *Nether*, the sacred core where the three ravines of the Labyrinth of the Night intersected. There were rings of suspended catwalks wrapping around the cylindrical cavity with holographic effigies lining the inner edge of each level. They were projections meant to honor all of the fallen Tribunes and heroes of the New Earth Tribunal. Around the outside were chapels dedicated to the Spirit of Earth and shooting up the center of the entire hollow was a system of elevators, which climbed to the upper city.

Located sparsely throughout were storefronts that served water and food if you had enough to trade for it. Amongst the lower castes of the New Earth Tribunal there was no true currency. People came from all walks of life to sacrifice food or possessions in exchange for any number of licentious pleasures. She had heard rumors that buried further behind these bars were secret brothels and gambling dens intended for the wealthier folk of New Terrene, though she had her doubts about their existence.

The tram came to a halt and she slipped off as if she had been a passenger the whole time. A couple of wives were waiting at the platform to greet their weary husbands. Her target didn't even pay them a passing glance. He rounded the walkway with his eyes fixed forward, as if on a mission. She kept a safe distance, pulling her cloak tight around her chest and keeping her head down. He had to be the one.

The man turned left, down one of the pathways leading to the central lifts—a massive metal shaft, which not only was packed with more than a dozen elevators, but also served as a sort of mega-pile supporting the transportation hub on the surface. Then he went down one of the branching paths, which led to the Core. A few people waited in line at the scanners. She was two behind him as he stepped through a tight grid of white and blue light-beams. The machine buzzed and the guard standing behind it stepped forward.

"Let me see your bag." The soldier gave a jaded sigh. Her target handed it over without a fuss. After the guard shuffled through whatever was inside and found nothing, he continued. "Turn around. Legs open." Her target followed the directions promptly. As he was being patted down, he held up his left hand, which gleamed beneath the overhead light.

"Prosthetic arm, huh? How'd you get that?" The guard tapped a few of the metal fingers before allowing him to stand upright. Sage looked down at her own right hand, the synthetic joints of her fingers folding flawlessly and without sound as she squeezed a fist over and over. It had been over seven years, but she could never get over the strange sensation of sliding her fingers along her palm and feeling nothing. There was only a slight tingle at her shoulder where her natural nervous system meshed with a manufactured one, but even that was hardly noticeable anymore. His was a chunkier construction, probably decades old and nowhere near as advanced.

"Shipping accident out in the Nascent Cell 'bout four years ago I reckon." Her target did his best to retain his composure. There was no way the guard would have noticed, but she saw the subtle indications of nervousness; his foot shuffling, the back of his neck sweating, the slight twitch of his human thumb between his index finger.

"Alright. You're good to go."

Her target sighed with relief before stepping forward. As she waited her turn, she began contemplating the possibilities. *Not in the bag. It could be waiting for him up top.* When it was her turn to pass through the scanner, the machine permitted her despite her arm. Tribunal security was programmed to allow passage of all acting Executors. Letting the loose end of her sleeve drape down over her right hand, she passed the nodding guard without making eye contact.

Dozens of elevator shafts shot upward, glowing white tubes that ran through the tall, empty space. It was congested, but she spotted her target heading into a nearby lift about to arrive. Trying not to appear rushed, she used her lithe figure to navigate the crowd.

The doors sealed shut behind her, but she made it, and there he was, a Ceresian wretch standing only a few feet from her. The elevator was well lit. No shadows for her to spring from. There were three pedestrians, a small price to pay in collateral compared to the thousands that would die if she failed. The ground trembled slightly before the elevator shot upward. The Ceresian stared at the ceiling. He seemed to be muttering something under his breath.

The bag is empty and it isn't strapped to his body. She scratched her head, the cold metal fingers running through her long, auburn hair. Then it hit her. *The arm!*

CHAPTER SIX
DUSK OVER NEW TERRENE

It was dusk over New Terrene. Cassius Vale stood beside Tribune Joran Noscondra at the foot of the Arbiter's Enclave. It was a daunting building, a fortress of rubicund metal rising without any windows or even a shift in the stark facade. The entrance was an enormous, deep chasm, permitting the steady flow of Mechs and soldiers in and out.

"Please forgive Tribune Vakari. He spoke before thinking clearly." Joran flashed his warmest smile as he rested his hand on Cassius' shoulder.

"He must learn to acquire a short memory. As I have," Cassius responded coldly. He removed the hand, using it to motion to the back of his head where there was a jagged scar running up from his neck to halfway up his hairline. "But some scars never heal."

Joran's eyes widened at the sight of the wound before he exhaled. "I hope one day we can put the past behind us, Cassius. I truly do."

"As do I, but know that my service is for the good of humanity."

"Then we serve the same party."

"Indeed." Cassius moved down the processional steps of the Enclave before turning around. "I will finish the rest of the modifications from my compound on Titan. Keep me apprised, and hopefully soon this little issue will be resolved."

"We haven't always seen eye to—" Joran began, before deciding it wasn't worth wasting his breath. He clasped his hands together and bowed modestly, looking from Cassius' eyes to the ground. "May the Spirit of the Earth guide your steps, Cassius Vale. For all our sakes."

The Ex-Tribune replied with the slightest nod possible before he turned and walked away. There was no reason to smile through his teeth at them any longer; no reason to bow and grovel his way back into their good graces. They needed him, and he relished in their continued ignorance. *Modifications*, he thought to himself with a chuckle. Of course he wasn't actually going to help them with their problem. The Vale Protocol may have begun with only the best intentions, but he would use it to his own ends.

There were shorter routes Cassius could've taken to get to the New Terrene Transportation Hub, but he enjoyed walking the city from time to time. Everything worked like a well-polished machine. Small crafts zipped by overhead within suspended rail tracks while pedestrian traffic flowed throughout the gridded system of avenues below. The streets were like plates hanging over the rifts of the Labyrinth of the Night, with narrow gaps along the edges opening to the darkness of the lower block. Pink flowered trees ran down their center, a testament to the fact that not all other life in the Circuit was dead. But they were the sole form of beautification. It was a place without much flare, but in its austerity there was a sublime nature, which rivaled the ancient cities of Earth.

No true outdoors existed in the city, for to be beyond the enclosure was to endure the biting cold of Mars' surface, the naturally low force of gravity, and of course the lack of breathable air typical on all the planets of the Circuit. Instead, ten stories above his head, an intricate, trellised ceiling spanned between the skyscrapers. It was the glistening, artificial sky of New Terrene, panels of metal plating alternating with those of glass in a pattern to mimic the movement of the sun in order to provide constant, ambient light. The tallest buildings seemed to dematerialize as they climbed beyond it, their mostly metallic enclosure shifting entirely to glass as they began to house soaring, vertical farms. There were no vast fertile plains in the Circuit, only contained environments suitable for growing crops. Nowhere were they more spectacular than the upper skyline of New Terrene.

Cassius turned down the main avenue of the city. The sun peeked in, casting a deepening brownish-red hue that was made even more magnificent as it glimmered off the ruddy metal of the city. He had no love for crowds, and the city was nothing if not bustling, but nobody seemed to pay attention to him as he passed. Anonymity was the name of the game in New Terrene, for anybody caught out of line would answer to the relentless military presence. Soldiers in the traditional black and green armor of the Tribune were always on patrol. Not to mention the Combat Mechs lumbering up and down the suspended streets, making them quake beneath each colossal footstep.

He could see the Hub rising through the Ceiling to take its place in the center of the skyline of New Terrene. Dozens of suspended rails crisscrossed through its opened base, with the more massive lines running above him. They cut axially along the main avenue of the city and eventually rose up Pavonis Mons to Midway Station, and then to the Conduit.

"Drop the bomb!" A voice suddenly shouted over the din of the city streets.

Cassius nearly slammed face first into a mob of frantic civilians, causing his eyes to snap down toward the commotion. He pushed through the crowd, eager to see what had caused such a panic. At the edge of the hub's lofty atrium, a semicircle of soldiers were facing something, their gaze fixed down the sights of their pulse rifles. Many of their arms were shaking, but he couldn't see their faces to grasp how nervous they really were.

"Drop it or we will fire!"

Cassius got on his toes to peer over the line. What he saw stopped him dead in his tracks.

Chapter Seven
Ascend, My Dear

"Fuck, fuck, fuck…" Sage Volus repeated to herself under her breath. She crouched over her target's corpse, blood oozing out of a laceration across his neck, his legs continuing to spasm. With her natural hand she aimed her gun at the three innocents across the elevator to keep them back. Then she analyzed the arm. Through the circuits on the bicep she could see the spinning core of some sort of bomb. It was built into the prosthetic, and a small timer within read three minutes and twenty-five seconds.

Making sure the civilians wouldn't be too bold as to try something, she quickly pressed a switch built into the black, metal wrist of her own synthetic arm. A concentrated, red beam fired out from beneath her forearm. It began to melt through the man's flesh at the base of his shoulder, and she made sure not to damage the root of the prosthetic and risk explosion. After she cut all the way down to the bone she turned it off and flexed her hand in a certain way that made a long, jagged wrist-blade slide out from above her wrist. The bone snapped as she swung down, blood spattering all over her face. With another hack she severed the arm completely from the man's side, drenching herself in doing so.

A woman across the room cried hysterically. The man at her side cradled her head to his chest and covered her eyes. The other civilian was a young boy, staring in awe as Sage rose with the bloodstained, fake arm dangling from her grip.

"I'm not going to hurt you." She attempted to comfort them, but she had never been good at such things. Nor could she speak for the bomb. She assumed the Ceresian was probably targeting the top of the Core where it punctured the conical atrium of the Hub. Judging by the size, it was a mini-nuke powerful enough to level the building's structure, closing up the main system of transport from the Lower Block and killing thousands with it.

The elevator stopped. The three civilians scrambled out screaming, "She's got a bomb!" She glanced around the exit. People were everywhere. There was nowhere to hide. She inhaled deeply and switched her gun to the unwavering clutch of her artificial hand. Then she made a break for it.

Half the crowd scattered as soon as they heard the word "bomb," the other half stared in sheer terror as they saw blood dripping from her cloak. She barely made it to the opposite side of the atrium when soldiers began converging on her. When a few more swooped down in personal hover-bikes she froze, looking straight down the barrel of around a dozen rifles. Her pistol waved in their direction as she held up the bomb so that the timer would be visible—two minutes and eleven seconds.

"Drop the bomb!" one of them shouted.

She could've yelled out and claimed who she truly was, but there was no reason for them to believe her. The Executors were part of an elite, clandestine entity answerable only to the Tribune's themselves or their respective Hands. Even the other Executors were a mystery to her and each other. It was their sacred duty to protect and serve the New Earth Tribunal at any cost, even if that meant taking the lives of its soldiers if left with no other alternative. She counted thirteen armed guards, with two Mechs approaching. If there were four or five she had no doubt she could take them out before they could land a shot, but not thirteen.

"Drop it or we will fire!"

I am the silent hand of the Tribune. She began reciting the Executor Vow in her head. Her heart pounded. It was time to finally see if all her training would pay off. Her trigger-finger slowly began to squeeze, until all of a sudden a familiar voice yelled out to break the tension.

"Hold your fire!" An older man wearing a violet tunic burst through the lines. "Hold your fire." He backed up toward Sage, facing the soldiers with his arms spread wide as if to impede a surging mass.

"Get out of the way you crazy bastard!" one of the guards growled as he charged and swung the butt of his rifle at the intruder's head. The aged man easily ducked out of the way. Then he delivered a few lightning quick strikes to the throat and one more which cracked the visor of the soldier's helmet, knocking him out in an instant. "I am Cassius Vale!" He held out his forearm so they could all see the lidless eye inscribed on his forearm. "Acknowledge if you recognize this as the truth."

The soldiers looked back and forth at each other anxiously until one decided to speak up. "I've seen him before, it's true," he said and a few of the others nodded in agreement, but none of them shifted their aim from Sage.

She noticed the long, jagged scar running down the center of the back of the man claiming to be Cassius Vale's head, which impeded his hairline. *It can't be*, she marveled to herself while masking her disbelief. He wasn't lying. She had only known one man in all of her life with a scar like that, but after so many years apart she had forgotten the sound of his voice.

"I was a Tribune!" Cassius declared. "This woman is an Executor and the next one of you who keeps her from her duty will have my wrath to suffer!" They began contemplating it, but none of them lowered their guns even as the Mechs arrived. "Lower your arms!" Cassius roared with authority, his stern features tightening. Most of them were still shaking, but one by one the soldiers finally backed down.

Sage panted—one heavy breath after another as she could sense the silent clock ticking. Then Cassius turned and they locked gazes. He wore a nervous smile, one it didn't look like he was accustomed to making. There was a sparkle in his eyes, and it told her everything she needed to know. Once again, the man who rebuilt her arm was there at a time of desperation. She opened her mouth to thank him, to say how much she had missed him, but he shook his head.

"Ascend, my dear," he whispered, and with a quick glance down at the timer she bolted towards one of the security vehicles.

Don't look back, she told herself as she pushed through the flabbergasted guards and jumped into one of the hover-bikes. She powered it on and zoomed upward, the blur of Cassius receding in the viewport's reflection. There was no time to reach the outer walls of New Terrene, only to go up. Pulling back on the controls with all of her might, she steered the vehicle through oncoming traffic. Ships swerved around her, most of them smashing into each other like the drums of thunder in a storm.

Her destination was one of the tiny maintenance ports leading out to the outer surface of the Ceiling. Once she was high enough she leaped out of the ship and grasped the latch with her metallic hand. Dangling, high above the ground and with a bomb in her free hand, she reached with her nose and switched on the laser. She took a deep breath and held it down as the lock was severed. Then she swung up, legs first, and kicked through the opening.

The sudden change in pressure made her ears feel like they were going to burst, almost knocking her off of her feet as she landed atop the Ceiling. There was no time to waste. *Twelve seconds.* She switched the bomb to her right side and hurled it with all of her might, aiming away from the tightest cluster of skyscrapers toward where the least damage would be done. The amputated arm soared across the air until it escaped New Terrene's artificial gravity field. Quickly, she slipped down through the opening, but as she went to close the latch, the bomb went off in a dazzling blast of purple and blue. The shockwave wasn't enough to shatter the Ceiling's glass but it was enough to launch her as the port closed behind her.

Air rushed by her as she plummeted, making it almost impossible to draw any air into her lungs. Tumbling, she reached out with her artificial arm, desperately hoping the Spirit of the Earth had a miracle in store for her.

As her vision began to go blurry, her hand slammed into the top of a small airborne craft. Her body came to a jerking stop, the muscles in her shoulder beginning to tear. The pain was unbearable. Her artificial fingers dug in so hard that they caved in the roof as it began to plunge toward the streets of New Terrene. She hung on for her life, and the last thing she saw before everything went black was the fading, affectionate smile of a man she could barely remember.

CHAPTER EIGHT

GENESIS

After making sure that Sage would survive her injuries, Cassius quietly departed Mars and, a week and a half later, the *White Hand* touched down within the hangar at his Ennomos base. He headed to the cargo bay and stepped out of the ship, surprised to find that he had beat ADIM. Worried that something might have happened, he thought about switching on the com-link in his ear to contact him, just to make sure. But after remembering how superior the engines of his ship were in comparison to a common Tribunal Freighter, he decided that the incident on Mars was fuddling his judgment. ADIM may have looked the same as the day he was powered on, but he was older than Cassius sometimes realized. Even out in the void of space he knew his Creation was safer than all the peoples of the Circuit.

He began to stroll down the hangar, running his hand along the smooth hull of the *White Hand,* his fingers grazing the elegantly inscribed name near the middle. He rarely took time to marvel at it. At first, the ship was a gift upon his inauguration into the Tribunal Council, before the Tribunes grew fond of their mammoth *New Earth Cruisers.*

It had the look of a pelican with half folded wings. The long, flat barrel of a rail gun ran through the ridged top between the wings and stopped just short of the sharply curved translucency. The exterior was clad in a pearlescent, silver coat, indicative of Tribunal nobility, with the edges of each of the ship's plates trimmed with white accents. The engines were built into the center of the thick, "L" shaped wings, able to rotate almost 360 degrees. As a whole it had a sleek style that made it almost impossible to tell where its weaponry and other systems were nestled.

Cassius had spent his early years as a Tribune tinkering with the ship. On the outside it appeared the same, but upgrades to its engines made it faster than almost any ship its size that he had ever encountered. Likewise, the stealth systems made it almost impossible to locate on any typical NET scanners, and it was outfitted with state of the art Plasma Shield defenses. But what he liked the most was his first foray into the realm of virtual intelligence and robotics. Gaia, though trivial when compared to ADIM, was an intricate program, which allowed him to run the ship entirely on his own. Such technology was considered blasphemous by the Tribune, but he always had an affinity for making things work beyond their expectations. He had visited experts in clandestine labs throughout the Circuit. They filled his mind with knowledge at the expense of their own work and sometimes lives, whatever it took to keep his affairs a secret.

He breathed in the sight of the ship in its entirety as they came around the front, remembering fondly the first time he had asked Gaia to power on the engines without even the flick of his finger. It began with her, and it ended with ADIM.

Again, he looked up through the roof toward space to see if a ship was approaching. There was nothing but blackness. It was the longest time the two had ever been physically apart since his conception. So, he took a seat on a container beside his ship, waiting. After a few minutes the soft purr of the station's many systems began to sooth him. His mind began to wander back to the day, almost four years ago that he brought ADIM into existence.

⁂

Ex-Tribune Cassius Vale stood at the edge of a three-dimensional map of the Circuit in his clandestine lab on Titan. His icy glare moved decisively along the bluish projections of the slowly rotating planets, those always stanch eyes narrowing as they fell upon that of Earth. A small HOLO-Projector, in the shape of a sphere, with fluted rifts of radiant, blue lights all around its circumference, rested in his upturned palm. Without looking, he twisted his thumb, shifting one of the offset planes on the device so that a splaying beam of pixelated light shot upward. The particles began to rearrange, the dusky likeness of a human head taking form.

His heart skipped a beat. He tried to steady his breathing, his hands beginning to tremble, but all the swollen emotions were only serving to drench his brow in sweat. It was the same as the year before, and the years before that when that fateful day inevitably would come to bring with it irrepressible pangs of grief and rage.

Once the projection was fully configured, the face of Caleb Vale was rendered with such realism that only a closely discerning eye would be able to notice the space between each floating fragment of light. But the image was frozen, the tip of Cassius' finger hovering over the blinking sliver on the device that would set the recording to replay for the thousandth time. The image had no background. It was as if the young man portrayed was there with the ex-Tribune, a living bust joining him at the viewport.

Cassius could usually fight back the tears, but on that day it made his eyes well. It was all he could manage to urge himself to switch on the message, cuing the lips of the hologram to begin speaking.

"Happy Birthday, Dad!" Caleb wished cheerfully, with only a hint of the vocal dilution inherent in a typical recording. The ex-Tribune's inventions were far from typical. "I bet you thought I'd forget."

Cassius released a pitiful sound, more a grief-stricken snivel than the reminiscent laugh he had thought would slip through his quivering lips. That face was so familiar to him, and yet stranger with each and every passing day.

"I can't believe how fast another year has gone." Caleb's expression dropped to a grimace.

"Look Dad. I know you're worried about me, but I'll be fine. You see, we did it, we finally did it." The hologram rearranged, zooming out to trace Caleb's full body. The floor of his environment was rendered, illuminating beneath his footsteps as he walked over to run the back of his hand along the surface of a glass chamber. At first glance it appeared to be filled simply with water, but swaying beneath the ripples was the straggly form of an aquatic plant. Its stem was wiry, almost pathetic looking, but Cassius remembered the shiver up his spine the first time he saw it.

"We moved it here from the lake. It's growing under the surface! A real, Earthborn plant. For the first time in decades, the purification process is taking a step forward. I...I—" the excitement in his voice was palpable, bringing to Cassius a twisted smile as his youthful son tripped over his own words. "I know it doesn't seem like much, but life on Earth after centuries...Dad, it's...it's a miracle." Caleb gathered his breath, and then chuckled to himself weakly. "You probably don't care, but it's everything to me."

Everything to me, Cassius thought to himself, his hand nearly slipping from the burnished sill he leaned on.

"Well, we're about to head out for supplies. And don't worry, I'll be safe. Earth isn't as vengeful as you recall. Anyway, you know I'll be thinking about you. We'll see each other soon, I prom—" Cassius' son was cut off as a powerful tremor knocked him off of his feet. A woman's voice shouted frantically in the background as he scrambled across the floor and reached out. Then the recording froze.

Bye.

Tears ran from Cassius' eyes in streams as he ran his thumb over the HOLO-Projector, replaying those last words over and over until he unraveled. The device slipped through his perspiring fingers, its impact drowned out by his angst-ridden groans. He hunched over the table, his insides curdling, his throat clenching as if he were being choked to death.

When his stomach finally settled, he turned, mustering his most regal stride as he followed the rolling device across the floor. It bumped against the foot of a console and began to play again, but Cassius bent over to freeze the message just as his son's face had fully formed. He went to deactivate it, but instead set it down on a table overlooking the laboratory.

"You'll want to see this, Caleb," he whispered as he moved in front of an array of HOLO-Screens hovering over a console. Each of the bluish-green blades set to compute and configure data was blank until he keyed in a command, which prompted the security protocol. He placed his eye against a retinal scanner and then typed in the password, 2AL3B82LE. Not too difficult for an outsider to figure out, but he always tried to maintain the guise that he held little information worth concealing.

The display lit up, hundreds of lines of diagnostics running across the large array of screens wrapping around the front of him. Among all of the images surveying the status of his world—the moon called Titan—and other data, he gravitated to the one showing a not quite human figure. Then he pressed a few keys on his bracer, causing the information to be transmitted to another screen rising up from it. He turned from the station and set it to begin recording.

"Recordi…" Cassius sniveled and wiped his cheeks one last time as to appear more his typically unflappable self. "Recording 243. March 15th, 514 Kepler Circuit. My birthday," he began as he strode toward a pulsating, red aura on the other side of the stark, dimly illuminated laboratory. "This will be my last entry regarding my first Automated Dynamic Intelligence Mech: codename, ADIM. What began in anguish as a project without intention, has become so much more to me. It has been four years, but now I, Cassius Vale, am on the verge of the greatest breakthrough in human history since the discovery of the element Gravitum deep within the Earth."

He stopped before a magnetically induced chamber where a small reactor floated at chest height. It seethed like magma, the light stifled as sharp fins spiraled around the volatile core of the complex sphere. His eyes unfolded over the device, in marvel of his work. The rapid whoosh of the churning blades matched the beating of his own heart as he grew close enough to feel the heat emanating even through its protective field.

"The fate which befell our beloved Homeworld was tragic, but we remain strong. Earth may be in our DNA, it may define us and where we came from, but even a master craftsman does not go back to alter his first masterpiece. We left our mark on that fading planet, and in its dying gasp reaped the secrets to evolve beyond it. We have not fallen to ashes alongside the frail life with which we shared her, but instead have ascended to greet all the vastness of the universe. I was counted amongst the fools who lost sight of what is out there for us to claim, but I have been enlightened. Here is the first step toward a new future, a brighter future for mankind.

"We don't need the battered husk of Earth any longer. There is no spirit wallowing deep within her core. The Tribune will call me a heretic, but with ADIM I will pave a new foundation for man. It was once believed by the Ancients that some divine being—some god—created man in his image. I believe today that we have assumed that role." He typed a command into the panel on his arm and a table tilted upright beside the reactor's chamber. Lying on it was the figure of ADIM. Bathed in darkness, his outline painted red by the oscillating light, the silhouette so like a man in height and scale that beneath the shadow, the difference was almost indiscernible.

"Just like the son I once helped bear to life, here is another to be guided by my will. An artificial copy, which will not perish so easily as…" Cassius' lower lip began to tremble before he closed his eyes and breathed to calm himself. "He is the first of his kind, an artificial conception able to adapt and evolve as we do. Not a virtual intelligence restricted to a console on a ship. Not one of the mindless drones bent on the pursuit of a singular task, which the Tribune sought to wipe off the Circuit. No, ADIM is a freely existing synthetic being ruled by the devotion inherent in any son eager to learn from a worthy father."

The table came upright, placing the figures gaping chest at the same height as the smoldering reactor. Cassius' finger froze over the command to initiate.

This was it. As easy as turning on the lights. He looked over his shoulder to see the face of his true son, frozen and lifeless. Four years of suffering and this was his gift to himself, progeny of metal and fission. When he turned again, his eyes were brimming with conviction. He was ready.

After setting the process to go forward, the whine of an alarm blared out. The field protecting the cylindrical chamber powered down. Then a mechanical arm rose up from the circular platform below the sphere, with a delicate claw-like apparatus on the end fashioned specially for grasping the potentially hazardous reactor.

"Together, we will reset the course of humankind. We shall assume the destiny we inherited when we survived the death of our homeworld. Together, we will rise beyond any of our wildest aspirations and take our place as mighty titans of this system and all others! This is the future I promise to you, Humans of the Circuit."

He proclaimed with the vigor of someone delivering a speech before a thunderous crowd. The only response was the alarm stopping, then the soft, undulant humming of the reactor as it was lifted by the mechanical arm. His glinting eyes watched without blinking as the source of power was conveyed into the android's hollow body. Once it was in place, all the inner workings of ADIM's chest coiled to greet it…all the wires and circuits, which traced the metal frame like our own veins. When that was complete, a series of ribbed panels closed to form a chest, the fiery glow of the core slipping through the narrow spaces between each armored plate.

The table glided across the room until it stopped directly before Cassius, rotating to a vertical position where ADIM's two-pronged feet landed softly on the floor. Branches of bright red diffused down his appendages, the light blooming through the gaps between all of the carefully articulated plates of its exoskeletal exterior.

Cassius powered down the screen on his arm and circled his creation in admiration. He followed the thick, reinforced circuits running between the shields on its neck as they pulsed with energy. Then tiny blue lights switched on, lining the outer rim of each piece of the dark-tinged, super-alloyed shell covering the entire body. It was one of the most beautiful things Cassius had ever seen. For the first time in exactly four years, a tear dribbled down from the corner of his eye that wasn't drawn out by memories of his son. *Perfection*, he thought to himself as he ran the back of his index finger over the ridged, blank surface where ADIM's mouth would be located if he was a human.

The eyes nested deeply in the crescent-shaped blackness between two plates of armor came on with a snap-hiss. The two blazing, red orbs were surrounded by a tight circle of smaller lights which slowly rotated around them like planets in orbit around a star. Cassius stepped back to observe the mouthless face, which he only then realized retained a markedly inquisitive demeanor. Then the magnetized table switched off and ADIM wobbled forward, innocent as a child learning to walk for the first time. But he was a quick learner. After only a few faulty steps, he found his footing and stood upright, so that both he and his creator rose to the exact same height.

"ADIM, can you hear me?" Cassius asked, leaning in until his noise almost touched the ADIM's neck.

"Processing commands." The smaller lights around ADIM's eyes began to revolve faster as his cognitive and optical functions worked in concert to access and comprehend his surroundings. "Are you referring to this unit?"

It was hard for Cassius to infer the statement as a question from ADIM's cold, apathetic voice, but he was able to detect the slightest subtle inflection. He did create him after all. "Yes, I am."

The robot looked down at itself, turning its hand over to inspect the back. All its limbs and joints moved with such fluidity that there wasn't a single noise emitted during motion as was typical in most robots, or even humans for that matter. "And you are the Creator?" It reached out and let the back of its long, sharp index finger graze gently along Cassius' cheek.

The ex-Tribune sniveled, his hand quaking as it wrapped around his creation's smooth forearm. The surface was cool, but beneath it he could feel a surging warmth desperate to escape its metal sheathing. He opened his mouth to speak, but nothing came out.

"Does this unit upset you?" ADIM asked. "This unit can assume a more familiar appearance if you desire." The small blue lights circulating ADIM's plating flashed, emitting holographic pixels that converged to envelop him in the image of his creator.

Cassius was made to look upon his likeness, standing close enough to barely see the red features of the machine beneath the projection. "No." He shook his head. Out of the corner of his eye he noticed at the hollow effigy of his son, looking on with the blithe grin Cassius so adored. "You are perfect."

· ⊶•◦❀◦•⊷ ·

Cassius glanced up with heavy eyelids. The spherical HOLO-Recording device was sitting in his upturned palm, glowing blue as it always did. Placing it back into his pocket with a yawn, he realized that there was still no ship approaching. He wasn't worried that ADIM might be in trouble, but he brought his hand to his ear to switch on the com-link anyway. There was no reason to deny it with nobody watching...he missed the android, almost as much as he missed his own son.

CHAPTER NINE
THE THINGS THAT BLEED

ADIM sat upright in the captain's chair of the Tribunal Freighter. A heap of bodies were piled behind him, their dried blood crusting along the tributary snaking down the shiny floor. He was in a state of stasis as the ship traversed a programmed route through the Ignescent Cell that would avoid contact with any colonies or mining facilities. On a screen adjacent to him was a live recording of the refectory. The six or so crew members locked inside it were seated sullenly at a table. It had been almost two weeks, but their defiance had faded shortly after the first day.

ADIM, I have arrived at Ennomos. Should I be expecting you soon?

ADIM sprung immediately from dormancy. He hopped to his feet, his orbicular eyes brightening as there was once again a reason for animation.

Creator. This unit will arrive at Ennomos Base in approximately 7 hours and 12 minutes. Was your business on Mars satisfactory?

Extraordinarily so! I will be awaiting your arrival.

The foreboding sense of detachment returned, but this time ADIM was not dismayed. There was work to be done. His Creator did not enjoy seeing the calamity of his undertakings, and so one by one he began hauling the corpses to the cargo bay. Once they were all neatly lined up in front of the access hatch, he secured the two containers of Gravitum to the floor and opened it. Air rushed around his metallic frame as the change in pressure forced the bodies out. He watched for a moment as they tumbled into the vastness of space to be lost amongst the stars. Then he resealed the exit and headed toward the refectory.

When he arrived, he placed his hand over the password pad and the door slid open. The captive's heads turned quickly only to see the android silently striding through their confines. Only one of them dared to speak.

"What did you do with them?" The engineer he had spared earlier sniveled meekly.

"They have been disposed of, as required," ADIM responded, not even bothering to stop and look as he passed to retrieve the cleaning supplies from the storeroom.

"Required by whom? What are you going to do with us?"

He got what he needed and headed out. "Your fate will be decided by the Creator." Without hesitation, he locked them in again and returned to the command deck.

Once there, he got on his knees and with meticulous attention to detail began scrubbing every drop of blood. He retraced every trail of every corpse, discarded all of the debris, and even performed some repairs. When he finally finished, the ship was left so spotless that it seemed as if he was never there.

ADIM resumed his position in the captain's chair where a ruddy glob of rock loomed through the viewport. It was Ennomos, a small D-class asteroid, part of the Trojan Formation orbiting along the inner rim of the Nascent Call. It was a fairly remote place. There were some mining bases in the region, but none of vast importance, and Ennomos itself had very little worth quarrying except for small traces of water ice. Regardless, the stolen ship couldn't be brought to Titan where the risk of detection by Tribunal eyes was almost guaranteed.

ADIM seized control of the freighter from autopilot, able to regulate every system simply by tapping through a single console where it would typically require an entire crew working in symphony. The station on the surface was discreet, built into a lengthy trough so that it would remain undetected by anyone who didn't already know it was there. The terminal itself appeared like a flattened tube with a sequence of articulated ribs running across the top.

The Freighter soared smoothly into the crevice and followed it until gliding through the mouth of the terminal. The reverse thrusters activated once it was fully inside, bringing it to a stationary hover. Then the massive entrance sealed shut with alarms blaring and the ship came down to land with a soft hiss.

ADIM wasted no time, rushing to the Cargo bay where he found his Creator already waiting.

"ADIM!" Cassius proclaimed as he stepped up the ramp into the opened cargo bay. "I am glad to see you in one piece."

ADIM paused for a moment to try and formulate a worthy response. "This unit is satisfied to see you are in one piece as well, Creator."

"By the Ancients!" Cassius turned his attention to the containers and ran his hand along the top of them. Each was a silver box with thin blue glowing insets. "This should be enough to finish, no?" Patting ADIM on the back, he turned to head out into the hangar.

"By my calculations, there is enough to re-supply a New Earth Cruiser two times over," ADIM agreed as he followed behind so closely that if he could breathe, he'd be doing it right down Cassius' neck.

"Help me bring them down?"

ADIM stared at them for a moment with his eyes churning. Then he reached underneath one, lifted it, and place it on top of the other. The containers dwarfed him, but he was able to bring them to his chest with such ease that one would have thought they were light as a feather. "723 pounds," he declared after only half a second. "This unit is capable of transporting 4.3 times more weight if you require, Creator."

"I know. So could I in my heyday," Cassius smirked, but ADIM proceeded out of the ship without responding. "I'll lead you."

Together, they meandered down the lengthy hangar. It was a brightly lit space with cambered supports curving like boomerangs to support the tall, half glass ceiling. Besides the *White Hand*, there were five other freighters parked throughout, similar to the one ADIM arrived on. Each of them was powered down and in different stages of being deconstructed by Gravitum Mining Bots that had been re-outfitted for assembly. They appeared like thickly plated spiders, with their many limbs extending from a blocky central body. Containment tubes were fixed at the bottom of their cores, used to hold the Gravitum they would siphon out in small quantities from Earth's mantle. Their many appendages made them perfectly suited for Cassius' needs. They were also far more efficient than trading to acquire proper shipyard machinery along with the manpower to operate them.

They reached a lift at the opposite end. Cassius used the retinal scanner to open it and they stepped on.

"The Tribunal Council is growing restless. A Ceresian attack on New Terrene was recently thwarted, and they suspect they are the ones who've been preying on the personal transports," Cassius explained as they descended deeper into the crust of the asteroid, a self-satisfied look smeared across his face.

"Will they make a declaration of war?" ADIM responded.

"Not so easily again. They will continue their attempt to bleed the Ceresians dry before electing for another war." Cassius stopped and placed his hand against ADIM's chest. It was warm to the touch from the reactor churning beneath his rib-plates. "It will be up to us to provide the necessary impetus."

The lift opened and they continued down a hall. They passed by a door with a HOLO-Screen out front that displayed a crowd of sickly looking people sitting inside. ADIM stopped and looked at the screen.

"There are nine others aboard the new freighter," ADIM said. "None appear to be a threat."

"We'll bring them down here next. Unfortunate souls. They'll be kept nourished enough not to die before we need them."

"Must they be alive, Creator? It would be easier to deal with them if they weren't."

"Corpses in the Cryo-chambers will teach us nothing. Once you see them, you'll understand."

"Yes, Creator."

They proceeded down the hall and stopped at a glass door. There was a clear vestibule beyond it with a dense enviro-suit hanging from the wall. Through there was a dark laboratory, illuminated by a bright, pulsing blue light on the far side.

"This should be fine, thank you," Cassius said, extending his hand to signal ADIM to place the Gravitum containers down.

ADIM dropped them and then quickly, but gently, grasped Cassius' hand. He noticed the half-healed scrapes along the knuckles. Taking time to observe and run his fingers over the wounds, he then glanced at his own arm where a seemingly fatal projectile had merely inscribed a shallow scratch in his chassis. "This unit does not bleed."

"Next time you return, the weapon will be..." Cassius paused and gazed curiously into the radiant eyes of his creation, bewildered. "No, ADIM, you don't bleed."

"The Creator has bled. The humans I must kill all bleed. But this unit does not. Is this what defines life?"

Cassius took a deep breath to gather his thoughts before he responded. "A tree doesn't bleed, but that doesn't mean it is lifeless. A system of mechanical parts does not bleed, yet that doesn't mean it's not rife with purpose."

"Yet, this unit is not alive as the Creator is."

Cassius stood with his mouth half-open. ADIM wasn't used to him being left without words. He immediately began thinking back through their conversation to analyze if he had said anything wrong.

"You need not think of such things," Cassius responded warmly. "We are all alive in our own way. Yours may differ from mine, but there is no denying your strength, your vigor. It doesn't matter to me what you are, ADIM, so long as you are by my side."

"Please do not doubt this unit's reliability." ADIM stepped forward, as if to help express the apprehension, which neither his face nor impassive voice could convey to a human.

"Never!" Cassius grabbed ADIM by the arms and shook them with conviction. "I just meant that this universe is a vast, endless place. Don't trouble yourself with the mysteries neither I nor any other can answer. For when this is all over with, we will seek them out for ourselves."

"Perhaps there are other units like this one?" The tiny lights around ADIM's red eyes began to spin as he considered the possibility

"Even if somewhere in the Circuit there are some that look the same as you do, there are none like you," Cassius admired. "You are unique, ADIM."

ADIM stepped back and his rotating eyes came to stop, satisfied with the response.

Cassius slid his hand to the android's back and began guiding him back toward the lift. "Now, let us go get the others before I finish our work on the Gravitum Bomb."

"Alone. Do you no longer require this unit's assistance?" ADIM asked as they stepped onto the lift, his eyes picking up to slowly spin as if to infer concern.

"I long for it. But at this stage, I can finish from a safe distance. And my suit will keep me safe from any chance of exposure. Instead, there is one last task I need your help with before we can return home to Titan together." The lift stopped and they moved out into the hangar where Cassius pointed left to a branching space where a small black and red ship sat. "You must take the *Shadow Chariot* to Earth and acquire the plans for a Plasmatic Drill for me. Only after testing Titan's core will I resolve to use that bomb."

ADIM said nothing at first. His innocuous face could offer no indication of how he felt, but it didn't matter. Though he may have valued the moments he shared with Cassius over all other things, in the end his existence was measured by a single directive.

"This unit is pleased to execute the Creator's will."

CHAPTER TEN
FOR THE TRIBUNE

Sage Volus' eyes blinked open wearily and she squinted from side to side with blurred vision. A sharp line of pain shot down the right side of her torso as she rolled to her back, but it was nothing compared to how much her head was throbbing. It wasn't unusual for her to wake with a slight headache as one of the minor side effects from the cybernetic implant latched onto her brain stem. Every Executor received one upon making their vows, and it served to improve such attributes as her physical reflexes and eye coordination. This time it was different, as if a ten ton vice were squeezing in on her frontal lobe.

It took a few minutes for her to acclimate to the bright, white room, but once she did she recognized it as the private medical wing of the Arbiter's Enclave. A HOLO-Screen over a console at the wall monitored her heartbeat alongside a projection of her body that displayed a live examination of all her biological functions. In it her right arm was missing, and she nervously glanced down.

From the neck down she was beneath a blanket. She began to peel it back nervously to reveal her pale, denuded body covered with electrodes and wires. She breathed a sigh of relief when she saw that the arm was still there, that elegant conglomeration of blackish metal and half-veiled circuits. With her other hand she traced the bumps of a new scar running over her right shoulder. When she willed them to, her artificial fingers wriggled in the same way as they used to. Only she no longer could feel the slight tingle at the nerve ending of her amputated limb. Whatever had happened to her had left her even more numb than before.

"Ah, you're finally awake!" Tribune Benjar Vakari said enthusiastically as he entered through a sliding door and locked it behind him.

He wasn't very impressive in stature, but his deep green tunic gave him a regal appearance. The emblem of the Tribune was stitched over his chest in gold and lighter green cloak draped over his left arm, which he never let fall to his side. Gaudy makeup made him appear young from far away, but the thin goatee wrapping his smirking mouth was peppered with gray hairs.

"Your Eminence!" Sage anxiously pulled the blanket up to her neck to cover her breasts. Then she struggled to reach the edge of the bed so that she could perform a proper greeting.

"Please remain seated." Tribune Vakari held out his arm to stop her.

Not sure what to do, she clasped her hands together and bowed her head as low as she could manage before it pained her. "What in the name of the Ancients is going on?" she asked.

"You don't remember?"

She furrowed her eyebrows and fought her aching head as she tried to concentrate. Images of blood and flame flashed through her memory. She recalled falling, and then blackness, but nothing more.

"Did I stop the bomber?" she asked as she shook her head.

"You left him dead in the Core after you discovered the bomb on his person. Guards attempted to stop you in the Hub, but..." He paused to analyze her face. Apparently satisfied with what he saw, he continued, "I was fortunate enough to have been there in time to restrain them, allowing you to trigger the explosive beyond containment. There was some superficial damage to the western vertical farms, but nothing we can't deal with before we lose the crops. What are a few plants compared to the thousands you saved?" Benjar sat at the end of the bed and put his hand on her thigh. "A shame that the loathsome Ceresian met his end so quickly. It would have been beneficial to have captured him alive, but I do not doubt the will of the Spirit."

As he talked, Sage noticed the fresh scars along the shoulder connected to her synthetic arm.

"That arm saved your life," Benjar said. "Most of the remaining tendons and muscles around your shoulder had to be repaired, but the surgeons took good care of you, my dear."

She sat up, the sudden motion making her woozy. "How long have I been out?"

"You suffered a fairly significant concussion and your implant was slightly impaired. You've been under close surveillance for four days."

"That explains the headache," Sage groaned as she reached behind her head to feel the faint scar beneath her hair. It hadn't been re-opened.

"No surgery was necessary. We just had to reboot it from the outside. Give it a spark. Once it kicks back in, your tolerance for pain will come back." Benjar shuffled along the bed until he was positioned by her head.

"I hope that's soon," she said as she squeezed her eyes shut to combat the soreness. "Thank you for helping with the guards."

"We got lucky I was nearby. You did well."

Suddenly, his lips came down to press delicately against hers. She didn't fight it. She never did, despite the way it made her stomach turn. Goosebumps rose along her skin as his hand passed gently through her hair. Hardly kissing back, she laid still as he positioned himself on top of her and began to caress her navel. She let her sight drift toward the light above her bed, receding into her thoughts as she always did. *I exist for the good of the Tribune,* she reminded herself of her vows. *Their will be done, for I am a servant of Humanity and the loyal progeny of the Haven Earth, Her spirit binding us in time and space.*

Then he began to slide her toward the edge of the mattress. Her shoulder got caught in the sheet, and the pain was enough to make her moan. He leaned the entirety of his weight onto her naked body, his elbow pressing against her ribs. She winced as he placed fervent kisses up her neck. "I can't," she wheezed as she scrambled further up onto the bed and pulled the blanket up over her. "I can't."

"Yes… sorry, my dear." Benjar pulled away panting. It took him almost a full minute to gather his breath. His cheeks were flushed and his lips were twisted into a scowl. "Even the mighty Sage Volus is not invincible," he sighed. "On to business then." He turned his back to her and began to observe the scans of her body on the HOLO-Screen.

She continued staring blankly until the light above her grew blurry. It didn't help the headache, but it was how she got through it. She could pretend she was sailing through space toward a distant star, or that she was standing on ancient Earth with the sun glaring down through a blue sky.

"There is no doubt that the bomber was the scum of Ceres." Benjar straightened his tunic and adjusted his cloak.

She looked down at him, but when she opened her mouth to respond she was immediately cut off.

"And you mutilated him before public eyes!" he snapped. His loose-fitting clothing was tossed violently around his body as he whipped around, the gust blowing back Sage's hair. "What happened to secrecy? You are meant to operate in the shadows, not confront a cohort of my men on the streets! Thank the Ancients I was there, otherwise half the Hub would be in shambles."

"I..." she whimpered and looked away. Her entire body began to tremble beneath the blanket. "There was a bomb in his limb." Fragments of what happened flashed through her mind.

"And you decide?" Benjar raised the back of his hand toward her and then froze. He took a deep breath to regain his composure, and flush the red from his cheeks. "Damned fanatics. Well it doesn't matter anymore. The crisis was averted, but you can't remain here."

"What?" Tears began to well in the corner of her eyes. She was hoping she hadn't heard him clearly.

"The entire city has heard what you did! How many stunning redheads do you think are running around New Terrene with pistols in their hands?" He sat down beside her again and ran the back of his fingers over her damp forehead. Then he shifted his tone to be more soothing as he continued, "You can't very well function efficiently under these conditions."

"But where would I go?"

"On another assignment while things here settle down here." He wiped her eyes with the end of his tunic. "You're one of the best we have. It breaks my heart, but we have no choice. You will traverse the Circuit to Ceres Prime. There you will pose as a dissident refugee from New Terrene in order to infiltrate the ranks of those Ceresian Pact bastards. I want you to find out the truth behind the attacks on our transports. There is a war coming, my dear, and I would not have us at a disadvantage."

Ceres, she thought without responding, *the lawless colony where even the hopeful glimmer of the sun doesn't shine through.*

Benjar's fingers slithered through the tangled strands of her hair as he began to gently cradle her head. "Can you do this for me, Sage? For all of the Tribune?"

Sage closed her eyes. She didn't want to leave. She was growing used to being able to see the sun outside. But she knew where her loyalties lie. "I will do what I must, your eminence," she conceded. "We serve the same Spirit."

"Excellent! May it guide you." He beamed and leaned over, placing one more soulful kiss upon her still-moist lips. She fought back the tears as he quickly turned to leave the room without another word, without even a second glance. She lifted her artificial arm and ran the cold, unfeeling fingers around the rim of her mouth, her jaw quivering as she continued watching the door long after his departure.

CHAPTER ELEVEN
WELCOME TO OLD TERRENE

ADIM lay flat in the narrow cockpit of the *Shadow Chariot*, a small ship designed to house little more than his own frame. It had the look of a headlong vulture. A ridge on top contained the ion-reactor, which powered the notched ion engines protruding off of the tail. It was the Creator's first gift to him. A personal vessel with stealth capabilities so advanced that none of the Tribune's dated scanners would ever see it coming. Most of the chassis was as black as space itself, with illuminated slivers of red slicing down the length of its wings and converging at the tip of the tapered bow.

The ship passed imperceptibly over the Earth's moon. On the craterous surface white lights shone from a sprawling complex, one of four Tribunal Citadels throughout the Circuit. Floating nearby above it was a station comprised of five massive rings with four, equally spaced inhabitable strips running along their edges like horizontal skyscrapers. It was one of the Conduits, the last gifts of the Ancients before Earth fell.

Dozens of transports were flocking to and from the construction, which served as a major trading hub. Every so often, one of the massive Solar-Arcs would pass through the rings in a flash. Though there were none at that moment, a complex system of gravity generators, magnets and moving parts conveyed cargo vessels to and from the ships as they moved at small fractions of lightspeed. The Conduits were the pinnacle of man's innovation, and by the beginning of the K.C. calendar, there were six of them placed above the major colonies of the Circuit, successfully delivering mankind from the depths of the second Dark Age.

This was not where ADIM was headed, however. He zipped by, his vessel too small to be noticed even with so many nearby. His destination was Earth, the very planet which had nurtured humans for thousands of years until it became uninhabitable. Nobody truly knows how long the ancients battled the wrathful world before the Circuit was founded, but what remained was a frightening sample. Cassius had told him of the once green pastures and blue skies, though of course he himself had never seen them. Instead, what ADIM saw as he rounded the Earth's Moon was a desolate wasteland. The planet was trapped in an ashen winter. The oceans were black like death. Beneath the brown smog of its atmosphere ADIM could only see the incandescent red of molten rock carving furrows across the dead landscape.

It had become the essence of perdition. The air was festering with radiation and poisonous fumes, unlivable without wearing protective suits at all times. Even when wearing one, however, visitors still chanced the volatile nature of the surface. The planet's plates were in a constant state of flux, resulting in violent earthquakes and unpredictable volcanic activity. The Tribune claimed it to be the results of the sins of ancient men. Scientists believed it was set off when curiosity drove them to start boring deeps holes through the crust in the pursuit of Gravitum. Nobody knows for sure, but it didn't matter to ADIM.

Humans were always sad when they saw it, but like his Creator he believed that the Earth could not be saved. All he contemplated as he approached was when it was appropriate to update Cassius. He had been sent to recover schematics for the Plasmatic Drills used in digging Gravitum mines. The Tribune was in control of all of them, but there were few who knew exactly how they worked.

Creator, this unit is just outside of Earth. ADIM decided to communicate when he was only a couple thousand miles away. A few minutes passed without him receiving an answer. He slowed down. Cassius was rarely late.

Sorry for the delay, ADIM. I was busy in the lab. The familiar sound of his Creator's voice eased his concerns. *Try to be discreet with this. I would rather the Tribune know nothing about this little endeavor.*

What if this unit is left with no other choice?

I leave it to your discretion. If lives must be taken, dispose of them swiftly. They'll chalk it up to the 'Vengeful nature of Earth.' Be careful of that yourself…I've lost too many sons to that wasteland already.

ADIM paused. Just as he was about to respond, the bow of his ship brushed aside the billowy atmosphere of Earth. The signal grew muffled as a loud clap rang out and the *Shadow Chariot* began to violently tremble.

Creator, are you there?

I...I'm losing you...I'll see... ADIM...Good Luck

The silence came and was as jarring as ever. ADIM would've turned around to finish the conversation, but he couldn't. It was rare when his awareness was hampered enough to distract him, but as he plummeted through the stratosphere it took him a few moments to regain control. It could've just been a manner of human speech he didn't yet understand, but the Creator had never referred to him in such a way.

Son. This unit is a son? ADIM pondered to himself, looking down at his arm as his Holo-Projectors cast the image of human skin up the limb. *Must ask the Creator if a son, by definition, must be human.*

The *Shadow Chariot* pierced Earth's grim veil as he contemplated the idea. He pulled up to extend laterally over an expanse of dark water far as the eye could see. Violent waves crested with relentless frequency hewed foam across the ocean like an incensed beast. ADIM kept his route at a low altitude, weaving a path over the liquid as he headed for the continent looming at the far end of the hazy horizon. Nobody was in site...not a ship, not a station. If he had been seen, the Tribune would already be on him, but he was never seen. With a few blasts from the reverse thrusters, he guided the ship to a gentle landing atop a low bluff.

The cockpit lifted back and the circuits linked to his forearms disconnected. He carefully switched down the engine and pulled a thicker chord out from his chest. The ship's Reactor Core was undersized so Cassius designed it to latch onto ADIM, like a symbiotic being. Together they formed a sort of Duel-Reactor-Ion-Engine, which made it unusable for anybody, or anything else. He vaulted over the side, the hard, frozen dirt cracking beneath his feet.

A stifling gloom hung all around him unlike any sort of night the other planets along the Circuit could muster. The stars were imperceptible, with only the silhouette of the moon shining faintly as it rose like a faded skull. He switched his vision to infrared and began sprinting across the countryside.

There was nothing. A few patches of petrified forests here, some rubble there, but nothing worth slowing down to look at. It was hard for him to consider that the muted stumps once held life. There were no heat signatures anymore, no cities with innumerable towers and with vehicles whizzing over paved streets. In half a millennium, no human had walked the Earth as he was then and lived to talk about it. It was his first time ever visiting the Human Homeworld, but to him it was as dead any other world within the Circuit. He began to realize that even though it had fostered its creations for more ages than he knew to exist, in the end it was as expendable as an obsolete ship.

When he came over a low hill, a group of heat signatures popped up. He was about a quarter mile out, but he had arrived at the N.A.412 Drilling Site right on schedule. Switching off infrared mode, he kneeled down at the summit and scanned the horizon.

A tremendous assembly sat in the clearing; an island of dim light within the oppressive darkness. The drill itself was a thick cylinder of layered shells that would pump out of the bottom, lowering the plasmatic tip deeper and deeper into the gaping crevice over which it hung. At the top of it was a sphere of offset rings that rotated feverishly around a radiant, red core much like ADIM's. Three towering, metal arms rose up to support it like a tripod, rising past the power core to hoist up a boxy structure, which not only served as living quarters for those who worked the mine, but that was fitted with jets underneath. In case of volcanic activity rupturing the excavation site it could lift off and safely carry the drill away with it.

Anti-air artillery was positioned on the ridge beside him. It posed no threat, but there was a time not long before when Earth was contested, when a violent crusade was waged by factions throughout the Circuit over who would control their Homeworld. The Earth Reclaimer Wars came and went, and in their aftermath only the Tribune remained. They promised to heal the dying world as man continued to puncture its surface in pursuit of the one element enabling humanity to subsist.

He neared the site, pulling up behind the turret. There were scanners left over from the war, but they were only searching for traces of life. The only thing ADIM had to worry about were the three, lumbering Combat Mech's patrolling the vicinity.

In the distance, molten rock began oozing out of a tall peak, glowing vibrantly like a trail of rubies where all else was obscured. He waited for a moment until the ground started to rumble from seismic activity. The timing was perfect. Each of the Mechs turned to observe the minor eruption. ADIM sprinted down the hill, his feet landing without a noise, and laid down in between the legs of the nearest one. Being that close would make his heat signature nearly imperceptible.

"How long you think this hole'll last?"

ADIM's enhanced auditory senses were able to pick up the pilot inside speaking to the others over his radio.

The Mech began to move with heavy steps that made the ground shudder even more intensely. ADIM sleuthed along, staying directly beneath the Mech as it neared the chasm.

"Yeah, you're right. I give it a month. Can't wait to get off this rock. Homeworld my ass. Give me the clean, glass sky of New Terrene any day."

ADIM quickly sprawled out and wrapped his limbs around one of the drill's massive supports. He activated the magnets on his palms and feet to remain secure against it. Then he waited there, making sure that none of the others took notice. A few mining bots scurried down the drill into the impossible depths of the mine like spiders down a web. They wouldn't take notice of him. They were inferior robotic constructs, built to perform only menial tasks.

There were lifts built into the outward facing surface of the cambered columns, but that was far too risky. When the Mech was at a safe distance he began to climb until all that was beneath him was an endless chasm cutting toward the core of the Earth. If he wasn't careful, even he would risk burning down there with long enough exposure.

After a long ascent he arrived at the bottom of the living quarters. The noise emitted by the layers of the drill rising and falling was deafening. The fusion core whirred, the rings around it revolving so fast they could cleave a man in half. Completely upside down, he crawled along the surface towards the core which was attached at the top by a thick duct. If he could heave himself toward the rotating blades and de-magnetize in time he would have direct access to the Drill's computer. But it would have to be perfect.

He got as close as he could, hung down by one arm and began to swing himself. *One Revolution. Two Revolutions. Three. Four...263 Milliseconds between.* The lights around his eyes whirled rapidly as he analyzed, and then, with no hesitation, he flung himself. His frame was barely able to twist through the tight space. The lower parts of his legs were slapped with such force that he was shot across the circular platform. When his imaging systems settled he scanned his lower limbs, but the plated exoskeleton was merely dented.

The inside of the sphere was as chaotic as the outside. The central core was comprised of even more revolving plates, all of them surrounding a smoldered reddish-orange core. Thick circuits were draped from it and weaved along the grated platform to more churning gears and blades below. The heat was excruciating, enough to boil a human without a highly protective outfit.

ADIM got to his feet. His balance appeared undamaged. He proceeded to approach the console at the base of the core. A HOLO-Screen popped up, prompting him to enter a password. As the Creator had figured, they were reserved for only the Tribune's master engineers in the rare case of a drill malfunction. They could scale down the small ladder falling from a hatch above him which led into the living quarters, but that was a rare occurrence. ADIM had all the time in the world to work.

Spreading his fingers wide, he placed them over the console. For him it would be no problem. Even cracking the Tribunes most complicated encryption was as simple as slicing through cloth with a hot knife. The screen flickered and his eyes began to stir as data streamed through him. It was only a minute or so, but when he pulled back, every ounce of information on what constituted Earth's Plasmatic Drills was transmitted.

He backed away and the screen faded. It was all too easy. *The Creator will be pleased that there were no casualties,* he thought as he grasped the base of the ladder and plotted his departure.

CHAPTER TWELVE
BINDING VOWS

Sage Volus waited in a seat on the main-tram rising up Pavonis Mons. It was mostly empty, not too many people heading to the Conduit that morning. She stared blankly out of the window, watching as the smooth, ruddy landscape rolled by. It wasn't that she cared much for New Terrene, but she hadn't ever been anywhere else for long. There were those few, all too short months on Earth, but she tried not to think about them. For almost all of her 26 long years of life, she had dwelled in the warrens below the city, and now she was being forced to leave despite saving thousands of innocent lives.

It was the path she chose, however. Nobody ever told her the life of an Executor would be easy, but when she took her vows death seemed all too enticing. She didn't crave it any longer, but Ceres Prime would be no vacation. She had heard that there was no greater haven in the Circuit for the base and corrupt. Not that it mattered. The Tribune needed her service and she would provide it as she always had, without reservation or doubt.

She glanced at the reflection staring back at her in the window. She hardly recognized the woman in it, probably because her hair was arranged differently to help disguise herself. Instead of wavy, auburn locks draping over her slender shoulders, she wore it in a short, straight style, temporarily dyed dark brown. But her pale, green eyes also seemed different, like they were sapped of their former luster.

She tried to force her lips into a grin, but it was hardly natural looking. From her hair, to the metal arm hanging from the stump of her shoulder, which was still throbbing with pain, she hated everything she saw. All she wanted was to smile one day again and mean it, but after so many years it seemed that day would never come.

"Miss…Miss…Miss!"

Sage snapped out of her trance. "What?"

"We've arrived at Midway Station. You gettin' off?"

"Yeah. Sorry." She rose to her feet and stumbled slightly. The sudden movement made her so woozy that she felt as if she were going to faint.

"You alright?" He tried to help her but she dodged him and caught herself on a seat.

Must still be from the blast, she thought as she shook her head back and forth a few times. "I'm fine." She shoved past him toward the exit.

She stepped out of the tram with her pistol hanging in a holster at her belt, alongside anything else she could possibly need… personal HOLO-pad, some rations, CP card, and of course the armor she wore. It was custom made for her, but unmarked as was typical of all Executors, a nano-armor suit with a composite plate fitted smoothly over her muscles. A set of double-layered pauldron's hung over her shoulders with armored sleeves that extended all the way down to her hands, covering her synthetic right arm. There was a day when it was probably a beautiful set, but time had weathered the white and amber ensemble.

She couldn't, however, go traipsing into Ceres in a suit of nano-armor without raising suspicion. Her masters took care of that. This time Agatha Lavos was the name prescribed to her, the orphaned daughter of a wealthy smuggler family working out of the Vergent Cell. She spent her whole life with her aunt and uncle working as a traveling merchant throughout the Conduit Stations. When they died, she requested a CP card and left it all behind to make a life on Ceres Prime. All the history was there, lovingly fabricated by the Tribune to make her identity as real as any other. Sprinkle in some facts about how her parents died and why she was drawn to Ceres Prime, and the character was complete.

Some of it was based on truth. She never knew her parents. Just that they died toward the end of the Earth Reclaimer Wars when she was an infant. But they weren't rich, and neither the armor nor the pistol were actual heirlooms. They were a gift to her from someone she loved before she ever came to serve the Tribunal Council directly.

This was the life of an Executor, to be as amorphous as a shadow. Even though they all served the same purpose, none of the others would ever know who she was and vice-versa. They were guarded by their anonymity. As far as the outside world knew, Sage Volus never existed.

Serena and Paulus Lavos. Killed in 494 K.C. by Tribunary forces outside New Terrene. She recited the story over and over in her head as she navigated the landing platform of Midway. *Agatha hates...I hate the Tribune and want vengeance for my family. The Ceresian Pact can help me.* It was a simple story, but sometimes that was better, less room to make mistakes. Although nobody in Ceres would probably care where she came from as long she could prove her worth with a gun.

She stopped to take a deep breath. The air was fresher than she was used to in the depths of New Terrene. It made her feel a little bit better. She couldn't tell whether or not her head was pounding from thinking too much, but she knew she had to relax. There was nothing to be afraid of. Expertly trained in the arts of combat and subterfuge, if she couldn't convince a few Ceresian grunts that she was worthy of their cause then she didn't deserve to be an Executor anyway.

A huge projection of Tribune Benjar Vakari suddenly rose through the tall atrium of Midway's northern spire like a bluish, semi-translucent statue and began speaking, "People of Mars. This is Tribune Benjar Vakari speaking on behalf of your Tribunal." Benar spread his arms and the rest of the Tribunes appeared behind him in a straight line.

Sage began riding up the escalators weaving throughout the massive station. Hundreds of people were strewn throughout, some of them waiting for the next Solar-Arc, most of them homeless. Guards were everywhere, most densely stationed near the mobile merchant stands set up at every level.

"Trust in the spirit which binds us, the Spirit of Earth dwelling deep in your soul," Benjar continued. "Together, we will deliver mankind to a new golden age, one of green pastures, of life outside these walls."

Wares from all corners of the Circuit were presented. People could come and barter with traders who tried their best to remain unaffiliated with any particular faction. They accepted almost anything, from food to possessions, but were mostly interested in acquiring what was known as Pico.

It was a currency which remained in existence amongst the Ceresian Pact and the fringe settlements lining the Vergent Cell. Since generating gravity was crucial for humans to be able to colonize the Circuit without being adversely affected, it was a credit system backed in a certain volume of Gravitum. One Pico could very literally be converted to one Pico-unit of the element. It was a system generally eradicated throughout the colonies of the New Earth Tribunal, reserved for only the wealthiest citizens who affiliated themselves with outside parties. It was, however, necessary to negotiate personal passage on one of the Solar-Arcs, making it almost impossible for most people under rule of the New Earth Tribunal to ever leave the settlement of their birth. Sage had a small amount wired into her counterfeited CP Card—the last of the wealth left to her by her fictitious parents.

Joran handed Benjar's projection a glass tube containing a wiry plant suspended in the water within. He presented it proudly. "There is hope," he said. "One day we will all return home. But we must remain faithful."

Her heart skipped a beat as she saw what was in the Tribune's hands. She almost tripped as she arrived at the platform where a small accumulation of people awaited the transport that would rise into the Conduit. Just seeing the plant made her short of breath. The memory was a haze to her, but she had been there the day it came to life. That tiny, pathetic piece of life was more than just a symbol of the Tribunal's faith to her, it was a piece of her that she could never reclaim.

The holographic Tribune placed the plant aside, causing Sage to almost bump into the man in front of her. "The cowardly dissidents of the Ceresian Pact will try to strip us of that faith," Benjar said sternly. "But I urge you to ignore their heretical rambling!" The face of the projection was at her level. The eyes pierced through her as if speaking to her directly.

I am a knight in the darkness, a vessel of their wisdom. I am the silent hand of the Tribune. I will not lose faith amongst the faithless. She repeated those words over and over in her head. It soothed her, made her forget that she had ever seen the image of that wiry plant.

"They raid and pillage our unarmed ships! They attempt to strike us at our very heart! But we will not be dismayed!" The walls vibrated as the authoritative voice rose to fill the entire atrium. "The New Earth Tribunal is here for you." Then it quieted to a passionate whisper. "Here for Humanity."

The transport arrived and the crowd began to file through doors. Sage almost missed it as she listened to Benjar's enthused message, hearing the last words before she fell into line.

"Together. We. Can. Not. Fail."

CHAPTER THRTEEN
AN HONEST LIVING

22 Kalliope was one of the latest M-Type Asteroids in the Circuit to begin being mined extensively. The craggy exterior was wreathed by deep channels and voids, holes cut so deep that they were like the eye sockets of a polished skull. After years of exploitation it seemed to have no more metal left to surrender, but the asteroid belt of the Ignescent Cell was fertile. In truth the surface had only barely been scratched.

"Let's tear this son of a bitch down, Julius," Talon Rayne, a Ceresian miner employed by the Morastus Clan, said over his com-link as he lifted his head up from a pile of explosives at the base of a gnarled pillar. He wore a clunky Enviro-suit with a bulbous helmet that was so filthy it made his cobalt eyes difficult to see. It was an older model, but it got the job done, providing sufficient air and protection in the inhospitable tunnels within the asteroid. It was weighed down enough too. So far from the residential block of the colony there was little gravity reaching from the generators. Exposure for too long could irreversibly affect the body.

"Roger that, Tal," Julius responded from the cockpit of a Mark II Quarrying Mech. There was static on the channel, typical for as far underground as they were.

Talon gave the pile another look before retreating around the narrow mouth of the cavern. A group of men in similar suits awaited him as the Mech positioned itself in front of them.

"Blow it."

A small explosion lit up the area around the rock pillar and caused the whole space to shudder. Fragments spewed out, peppering the armored front of the Mech harmlessly. Then the sound of widening cracks came like rumbling thunder before the far ceiling came crashing down. The miners stumbled a bit, wincing as even their suits couldn't drown out the thunderous clamor.

"You girls havin' fun listenin' from back there?" Julius quipped as his Mech slogged forward over some debris. The cloud of dust quickly began to vanish into the vents of a vacuum on either side of the vehicle's midriff.

"Gets louder and louder every time," Talon remarked, wearing a smirk as he wiped the grime from his visor.

"Never get tired of watchin'."

"How's it look?"

"Scanners goin' wild. Looks like we knocked the vein down right on top of us."

"Well boys, let's get to it."

It was all in a day's work. A hauler drove up from the back loaded with machinery and smaller carts. The Mech would do most of the heavy lifting, utilizing the two powerful drills built into its arms. The rest of the crew of six operated the smaller pieces of equipment, which served to further break up pieces, sift out undesired materials and transport the extracted ore. That was pretty much all there was to it. It was arduous work, but an honest living.

Talon had gotten used to the clamor of churning drills echoing throughout the yawning caverns by then. He approached the site where debris flew at him in a constant drizzle. Crouching down, he began loading up one of the pushcarts no differently than he had done a hundred times before.

"Nice and steady now," Bavor, the miner balancing the barrow, shouted over the racket. He was a tall, impressive specimen of a man. What he lacked in intelligence he made up for with a hulking frame fit to labor for hours at a time without tiring. Talon noticed him eyeing him with an irritated glare as he moved sluggishly. It was no secret that there was bad blood between them.

"I got it," Talon panted. He hoped nobody could notice, but his arms were trembling so intensely that it was fairly visible, even through the hefty sleeves of his suit. The muscles up the length of his limbs began to burning as they hadn't since his first day working the mines.

A thousand times before he'd lifted similar chunks of cold rock, most of them heavier than the one resting on his forearms at that moment. *It's happening,* he thought just before the rock suddenly tumbled out of his grip, slicing across the side of the cart and tipping it over.

Bavor fell backward, cursing. When he was able to get to his feet he charged over the spilled rubble, hoisting Talon up by the chest-plate until their eyes were level. His face beneath the dusty visor was boiling. "You fuckin'..." He strained to think of an insult before tossing Talon aside like a doll out of frustration. "We don' get paid by the hour!"

Talon growled. After almost a three month shift he was growing tired of Bavor's brazen nature. His legs were quaking, but they had just enough energy to spring him forward. Right before he made his move a massive metal arm came between them.

"Enough out of you, Bavor!" Julius threatened over the com-link, his baritone voice immediately commanding respect. "Tal, you alright?"

"Yeah I'm good. Just slipped." Talon grasped the metal arm, which heaved him up to his feet.

"Man's too weak to be liftin'!" Bavor growled and began tossing the spilled rocks into the cart to show how easily he could do it alone.

"Shut it." Julius urged his Mech forward with a few colossal footsteps until Bavor stormed away in a huff. Then he turned so that the cockpit viewport was visible. Talon looked through the murky glass to see the dark skinned face of his oldest friend. They couldn't speak it on an open channel, but his tightened expression seemed to be asking, "*It's happening again isn't it?*"

"Son of a..." Julius murmured under his breath as Talon nodded meekly in response to the look. "Take over the hauler from Vellish."

Talon didn't say anything. He stood in place with a blank stare, trying to ignore the throbbing sensation running up over his shoulders.

"That's an order."

He wanted to protest, but Julius was right. He'd be of little help doing the manual labor, especially with Bavor on his ass. Kicking a bit of rock, he headed toward the hauler waiting at the mouth of the cavern.

"Lil' girl can't handle a day's work." Bavor nudged him in the chest as he passed.

Talon clenched his fists, but he didn't bother looking back. The two of them had shared many scraps before, but with his muscles failing him he knew it wasn't the right time.

Chapter Fourteen
More Than a Face of Stone

It had been weeks since Cassius dispatched ADIM to Earth in order to acquire plans for a Plasmatic Drill. He stood on the glass-enclosed terrace of his compound, looking out upon the landscape of Titan. It was said by scientists that the world resembled how Earth may have appeared long before life walked its plains. Cassius didn't see it. On the surface it was fatally cold and dim, and dead as the Ancients had left their homeworld. A dense, bluish-brown haze hung perpetually overhead, with the shadowy profile of Saturn and its ring darkening half the sky. The sun was barely visible during the day, and at night the stars were obscured by the shadowy bodies of half-a-hundred small moons.

His compound was built into the shallow ridge wrapping around the rim of a relatively small impact crater known as *Ksa*. The floor of the rounded basin was a darkly colored plane of frozen dirt littered with small ice rocks. It was hazy, a strong wind churning around the bowlish void to stir up the precipitation falling from a thick, greyish cloud. In the center there was a peak and through the murk he could see a tower rising from its crest, tapering up to a silvery point. It was the Hub of Edeoria, the first colony settled in the Nascent Cell by Cassius' ancestors. Beyond it a Conduit Station floated out of view, servicing all of the moons of Saturn.

Unlike New Terrene, Edeoria did not rise in glass spires to scrape the sky. There was an inadequate amount of sunlight to make such a strategy necessary. Instead the Ksa crater was stippled with dozens of earthscrapers. They sunk into the ground like reverse towers, creating hollowed out atriums wrapped by program dug into the sides. At the top of each of them was a sequence of metal jaws, which sealed them from the frigid environment. Blue lights dotted their rims, mirroring the look of a clear night sky as they glittered throughout the basin.

Cassius took a deep breath as he looked upon all which was left to him. He had run from it for so long, but in the end he wound up in the same exact spot as his father before him. Unwrapping his fingers from the rail, he stared for a long moment at the spot beneath where the metal had been slightly tarnished over the course of centuries. Millions of souls resided in the tubes beneath the surface stretching out before him, but he never considered it a home.

He remembered what his father used to tell him when he was a boy, how in the early days of the Circuit, when humanity's continued existence hung on by a thread, settlers arrived to colonize the satellites of Saturn. It was an exciting time for them, when worlds such as Titan and Enceladus with known regions of water were to be seen under closer scrutiny. There was hope that perhaps humans could one day live in such places without enclosure, or even that life itself might have lain dormant beneath the surface. But like most discoveries throughout the age of the Kepler Circuit, good news was an unwelcome guest. From Venus to Pluto, no worlds were suitable for men to walk. There was not even the smallest microbial organism to be found.

"Creator, this unit has arrived undetected." ADIM's voice announced through Cassius's com-link to snatch him from his reverie.

Cassius had been waiting there with the intention of trying to spot the *Shadow Chariot* as it pierced the veil, but apparently his gift to ADIM had slipped right by him. It didn't dismay him at all. Despite Joran Noscondra's endorsement, the frequency of Tribunal patrols around Edeoria had increased in recent days. Nora Gressler may have been the overseer of his region from her citadel on the nearby moon, Enceladus, but Cassius knew Benjar Vakari was the one coaxing her to keep an eye on him. He imagined it would be better that they hadn't yet discovered the android, ADIM, whom he had built in secret against Tribunal Law.

"ADIM, I'll meet you at the docking bay," Cassius responded before exiting the terrace into his personal chambers.

It was a spacious room, the smooth, metallic enclosure bearing a shimmery, white tint. A wide bed with sheets of silken, red fabric rested in the corner. It was made cleanly, as though it had never even been used before. Other than that, the room was empty. There was nobody else inside. There were no pictures on the walls. It was just how Cassius liked it, completely silent, desolate.

He turned out into the adjacent hall which was lined on either side with soundless, holographic busts of his ancestors. Two shallow troughs of water ran beneath the podiums, the water sitting still as stone.

When he arrived at the corner of the next hallway, he was surprised to see ADIM already standing there. The Docking bay was further down through the complex, but there ADIM was, standing in front of a sealed doorway with his eyes spinning rapidly.

From only listening to ADIM's voice, it was almost impossible to tell the connotations behind his words, but Cassius had learned that the manner in which the smaller lights rotated around his red eyes was an indicator. The faster they spun, the more tirelessly his cognitive functions were working to fully comprehend the situation. The slower, just the opposite. But there were thousands of variations in between. He wasn't always sure, but Cassius imagined what he saw to be vexation.

He approached slowly, but there was no reaction. ADIM's sensors were fixed on the stark door nested unassumingly into the wall. There were no words on the serrated metal, but through it was a shaft descending into the depths of Titan where an underground lab resided. He had forbidden ADIM from ever seeing the contents of that place, where he claimed all the recorded memories of Caleb resided. In truth it was where heartbreak drove him to create ADIM, and where the mechanisms required to construct more, similar androids remained very operational.

"This unit would have desired to meet the creator's son," ADIM stated without averting his gaze.

Cassius made a concerted effort to ignore the comment. "ADIM, are you alright?" he asked. He placed his hand on ADIM's back in an attempt to guide him away from the door. It wasn't the first time he had caught ADIM standing vigil at the one place in the compound from which he was prohibited. Cassius wasn't sure if it was frustration that drew him there. He wasn't even sure if ADIM could truly get frustrated. Instead he often figured it was the same type of curiosity that draws a child to defy what he is told to do, just to gauge the consequences.

"Yes Creator." He turned his chaste face to Cassius. It was without expression, but for those stirring, red eyes. "This unit was merely curious as to whether a son, by definition, must be human?"

Cassius pulled ADIM away and they began walking down the corridor. "What do you mean?" he asked, unsure why his voice suddenly held a hint of apprehension.

"Before losing transmission within the Earth's atmosphere, the Creator inferred that this unit may be a son, as Caleb Vale was to you."

Cassius took a moment to consider his response. *I'll have to be more careful with what I say around him. Sometimes I forget how malleable the mind of a juvenile is, whether metal or flesh.* "Biologically, no," he answered, "but we humans are so much more than meat and blood. A son, you cannot be, but my child, yes you are."

"But not like Caleb," ADIM inferred as they turned into the hall of holographic busts.

Quicker than a human child, he sees right to the depth of my words, Cassius thought before saying, "You may have not been birthed from the womb, ADIM, but I created you, nonetheless. I loved Caleb more than I can ever convey—"ADIM stopped moving, and the abruptness of it made Cassius forget his train of thought. He was staring toward the tall window at the end of the passage, the images of generations of Vales lined up down his peripheries.

"Do you love…" He held out his hand and rotated it to examine both sides. "This unit?" Trying not to get choked up from the talk of his son, Cassius turned to ADIM and offered the only answer he could think of. "I gave birth to you. I am your Creator, and you are my Progeny. No mere word can express my devotion to you."

"Is that what love is?" ADIM's eyes began to churn more wildly than Cassius had ever seen them before.

How can I explain such a thing? Cassius wondered. It didn't take long for him to realize that he couldn't. An emotion so powerful that it stirred up tears and blood and war without relent. An emotion so profoundly Human. He settled on the truth. "As best as I can define it, ADIM, yes." Then he turned and placed his hand on the podium above which the effigy of his father, Nihlus Vale, was projected. "All I know is that the significance of blood is a manmade conception."

"A man can feel love for whomever he chooses," ADIM said categorically as he glanced at the bust.

"Or whom he chooses not to," Cassius grunted, steering his gaze away from his father with a sneer.

"Did you not love your creator? Your biological father?" ADIM used his holographic camouflage to cover himself in the very image of Nihlus Vale.

"I remain indifferent," Cassius said, immediately realizing how the bitterness in his tone betrayed the words he thought he meant. "I can't say that I hate the man, only that he was unworthy of this great gift our ancestors left for us. When the Tribune arrived to occupy Titan, when they came with their massive fleet before the height of the Earth Reclaimer Wars and demanded our unwavering patronage, he handed over this place without so much as picking up a gun."

"This Unit has learned much of the wars from you. Based on the size of their fleet this seems like the proper course. Probability of victory was minimal." ADIM deactivated the projected skin of Nihlus and leaned forward over the bust. He reached out into it with one finger, the tiny pixels of light splaying around it and painting the metal of his arm with a blue sheen.

The response slightly irritated Cassius, but he did his best not to let it show. "A human does not simply lay down his rifle and kneel before his enemies without a fight. That was the day I witnessed the cowardice of my father. The colony of Titan died that day. It became just another righteous arm of the Tribune, and so did I. Once we see our parents' failures, there is no room to remain a child. I chose to serve those strong enough to take all that he had, and I didn't see him again until his body was burning to ashes, rejoining the Spirit of the Earth, or whatever it is they call it these days." Cassius sighed and patted the altar of the effigy a few times. The memories alone were enough to make him weary.

"Is this why many of the humans aboard the Tribune vessels combated this unit? They must have known death was inevitable, yet they too raised their weapons." ADIM tilted his head around, his neck twisting so far that it chilled Cassius. He had killed many a human in such a manner.

"We are often not rational beings. The best of us can balance that emotion, use it as both a shield and a pointed edge to overcome our enemies. It has taken me a long time to do so, and I realize now that my father's cowardice may also have saved thousands of pointless lives. But at what cost? The culture of Titan died with his memories as it has long escaped mine. A miraculous victory or even a narrow defeat, and our names could have been celebrated for centuries to come." Cassius paused. The silence from his creation could only mean that either he understood, or was waiting to process more information before judgment. "One day my bust is meant to be featured in his hall amongst my ancestors. To be seen by nobody. I would not have it here."

"The Creator does not wish to be remembered?" ADIM watched curiously as Cassius moved down the hall to the bust of Caleb Vale, where his lips began to purse in repressed rage.

"I do!" Cassius affirmed, his words coming out sharper than he intended. Then he looked back at the bust. *Caleb, you don't belong here,* he thought sullenly as his eyes unfolded upon the projection of his human son. Just looking at the static face made his blood boil and the hairs along his arms stand on end. He turned back to ADIM. "I just want to be remembered as more than a face of stone or a painting on the wall. I want them never to forget."

"This unit will never forget." ADIM moved in front of the statue and assumed its identity; the youthful, expressionless face of Caleb Vale. "This unit will make sure all humans remember."

Cassius turned to his creation and grasped him by the wrist. "We will together," he said earnestly, trembling as he looked upon the image. ADIM quickly shifted back to his ordinary state when he noticed the pulse of his Creator hastening.

Cassius let go and staggered backwards, as if snapping from a deep stupor. He wiped his eyes before quickly turning ADIM around and heading back toward the docking bay. "Now, let me show you the fruits of your work on Earth."

CHAPTER FIFTEEN
STRENGTH ENOUGH TO FIGHT

The Elder Muse wasn't much in the way of luxury, but the mining colony of 22 Kalliope had little to offer in such regards. It was literally a hole in the wall. The cold metal shed was half-submerged into rock beneath the asteroid's stony, upper crust, with walls so austere that it looked like it was never intended for use. The hanging lights fizzled and chattered as the tremor of miners working deep below resonated. It was like something out of the old world, but for the miners it was a second home.

"Another fuckin' ace?" Julius flicked the cards out of his hand in obvious frustration.

"I'd say that makes two of a kind, eh Talon?" Vellish smirked, twiddling a pick between his teeth.

"By the end of the night you're gonna' be a poor man," Talon snickered. He took his time placing the winning hand down, enough to rub it in.

"Night's keep endin'...I still wake up poor," Julius grumbled as he leaned over the table to haul in the cards.

"Don't we all?" Vellish lifted his drink and everyone at the table clanked their mugs together.

There were four of them, each dressed in their casual garments with creases forming along their eyelids from a long day's work. Julius sat across from Talon. He was a tall, burly man with big, expressive eyes and skin as dark as charcoal. The others were Ulson and Vellish. They were fairly generic looking men amongst miners with not much to distinguish them apart from Vellish's crooked nose and Ulson's neck-length hair.

They were playing a game of cards, one of the few sources of entertainment available in a mining colony. There were no women except for the few brazen enough to work the pits, and they were rarely considered worth looking at. Gambling made the days go by. A slot in the table in front of each of their seats allowed them to place in their CP Cards. There they could access their Pico Credit and put money on the games. Big bets were prohibited so nobody got rich, but a good player could double his profit from a single mining cycle if he was careful. Talon was that player, so crafty he could hardly get a game outside of his own crew anymore.

"Aye, bot!" Julius signaled to a rusty android strolling around the bar with a tray on its outstretched palm.

It was fairly archaic in appearance, built years before the Tribune's genocide of unpiloted automatons during the Earth Reclaimer Wars. Afterwards, robotics had become a mostly forgotten art. The colonies of the Ceresian Pact made use of the few models that managed to survive the Circuit-wide cull. Their simple programming, however, only allowed them to fulfill basic services.

"Another round over here. On me." Julius tapped the table a few times as the robot took its time reaching them.

"Fucking things take forever," Talon groused. Watching the bots work only ever made him irritated. Worse now that he knew his lease on life was steadily hurdling toward its end. They moved stiffly, like they were being worked by talentless puppeteers, and always stared forward with impassive, white panels for eyes.

When it finally arrived, Julius handed over his CP Card and the machine read it with a scanner fixed into its wiry chest before rigidly placing down five drinks.

"Thank you for your purchase at *The Elder Muse*." It played an aged recording of a man reading the name before its hips swiveled and it proceeded to another table.

"Cheaper than a man I suppose. But ain't no way one of them could ever handle the mines." Julius wasted no time snatching up his drink. Everybody else followed his lead and lifted their glasses to say cheers to the sentiment before bringing the glass of bluish liquid to their lips.

It was Synthrol, water infused with a certain synthetic toxin that mimicked the effects of liquor. Alcohol was one of the rarer commodities throughout the Circuit, so much so that Talon was sure none of the men sitting in that room had ever been fortunate enough to try the real thing. But Synthrol did the job well enough for them, and for a small fraction of the price.

"Couldn't have said it better myself," Talon said. As everybody else took a hearty gulp of their drink, he barely took even a sip. He didn't want any more. One sip was enough to take away some of the ache from his muscles, but he had to make sure he kept his edge mentally. Everyone around the table may have been his friend, but he desperately needed the credit.

"Alright, my turn to deal." Talon grabbed the deck from in front of Julius and began to dole out cards in as nonchalant a manner as possible.

"You hiding something under those gloves?" Vellish joked before straining to swallow too big a gulp.

Talon froze for a moment, squeezing on to the stack of cards as he nearly forgot where he was in the order. Across the table, Julius almost choked. The whole room was reduced to a lonesome hum. He wanted to come clean and it was only a matter of time before someone besides Julius pressed the matter. Nobody was a stranger in the mines, but what they didn't know was that he was dying. Slowly and surely his body was withering away from the Blue Death. The effects were beginning to show themselves on his hands, so he had been wearing gloves daily for the past few weeks.

"Tal?" Vellish snapped his fingers in front of Talon's eyes.

He snapped out of it and the familiar din of *The Elder Muse* filled his ear drums. "Nothing but hands," he affirmed and began dealing again, trying not to make eye contact with Julius, who was solemnly shaking his head. "I promise."

"Bet he's got his girl watching us from the rafters or something," Ulson chimed in.

"Or maybe I'm just better." Talon placed down the remaining cards. "Enough talk. You guys still have credit for me to steal!" He took a long sip of his Synthrol, throwing aside his original strategy in favor of peace of mind.

"Not this time," Julius declared before peeled back the corner of the cards to see what he was dealt. What he saw made his eyes droop. "I hope," he sighed.

The game went on. The drinks kept flowing, and for once Talon didn't seem to have an edge on his competition. He didn't care. It was a small price to pay for how good his body started to feel and how clear his oft-troubled mind grew.

Suddenly the door of the Elder Muse burst open.

"What a surprise!" Bavor scoffed as he stormed through. "Too weak for your shift, but here as usual playin' mindless games." His face was still caked with grime and his brawny chest seemed ready to burst through the fabric of his boiler suit.

"Leave 'im alone, Bavor." Vellish shooed him away without bothering to look up.

His head dizzy from too many drinks, Talon decided not to back down a second time. "It's a game of cunning and percipience. Seeing as how you probably don't even know the meaning of those words, we'd all probably be better off if an *intelligent* man such as yourself stayed out." Talon took a long sip of his drink, swishing it around in his mouth before slamming the glass down on the table. "You know. Just to give us a fighting chance. "

The Synthrol may have eased the soreness, but it didn't make him any faster. Before he knew it, Bavor had hoisted him up by the chest.

"What the fuck did you say?" Bavor growled, his nostrils flaring as his nose pressed against Talon's. His breath smelled as foul as the very depths of the mines. The rest of the table quickly got to their feet and it seemed like all the others throughout the *Elder Muse* were caught in a collective gasp.

"Comon' Bavor. We're all just trying to have a good time after a long day." Julius put his hand on Bavor's shoulder, but was immediately shrugged off.

"Didn't realize your hearing was just as poor as your brain," Talon sneered, and as he went to grin, a heavy fist crashed into his jaw. Before he could fall back he was flung across the table, tumbling onto his stomach with the wind knocked out of him.

"He was just kidding!" Ulson shouted as the rest of the crew grabbed Bavor to hold him back. The entire room jumped to their feet, crowding around the spectacle.

"What? Little girl can't take a proper beatin'?" Bavor broke free of the others with an amused grin. "Bet his bitch'd be tougher than him. I ought to give her a run back home."

Talon snapped. Growling like a mad man, he jolted forward

from his knees. Another blow met his ribs, but intoxicated and in such a blind rage, he felt nothing even as they crunched. He grabbed a mug and smashed Bavor across the temple with it so hard that the big man howled and lurched over. Then, evading a wild swipe, Talon grabbed him by the head and slammed it into the edge of the table. Blood spurted out. Frantic hands pulled at Talon before he could hit the head again, causing him to stumble backward onto a pile of squirming bodies.

"Tal?" Julius whispered into the ear of his friend softly as everybody scrambled to get their bearings. It was the only noise in a room that seemed frozen in time.

Talon said nothing. He panted like a wild beast at the end of a hunt. Bavor was slouched against the table, the side of his head split open. Blood percolated over mashed skin and splintered bone, dripping down over his still twitching eyelids.

Talon stared at the corpse. He had seen enough dead bodies in his time to know Bavor's time had come. He hadn't meant to kill him, but that wasn't what caused his initial astonishment. The Blue Death may have weakened him to the point where carrying out his job was nearly impossible, but there was still strength enough left to fight. Just that small recognition was enough to bring the slightest smile to his lips. That was until he realized exactly what he had done.

Chapter Sixteen
Secrets Beneath Edeoria

The *White Hand's* vertical thrusters brought it to a slow hover over Edeoria: Shaft 23, a sunken residential zone near the edge of the crater. ADIM guided it down slowly as the first of the metal jaws unfastened. Wind and dust battered the hull, but he kept it steady as the ship lowered into the hollow. Once through, the first entrance resealed and a second one below opened up to the contained area of Shaft 23.

Illuminated terraces wrapped the cylindrical void with wide streets of circulation receding back to hundreds of residential unit entrances. Each of these levels was uncharacteristically over-crowded with people, however. Hammocks were slung along the railings and people huddled around happenstance shanties. These displaced citizens were an unfortunate side effect of Cassius' plotting. He took a moment to analyze their grimy, sullen faces. It only strengthened his resolve.

ADIM steered the ship further down and into a gutted hangar at the lowest level before another sealed, shaft entrance. Cassius looked out of the viewport to see a unit of Tribunal Soldiers waiting on the surface beside a small transport. All of them wore oblong helmets with shiny, black visors except for the apparent leader.

Cassius sighed. "Make yourself scarce, ADIM. I'll try to get rid of them," he ordered as his ship's engines powered down.

"Yes, Creator. This Unit will be watching."

Cassius headed out to the hangar, already fairly confident about why the soldiers were present. He tried practicing his most convincing smile before the *White Hand's* exit peeled open.

"Friends. What brings you to Edeoria?" He settled on his

usual, grim demeanor.

"I am Hand Belloth. We come on the behalf of Her Eminence, Tribune Gressler," the handsome leader pronounced as he took a step forward. He spoke with an unfettered sense of self-importance. Ribbons of green and gold decorated his armor of similar coloration, the gold hand printed on his shoulders indicating that was a Tribunal Hand. "Just standard patrol," he continued. "The area below has been quarantined for quite some time. Her Eminence wishes to inquire why. You will allow us to survey the area."

The move was too bold for Nora Gressler. A Hand was far too high in position to be sent for ordinary surveillance. There were only four of them, one assigned to each member of the Tribune. Where the Executors were the clandestine agents stationed around the circuit, the Hands served directly as an extension of the Council's will. They were advisors, commanders and diplomats, amongst other things, and answerable only to the Tribune. Cassius could sense Tribune Vakari's hand behind his presence on Titan.

He looked around. There were a few Edeorian guards around the hangar, but they would do little in a firefight. He wasn't even sure that they would side with him, being that his quarantine had forced thousands from their homes.

"I will allow nothing," Cassius responded coolly. "You can tell your masters that the area remains confined for good reason. That will have to do, Hand Belloth."

"It won't." Belloth placed his off hand on the stock of his rifle, making sure that Cassius would see. "I'm on strict orders from Tribune Gressler. You will provide access."

"Or what?" Cassius scowled. He returned the favor by slowly sliding his hand toward the pistol hanging from his belt.

"Or you will waste more of Her Eminence's time! What are you hiding down there anyway?" It was becoming evident that the Hand was looking for any excuse to goad Cassius into a firefight.

Cassius went to speak, but then he heard ADIM's voice in his ear. "Shall this unit rob them of their lives?" He glanced from side to side, but there was no sign of the android anywhere. Then he looked to Hand Belloth and responded, "Nothing," while shaking his head to signal ADIM not to strike. "But I doubt you and your men want to enter a district with a severe Gravitum leak. Unless you do." He moved around the soldiers with a spry gait. "In which case I'd be happy to send you wallowing back to your masters with the Blue Death."

"Gravitum leak?" Those words garnered Belloth's attention. He took a nervous step back. "Are you sure?"

"No. As the purveyor of this colony, I want to rid these fair citizens of their homes. In fact I'm hiding a bomb down there just to kill them!" Cassius laughed heartily and placed his hand on the Hand's shoulder. "Now please. I must meet with the maintenance officers to discuss the matter and I'd rather not have Tribunal soldiers scaring the color from my people's cheeks."

Belloth quickly shook the hand off with a grunt and lifted his rifle in a threatening manner. "Fine. But we'll be watching, Tribune Vale," he grumbled irritatedly before signaling his men to return to their ship.

Cassius waited until they were all inside before shouting out to the Hand just as the hatch was shutting. "Oh and do give Benjar Vakari my regards!" Then the vessel powered on and lifted off. He breathed a long sigh of relief. After so many years of planning, it was too early for any drastic measures to be taken.

"Forgive me," the head engineer running the hangar apologized as he stepped out of an adjacent room. "They had Tribunal clearance codes."

"It is no matter. Next time send them directly to me."

"Yes, Your Eminence." The engineer clasped his hands together and bowed.

"Now open the access hatch. I must inspect the quarantined area."

"Are you sure it's safe? With the leak and all?"

"I said open it, and do refrain from questioning my motives in the future," Cassius said with a harsh edge creeping into his voice.

"Forgive me, Your Eminence. I hope the matter can be resolved soon. My family—" The engineer stopped, his eyes widening fearfully as Cassius's hard expression didn't budge. He backed away with a succession of bows before hurrying back into his quarters.

After making sure the *White Hand* was locked, Cassius headed toward the back of the hangar. The handful of Edeorian guards in their shoddy, gray armor tried not to stare as he disappeared around a corner.

"My sensors indicate that there is no Gravitum leak," ADIM said, but the voice wasn't directly in Cassius' ear.

Cassius flinched as all of a sudden a section of the wall began to move and ADIM came walking forward. His holographic camouflage had allowed him to blend in flawlessly.

"Do refrain from doing that," Cassius begged. He took a few lengthy breaths to steady himself before responding, "No, there is no hazard."

"So you are not in danger?" ADIM questioned, moving himself in front of a maintenance door, which led down into the quarantined area. The engineer had already had it opened.

"No, ADIM, but the Circuit cannot yet know what it is we are doing. We must hide the truth until the time is right."

"This unit understands. We must lie to them, to protect them from themselves."

"Exactly. So that we can offer a brighter future."

They descended the cramped stairwell, emerging into a space very much like the one above it. Only this area was completely uninhabited. It was silent, the dull buzzing of light fixtures the only sound to fill the many terraces plunging toward blackness. Three massive stilts of metal rose from the unseen bottom to the level on which they walked to hold a cylindrical casing in their center.

"That is the same as the drills on Earth." ADIM expressed as he looked over the rail to see how enormous the construction was.

"Not yet entirely. I'd been working on it while you were infiltrating the freighters, but I had some trouble configuring the Plasmatic Drill. With the data you recovered, however, it shouldn't be too hard to finish."

ADIM held out his hand and a projection of the drill on Earth, broken down to its smallest components, began spinning slowly above his palm. "Where are the construction units?"

Cassius joined his creation at the edge of the precipice and stared at the hologram. "You have been very busy lately. I was hoping that we could work on it together, like old times."

"As on Ennomos?" ADIM looked to his Creator and if that

blank plate stretching down from his eyes could wield a smile, then Cassius imagined it would have.

"Yes ADIM. Soon our work there will be revealed, just as it will be here. Our time is coming swiftly. We must be ready."

"This unit would be—" ADIM glanced down at his hand and then, as if mimicking Cassius from earlier, grasped him gently around the forearm. "Honored. Humans use that word in similar circumstances. Is this Unit's application correct?"

"Yes." Cassius reached down to touch the metal limb. "Yes, it is. And the honor is mine... my son."

Chapter Seventeen
Pawn of the Morastus

The tops of Talon Rayne's feet scraped along the coarse ground as he was hauled through a tunnel somewhere in the depths of Ceres Prime. Lines of clear, sharp pain shot up his torso, with a dull ache pulling at his sides every time he breathed. They had hardly asked him anything during the interrogation. They knew he had nothing of value to offer, but a few more cracked ribs was an easy way to get a message across.

He tried to focus on the confusing mass of dark shapes shuffling by but his vision was too blurry. Only when the floor transitioned to smooth metal did he know he was almost there. He squeezed his eyes a few times to try and sort out his aching head before he was uncouthly shoved into a seat. Hunched over, his bound hands resting between his legs, he looked up through a mess of tangled hair to see a familiar face.

"Talon, Talon, Talon," a man repeated with a sinister delectation. "After all these years we're right back where we started."

Talon had to squint to get a good look at him. He was handsome, with a young face that had neither a scar nor a blemish. His primly feathered blonde hair fell down below the nape of his neck. Hungry blue eyes protruded against his typical Ceresian, pale skin.

"Zaimur Morastus, did you really need to beat me half to death first?" Talon grumbled, licking some dried blood off of his lower lip.

"It is the only way some men learn." He grinned and nodded, signaling the two guards flanking Talon to lower their weapons and step to the side.

Talon didn't know much about Zaimur personally, only that he often flaunted his riches for all of the Circuit to see. Denuded, beautiful woman sat on either side of him on a plush couch, sensuously fondling the inner collar of his clothing. He wore a long, silken tunic stitched with a colorful assortment of golden yellows and blues, and with pronged pauldrons swooping up from either shoulder like crests of iron feathers.

Even as the women caressed and patted his neck with kisses, he paid no heed. They were mere props. Instead he kept his eyes fixed on Talon, his hand tenderly stroking the snout of a long-legged dog, its icy glare fixed just the same. The beast was probably worth a hundred of the woman. Talon had seen only a few in his time, but no specimen so strikingly laced with muscle. Few species of life escaped Earth but for man, and that dog was probably worth an entire mining colony to the right buyer.

"Magda is beautiful, isn't she?" Zaimur ran his hand over the one of the dog's pointed ears. He then planted a kiss on the top of her lean head, causing the two women on either side of him to frown slightly in their desperate pursuit of affection. "Won her from a nasty pirate out on the Vergent Cell. Bastard put up quite a fuss, but she has a tremendous appetite." He grabbed her beneath the jaw, causing the beast to bare her unsettling fangs.

A shiver shot down Talon's spine. If the Morastus Prince's reputation wasn't exaggerated then it was very likely he could wind up as dinner if he wasn't careful. "I've never seen one this close before," Talon marveled. Magda's ravenous eyes glinted like pearls with the light, and he couldn't help but stare into them as he gripped the arms of his chair tighter.

A severe look washed over Zaimur's face." Always so serious!" He broke into laughter and leaned back on the couch, allowing the women to continue their massaging. "I would never let her eat your tainted body. Though I have no doubt she could."

Talon released the gulp of air he hadn't realized he'd been holding. "If you're not going to kill me then why am I here?"

Zaimur leaned forward and grabbed a glass goblet. As he brought it slowly to his lips, the cubes of ice inside rattling, the pungent aroma of real alcohol stung Talon's nostrils. It almost made him tear up a bit.

"Bavor may have been a slow-witted oaf," Zaimur began in a surprisingly calm manner, "but he was as strong as a machine and ignorant enough to want for nothing. Perfectly suited for the mines. I don't care why you killed him. I don't care if he deserved it. He was an asset to my clan, my father's clan, and you will make us whole again."

"If it's money you want, I can take another shift, or—" Talon stammered before being cut off by Zaimur shaking his head.

"We have enough miners. Hell, if it were up to me we'd have replaced all of you with robots if they were good for anything but looking intimidating or working bars! Damn, Tribune's cull set us back a century," he grumbled and took a sip of alcohol. "Anyway, on your way over I was thinking, 'maybe we could throw him into the arena and see if the Talon Rayne of my father's memory is more than just a tale.' But I fear you're too worn to be of any use down there."

"He still talks about me, eh?" Talon sat up, trying to illustrate some semblance of the bravado he wielded those many years ago.

"My father is barely a shell of his formal self, a vacant shadow waiting to die. But know that if you weren't so highly regarded for your past services to him then you would have never left Kalliope alive."

"You'll have to extend my gratitude."

Zaimur almost choked on his drink as he snickered, "You were once an enforcer for my father, leader of the wealthiest clan of the Ceresian Pact. Was the offspring of some worthless tramp worth giving up all that you had earned?"

"She is worth everything!" Talon roared, lurching forward before being promptly slammed back into his seat by the guards.

"There he is. I knew he couldn't be too far gone." Zaimur placed his drink down with a loud clank and smiled.

"If you hurt her!" Talon pulled on his bonds so hard that it made his wrists sting.

"Relax. I don't know what kind of monster you think I am to harm a child. I merely wish to offer a proposal that will end all of this conflict. One I believe can benefit both of us."

Talon let his muscles slacken. "I'm listening."

"I assume you've heard of the attacks on Tribunary Transports passing through our Cell?"

"Just rumors in the *Elder Muse*. Nobody could say for certain who it was."

"That's precisely the problem!" Zaimur got up from his seat and walked over to look at a holographic map of the Circuit in the open space adjacent to them. "Those ships are tracked and encrypted in a way I have understood could not be broken! No matter who I pay, nobody can seem to tell me where on this damn map the ships were taken. Circuit Gravitum shipments are hardly enough to keep the generators up and running sufficiently around the Cell. The Tribune needs our ore and water, sure, but nowhere near as much as we need the element they now control."

"It seems like you're going to ask me to start another war."

"War has been brewing again since the Tribune won Earth three decades ago, whether any of the clans want to admit it or not." Zaimur stopped and pointed to a location on the map along the far reaches of the Ignescent Cell. "We have discovered a small asteroid here. It is rich in iridium ore, a rare metal that will help protect our ships should it come to that. It is also in an optimal defensive position if they decide to attack from Mars or anywhere else in the Renascent Cell. I need that Gravitum in order to set up a station there."

"You want me to rob a personal transport of the Tribune?" Talon's eyes widened, though he wasn't sure whether it was out of excitement or dread. There was a time when he would have jumped at the chance to take on such a mission…a suicide mission in all likelihood.

"In so many words… yes." Zaimur whistled and the dog ran to his side.

Talon looked to the floor and exhaled, "I gave up on that life."

"Yes I know. To survive! Because every child should grow up with their father." Zaimur approached Talon and lifted his arm to carefully inspect it. He pulled back the sleeves, revealing the faint, abnormally blue veins branching over his bicep like a strand of twisted vines. "But the mines have failed you in that regard, have they not?"

Talon didn't say anything. His heart began to beat so rapidly that he thought it was going to burst from his chest.

"When that Gravity Generator exploded on Kalliope, I'm guessing. When was it, a little less than a year or so ago?" Zaimur traced the veins up to Talon's shoulders. Talon didn't nod, but his eyes divulged the truth. "Someone always leaves with the Blue Death when that happens. My father got it that day as well, you know. A slow moving affliction, though it took his old body quicker than it's taking yours. The poor man was once a general and now he can't even get up from his own bed to take a piss. He would have spent anything to find a cure, but some fates have no remedy. As you know."

Beads of sweat rolled down Talon's forehead, and it was all he could do to keep himself from tearing. *How could he have known?* He kept denying it to himself.

"Don't act like it's a surprise to you. I heard what happened down there, plus I don't think those tired eyes are just from them." Zaimur gestured to the guards. "I'd say you have two years or so left at best. You're still young. Is that long enough with your precious daughter? Is that long enough to keep her from the couch of another rich man? I didn't kill you earlier, Talon Rayne, because you're dead already."

"Then why would a corpse help you!" Talon whimpered. The face of his young daughter filled his thoughts. "The Tribune is sure to add to the defenses of their ships with so many stolen recently. Why hasten my death sentence?"

"Because I have something that you cannot offer her." He leaned down to whisper in Talon's ear. "A chance to become more than those two beautiful woman over there. Look into their eyes."

Talon hadn't really cared enough to analyze them earlier, but their faces were scarred and their eyes sunken as if they had surrendered their will to live. His lip quivered as he transposed her face onto theirs with his mind.

"Get that Gravitum for me," Zaimur continued softly, "and I give you my promise to provide her the chance to serve me honorably, as you once did my father."

"I trusted Zargo. How do I know I can trust you?"

"We share the same blood. Plus, there are plenty of pretty girls out there. It is no expense on me to help her, Talon. You killed Bavor and owe me a debt, but I bear no ill will toward you personally. I could just as easily send you off to the Keepers as I should, but I offer you this opportunity in good faith. My father trusted you to get the job done. I will trust you to do the same. Succeed or fail, I will make sure she is taken care of. I reward the men in my service well. Perhaps, had my *distinguished* father done the same you would have never left him for the mines." Zaimur patted Talon on the back and returned to his seat, the supple legs of the women immediately wrapping over his thighs as if a part of a living throne.

"I don't really have a choice, do I?" Talon sighed, slumping back in his chair and staring at the slowly rotating map of the Circuit.

"I'm not so generous with those who spur my kindness," he said calmly, but his face was stern, those fierce, blue eyes boring through Talon like daggers.

"I'll do it. But we're gonna do it my way."

"Excellent!" Zaimur's expression lightened. "Recruit whomever you trust, and ensure them that they will be paid handsomely. I will provide all the resources you may need, just try to keep my involvement as quiet as possible."

"I'll try, but people usually like to know who they're working for before they like give up their lives.

"And they will. Once you're ready, I will personally review all of them. I'd like them to know that the Gravitum is for someone important. Just in case." Zaimur put on a crooked smile.

"Of course." Talon nodded and returned a similar expression. "One problem. I don't know if I'll be able to deactivate the tracking systems. Tribune will probably disable the ship."

"I don't care about the ship! Just get me what it's carrying. And who knows, maybe our little venture will unveil which of the other clans has been licentious enough to take half a dozen transports in the shadows." Zaimur snapped his finger for one of the girls to get up and refill his drink. "Bring him one as well. I see the makings of a beautiful partnership." He grinned widely and nodded at his guards, signaling them to unbind their prisoner.

Talon sat still as the cuffs came off, half staring into space and half trying to judge the quality of his new employer. A drink was placed in his hands. He had tasted alcohol before with Zaimur's father, but at that moment he didn't want any. All he wanted was to go and see his daughter again—to hold her in his arms for as long as he could. But at least he was still alive, and as he brought the rim of the glass to his dry lips, he knew that was a notion worth drinking to.

CHAPTER EIGHTEEN
THINGS CHANGE

After leaving Zaimur's chambers, Talon headed to the Underpass, the network of underground mag-rails which traversed the sprawling, subterranean conurbation that was Ceres Prime. When Earth fell, the asteroid Ceres, the largest in the solar system, was found to have a surplus of water. Beneath its porous outer crust was a layer of water ice so thick that the colonies of the asteroid belt thrived even before the establishment of a Conduit. There was little in the way of ore, but the countless cavities beneath the surface made it a perfect specimen for controlled, underground environments. Tunnels and caverns, some man-made like the Underpass, crisscrossed the subsurface to form a city second only to New Terrene in population.

It was mostly empty by the time he arrived at his line, which took him to West 534, a housing district known mostly for producing savvy mercenaries and prostitutes. There were more indecent places to live on Ceres however, where even the gravity generators were so obsolete that over generations, the people there had grown slightly taller and lankier to make up for the deficiency.

That was how most Ceresians lived, toiling in their own filth as they scraped for a living extracting water in the depths of the asteroid or working what small underground farms were possible. It was getting worse though. As the rift with the Tribune widened, only the bare necessities came in or were sent out along the Circuit. Talon could sense the apprehension every time he was home. People were beginning to fear that the Tribune was even gaining control over the Keepers of the Circuit.

The housing district itself took up a massive cavity filled with an agglomeration of small, metal shacks piled in no real order.

There was a sort of sublime quality, with shafts of corrugated metal weaving in and out of crags and outcrops of natural formations. It had the look of an industrial hive with a tall domed construction popping up in the center where his tram was headed. Neon lights poured through the openings in its latticed structure, painting the whole district in an undulating aura of shifting colors.

Dome 534 was its unimaginative name, and where the people of that district and many others congregated at night to lose track of time. It wasn't the finest club in Ceres Prime, but it was by far the most entertaining…a home to weary souls, degenerates, addicts, gamblers, strippers, synthrol, and last but not least, gladiatorial combat. Even some of the leading figures of the banking clans ruling over the Ceresian Pact would make an appearance from time to time.

Talon got off at the station in front of the club, beneath a twisting canopy of iron peeling away from the dome. He brushed some of the dust off of the dark-blue tunic Zaimur had provided for him then he followed a small crowd to the oversized, triangular entrance with only a loose canvas hanging down to serve as a door. There a human guard was flanked by three robots. The guard himself wore a bland suit of light, composite armor with a tarnished blue and gray color pattern, the colors of the Morastus Clan, the faction of bankers who regulated *Dome 534* and its district. They were run by Zargo Morastus, Zaimur's dying and increasingly incapable father. It was a well-known fact that he suffered from the Blue Death like Talon, and though anybody who was discovered to have the affliction was to be sent off to serve the remainder of their days as a Keeper, wealth was a powerful ally.

"CP Card," the guard groaned from beneath his tinted visor. With his unarmed hand he held out a scanner bearing a small HOLO-Screen.

Talon pulled his card out of his pocket and handed it over. It didn't cost anything to get in, but in the colonies of the Ceresian Pact, the card carried more than money. It was a person's identity.

"Talon Rayne." The guard nodded and began stretching his gun-wielding arm. The loose parts of his battle-worn pulse-rifle clanked together.

"Welcome to Dome 534. Please remain orderly or force will

be necessitated," one of the robots advised with its monotone voice.

They were newer machines than the ones on Kalliope, but it was hard to tell from their shoddy construction. Each of the three wielded a Pulse Rifle, though they were no good in a firefight. Every Ceresian knew that. They could hardly move without causing a racket as loud as a group of shooting pistons, and outside of serving bars and other menial tasks, they were essentially useless. They weren't quick enough to avoid fire, nor were their targeting systems efficient enough to hit a moving target. But they lasted long enough, and were content doing the grunt-work humans didn't care for.

He remembered what Zargo Morastus used to tell him whenever he lamented about one of the hunks of metal standing guard. 'The Tribune's genocide against robotics set us back a hundred years in the science. There are a few experts here and there, afraid of what to do next until we see who'll rule this Circuit of ours.'

"Move along."

Talon winced as he was nudged on one of his bruises by somebody pushing past. He was going to say something before deciding it was better not to start another brawl so soon. Instead, he took a deep breath of the musty air before peeling open the sheet enough so he could squeeze through.

The pungent stench of sweat, blood and sex greeted him like an ephemeral wall. It was probably enough to make newcomers nauseous, but after the first inhale, Talon grew accustomed to it. Sometimes he feared that he even liked it. Everywhere else he had been all over the Circuit doing Morastus' bidding, the air was equally stale and artificial.

The club was alive. People were shouting, drinking, dancing, fighting and fucking. Electronic music pulsed like a hastened heartbeat with vibrant lights following the beat. Talon felt the heat emanating from all the hundreds of bodies, a stark contrast from the frigid mines.

"Tal!" Julius yelled from the bar with an ear-to-ear grin as he saw his friend pass through the noisy dance floor. His tall frame made him stick out over everybody else.

"Julius." Talon returned the grin and gave his friend a light embrace. "Where are the others?"

"All turned in already. Buncha' pansies. But there is somebody here for you." Julius stepped to the side, revealing a young girl, no more than six, waiting patiently behind him. She was small but well fed, with rosy red cheeks accentuated by her dark, messy hair. On her face there was the innocent but smug expression a child wears when they know their plan worked.

Talon's eyes lit up before he rushed to her. He fell to his knees, and threw his arms around her, pulling her to his chest until her small voice became muffled. Her tiny hands struggled to wrap around his sides, but she reached as far as she could. It didn't matter how much his bruised sides hurt from her efforts. His arms began to tremble and his eyes began to well, but he held her for as long as possible, and imagined that he was the happiest man in the Circuit.

"Her mother's been takin' care of her. Hasn't she, Elisha?" Julius asked her playfully.

Talon could hardly hear a word she said as she began muttering endlessly into his chest. When she was done he held her at arm's length and stared into her beautiful, blue eyes.

"How was the mines, daddy?"

"Its... uhh." He flashed a grim look up at Julius. He had done what he could to make sure none of the contusions across his body were showing and that the blood was washed off his mouth. "It's great, Elisha, but I missed you." He pulled her head closer and kissed her forehead gently. The cut on the inside of his lip still stung a bit.

"Where've you been?" Elisha's brow furrowed as she crossed her arms. "Julius said he'd teach me how to play cards."

"I said I'd let you watch!" Julius laughed and hopped back onto his stool at the bar. "I swear, Tal, the girl's as crafty as you sometimes."

"He said that did he?" Talon sat down next to his friend and lifted Elisha up onto his lap. "Trust me, you don't want to learn from him," he whispered in her ear. "He's terrible."

Elisha giggled loudly. "You teach me then! I'll take all his Pico like you do."

Talon hurried to shush her, but looked up to see his friend

with a crooked smile. "Steal my money do you?" Julius said. "How 'bout you use some of them to buy me a drink then! I'm parched."

"Fine, fine." Talon motioned to one of the robots behind the bar. "Two Synthol's, a water, and what kind of pills do you have today?"

"We have Nutrient Supplement A2 and 3 at the moment," the robot's metallic voice responded from beneath its static face.

"I'll take two of each." Talon place his CP card in a slot on the top of the bar. When he pulled it out there was a soft, accepting 'bing,' and the robot went to retrieve his order. He watched it move with aversion, tapping his finger on the bar as he thought about how much faster he could have readied the simple order.

"Did you eat today?" He turned to his daughter after he saw that the robot was finally finishing.

"With mommy before her shift," Elisha responded.

"That's hours ago." He took the glass of water from the robot's grasp and gave it to her. Then he picked up two elliptical pills from a small tray, which rose from a duct in the bar. "Take these."

She wrinkled her face and shook her head defiantly.

"Comon' Elisha, it's good for you," Talon insisted. "I'm too tired to argue."

Reluctantly Elisha let him drop them into her palms and he watched as she took them one at a time with exceptionally long sips of water. The glass was so big that she needed two hands in order to lift it to her mouth.

The robot placed down two shots of Synthrol. Talon put his pills in his mouth and snatched his shot up. Then he and Julius clanked their glasses together before quickly tossing the bitter tasting drink back.

"Not often that Talon Rayne buys me a drink," Julius said as he wiped his lips. "How much *did* you win back on Kalliope?"

He stroked Elisha's hair, wishing he could remove his gloves to feel it. He wasn't sure how to tell Julius the news, but decided to come right out and say it. "It's not that. Zaimur made me an offer."

"I thought you were done with them?" Julius tried to pretend he didn't notice the bright bruises running around Talon's wrist as his sleeve pulled back.

"I am. I mean, I was. But..." he lowered his voice so that his daughter wouldn't hear him over the music. "Julius, I don't have that much time."

"Don't talk like that!" Julius said with a sharp whisper.

"I'm just being honest with myself, finally. I guess it took what I did to Bavor to realize that."

"The bastard got what was comin' to him. You know that. We all know that."

"I don't care about Bavor!" Talon snapped. "I care about her." He looked down to see Elisha falling asleep on his lap with the glass balanced between her hands and legs. He gently pulled it away and let her head fall to rest on his forearm.

"Ain't that why you stopped servin' his father in the first place?" Julius attempted to urge one more drop out of his drink, probably to mask his worried expression.

"Things…" He glanced over Julius' shoulder to see Elisha's mother, Vera, approaching in a skimpy leotard that she might as well have not been wearing. "Things change. We'll talk about it when we're alone."

Vera smoothly swept around Julius to place a kiss on Talon's lips before he could deny her. She had an undeniable grace, and even though she was so thin that her ribs showed there was no questioning her beauty. Short, tidy black hair fell just above her shoulders to frame her soft face. But as lovely as she appeared, her outfit told the whole story. She wasn't Talon's wife. The only bond they had was the daughter they made, despite their best efforts not to. She was a professional prostitute and a good one too. Truthfully Talon hated leaving Elisha with her and her capricious ways, but he didn't have a choice. All he could hope for was that the miracle sitting on his lap wouldn't grow up to be some fleshy toy like so many Ceresian women.

"Hey handsome. Didn't know you were back so soon," Vera said before kissing Julius' cheek. The giant man couldn't help but blush and Talon couldn't blame him. Her touch was as addicting as Synthrol and as toxic Gravitum.

"Vee. I like your outfit."

"Shut up!" She slapped him playfully on the arm and then embraced him around the back. She brought her moist lips close enough to his ear to send a shiver down his body to the tips of his toes. "You fuckin' love it."

Talon tried not to smile, but seeing Julius' attempt at trying not to get caught staring got it out of him. "Comon' Vee not in front of her."

"Don't think you were gettin' lucky cause you just got back." She let go of him and slid over to place herself between him and Julius. "I'm too tired anyway. Those Morastus thugs sure know how to handle a lady." She re-adjusted the bottom of her leotard.

"Better than me?"

"Always fishin' for compliments." She leaned over seductively and stopped just in front of his face, biting her lower lip. "You were the best." She pretended she was going to kiss him before reaching down to pick up Elisha who was fast asleep. "Now let me take her off your hands. My shift is over. I'll let you two lovebirds enjoy your first night in paradise. "

Talon brushed his daughter's hair. "We won't stay long." He placed as lengthy of a kiss on her forehead he could manage with his cuts before hesitantly releasing her into Vera's arms.

"Stay as long as you want. And don't be shy with the rest of the girls." She gestured with her head to the cages from the ceiling throughout the club. Half-naked women danced suggestively inside of them—all of them for hire. "I'm sure they'll be gentle." Then she sauntered away, leaving all of the men along the bar who happened to get a glimpse of her salivating.

"Damn." Julius marveled until she disappeared through the reveling crowd. "When are you gonna tie that girl down?"

"She's all yours if you want her." Talon was already facing the bar, staring into his empty glass.

Julius laughed and wrapped his arm around Talon's shoulders. "Have I ever told you you're the best friend a man can have?"

"Not enough. " He flashed a grin as he motioned for the robot bartender to come over. "I'll get us another round. We can talk about business tomorrow in private after we've settled in. See if you can get Vellish and Ulson to come too."

"Sounds good to me."

CHAPTER NINETEEN
ANOTHER END OF THE CIRCUIT

Sage stood on the Conduit Station above the asteroid Ceres, watching as the Solar-Ark she had arrived in faded into the void of space. Her head was still throbbing so excruciatingly from the disembarking process that she had to stop on the landing platform to lean on the railing. Her human thumb and forefinger were wrapped around her temples, squeezing ever so gently to try and alleviate some of the pressure.

It wasn't her first time aboard one of the Solar-Arks interweaving the Circuit, but it had been many years, and she had forgotten how strenuous it was to get on or off. The ships went so fast that they could reach Pluto in nine days from the sun, so she wasn't surprised that her brain felt like it was going to tear through her skull. All the other passengers were complaining about the discomfort as they walked past her, but the technology the Ancients produced to sustain a human through the transition continued to amaze her despite how much it hurt. Somehow magnetic and Gravitum induced systems had brought her from a fraction of the speed of light to a complete halt alive. The concept was enough to make her head spin if it weren't already pounding so intensely.

She waited until the shimmering-golden solar sail of the Solar-Ark appeared like the faintest star in the blackness. Then she slowly began to make her way toward the terminal where all of the other passengers were headed.

The newly repaired Executor implant inside her dulled some of the pain, but only enough to make it somewhat tolerable. It couldn't help the fact that her legs were sore from remaining still aboard the Solar-Ark for almost five days. They weren't much in the way of luxury, and being confined to a tightly secured seat didn't make her shoulder feel much better either. Every time she moved it too much it stung as if someone was gradually sliding a thin blade into the muscle and trying to pry it apart from the artificial arm.

"Please proceed to the Ceres Spaceport as quickly as possible," a soothing, female voice spoke over the speakers. "The Landing Terminal air-lock will be released in five minutes."

As much as she didn't feel like rushing, Sage had no desire to be sucked out into space. She used the sill to pull herself along, wincing with every step until she caught up with the crowd. The doors sealed shut behind them as they passed into the Ceres Spaceport.

It wasn't as clean or polished as Midway Station, but it was at least double the size. A similar massive, airy room was filled with at least a dozen floors, but there were no projections of the Tribunes rising through the many atriums to instill hope in the Ceresians. Like Midway, each level was bustling with merchants from all over the Circuit, but unlike it they also branched into other subsidiary terminals with localized shuttles. For Ceres, Spaceport wasn't just the hub of a single planet, but for all of the Asteroid Belt and Ceresian space.

She wasn't sure which way to go, so she stayed close behind the largest group of travelers that broke away, assuming that most people would be heading toward Ceres Prime. Merchants desperately tried to show off their wares, but she kept her head down and ignored them. She figured that if she was going to be playing the adopted child of Conduit Merchants then she'd be better off staying away from their kind. One wrong slip of the tongue and she had no doubt that any worthy trader would be able to see right through her guise.

One of them pushed his stand out in front of her to offer custom made silverware. She almost banged it, but the pain throughout her body was lessening with each step and she managed to avoid it. Another offered chairs fashioned from fused together scraps of broken down ships that she couldn't even believe stayed upright. In fact all of the wares she saw being sold were unequivocally mundane, but they were things she never imagined could be purchased—a plate to call your own, or even a strange looking statue made out seemingly useless materials. In her shack on New Terrene she had a mattress, a light, and a locker to keep her belongings all provided by the Tribune. Everything she saw seemed like such a waste, though even she couldn't help but be impressed by Ceresian ingenuity as much as she didn't want to admit it.

The group led her down a wide set of elevators, presumably leading toward the Ceres Prime Terminal. At the landing there were more merchant stands, but those ones didn't seem as harmless to her. She stopped in her tracks. Hanging from racks were the powered down chassis of robots. Before she knew it she found herself standing right in front of one, analyzing it from every angle.

"Aye. That one there is an old service bot. Won her in a game of cards out in the Vergent Cell. Probably been around since decades before the Earth Reclaimer Wars, but she can still help you with repairs. I'll tell you that," the merchant out in front proclaimed.

Sage didn't bother responding. Just the look of it sent a shiver down her spine. She had heard that there were robots which survived the wars and the Tribunes warranted cull, but she had never seen one before. The way its metal, rusted frame tried to mimic a human body—the way its mouthless face seemed to be staring at her with dull, white-panel eyes as if it were innocent. It was enough to make her feel sick.

"You interested? She's yours for 10,000 Pico."

She? Sage thought to herself. She wanted to smack the man for referring to the abomination as if it was alive, as if the Spirit of the Earth possibly ran through hunks of metal and wire like they were human. The only thing she was interested in was doing the work of the Tribune and tossing the merchant's entire store over the railing.

She reached out with her artificial arm to grab it by its artificial neck, but then she stopped. The metal of both her hand and the robot were of the same shade. Her lips began to tremble.

"Say something or move along."

"Just looking," Sage growled as she pulled her arm back to her side and brushed passed the merchant. *Destroying them would just get me caught.* She justified it to herself, but as she continued onward she couldn't keep her eyes from drifting toward the synthetic hand sticking out from beneath her armor. *I will not lose faith amongst the faithless.* she repeated to herself, shaking her foggy head as she followed the group through a wide entrance into the Ceres Prime Terminal.

There was a small transport ship at the opposite side of the long line the group she had been following began to form. It wasn't moving too slowly. She found that it was much quicker for security to scan a CP card than to take retinal scans, as was the Tribune's protocol.

She fell into it, making sure to appear like she had done it before a hundred times. She didn't want to risk exposure again by addressing how strange everything was to her, but that didn't keep her from carefully analyzing her surroundings. The people who hadn't arrived from New Terrene were incredibly pale—as white as the tundra of Mars' poles. They were noticeably longer too. Not that they were all taller than the people she was used to, but they were lankier, as if someone had tied two ropes to their arms and legs and pulled. She had always heard that the Gravity Generators in the lesser regions of Ceresian colonies were meager, but she had never seen the proof firsthand.

The man in front of her, however, was as hulking as anybody she'd ever seen. He was a tremendous specimen, with a neck as thick as a tree trunk and muscles bulging out of the short sleeves of his tattered shirt. It wasn't just her who noticed either. As the line moved forward a child nearby seemed to notice who he was and came running over.

"You're Culver aren't ya? The Hammer of Pallus Major," the boy said excitedly.

"What's it to you?" Culver responded gruffly.

With her head feeling as close to normal as it had in days, Sage listened closely to their conversation.

"I've seen you fight in the arenas a dozen times! Please, please tell me you're headed to Dome 534 this week?"

"Course I am, kid. Now bug off." He gently shoved the boy forward toward the security guard at the entrance of the transport.

Sage wasn't sure what would greet her on Ceres Prime, but the word 'fight' was all she needed to hear. She knew that no Ceresian had any chance against an Executor.

The man called Culver presented his CP card to security before stepping onto the transport. She pulled hers out of the satchel on her back and did the same, half-ignoring whatever the guard said as she watched to see where Culver was going. She had no doubt that the Tribune forged card would work, and it did without a hitch. When the guard had finished looking her over, she stepped onto the ship and strapped herself into a seat as far away from Culver as possible where she could still keep an eye on him. If what she had heard about Ceresians was true, then she knew that they were a rugged people. There was a great amount of respect to be earned by proving you could handle yourself in a fight, and she intended to put the rumors to the test.

CHAPTER TWENTY
SIMPLE ENOUGH

Talon was sitting on the edge of a precipice, which overlooked the entirety of the West 534 Housing district. It was a spot carved into the rockscape at the lower end of the blocks, secluded enough by two perpendicular walls of metal shanty that few other people even knew it was there. His parents used to take him there when he was a child and for whatever reason he kept coming back. It was quiet enough, far above the vibrant Dome to escape most of the hubbub. It gave him a place to be alone with his thoughts, but at the time it was a place where no prying ears would hear his conversation.

"So, what is it you brought us here for?" Vellish asked as he took a seat on a ridge of rock across from Talon. Julius was sitting next to him with sleepy eyes. It wasn't morning, but it was hard to tell the time of day in the dim, subterranean light anywhere in Ceres Prime. Not to mention that the lights of the Dome were always flashing. "And where's that beautiful little girl of yours?"

"She's with her mother for now. Where's yours?" Talon smirked.

"Mine?" Vellish looked to the craggy ceiling of the hollowed asteroid as he tried to think.

"Common Vellish. Really?" Julius gave him a playful slap on the back of the head.

"Oh I get it...Ulson." His face reddened as he chuckled meekly. "Very funny, Tal. Just cause Julius here ain't as tender don't mean you gotta be jealous." They all shared a laugh before Vellish caught his breath and answered the question. "He's with his real wife. I suppose we should all *actually* be jealous of that."

"I don't know. Things got pretty rowdy last night," Julius

responded. "Not sayin' I can remember all too well, but there were some beautiful ladies down there."

"Yeah, but he don' have to pay for his," Vellish cackled, taking the easy opportunity to try and make somebody else blush.

Talon struggled to hold back his amusement. "Alright, alright guys. We don't want to end this partnership before it even begins. Besides, who said that Julius needed to pay for anything last night."

Vellish's eyes widened as he looked at Julius. The big man only offered him a wink before his lips pulled back into a toothy grin.

"You guys are both fuckin' liars," Vellish said jokingly. He shook his head and leaned back against the rock. "Okay, that's enough of that. Spill it Tal, I plan on heading down to the Dome sometime before I die."

Julius flashed a nervous look at Talon. Death had been a shaky subject around him since he found out he had contracted the Blue Death. Talon nodded at him as if to say 'it's fine, he didn't know,' and then he carried on. Julius leaned in attentively to listen.

"I told a little to Julius already. The Morastus Clan has made me an offer to make things right after I deprived them of one of their best miners."

Vellish rolled his eyes at the thought of Bavor.

"I know," Talon agreed, "And if I had any other choice I would have told Zaimur to shove it up his ass. But you both know that's not an option."

"Hell if I ever got a chance to meet him personally, I'd sure hope that I wasn't still slavin' away in the mines..." Vellish said matter-of-factly before Julius nudged him in the arm. "No offense, but not all of us chose this life."

"I know. And you both know why I did, but this job may keep us all out of the mines for the rest of our lives."

"Now you have my attention."

"He wants us to intercept a Tribunal Transport on its way from Earth to Mars, and bring back all of its cargo."

"Now you're fuckin' lyin'!" Vellish exclaimed with a sideways glare. "What the hell is it carryin'?"

"Gravitum," Talon pronounced, accentuating each syllable. If Vellish and Julius were leaning in close before, that word almost made them fall forward off of their seats. "Most of the New Earth

Tribunal gets their stores from the Circuit, the same as we do," Talon continued. "Now I don't know how much you two know about it, but the clans are beginning to think that the Keepers are leaning in support of the Tribune. Every year since the War, our shipments have been getting smaller and smaller, while they thrive, and the Tribune's themselves have the nerve to personally attain Gravitum from the mines on Earth that they now control."

"I've heard rumors. Never thought anything more of it," Vellish admitted with a shrug.

"Well that's the truth of it. We have tons of natural resources the Tribune needs, water not being the least among them, but it's nothing they couldn't figure out how to acquire without having to trade with us anymore. We need Gravitum to survive, and they control the only source." Talon noticed them trying to mask their skepticism. "I know it seems impossible, but if the Solar-Arks stopped trading with the enemies of the Tribunes then we would be as fucked as the Earth."

"That's a big if, Tal," Julius finally chimed in. "In half a millennium no faction has ever been able to turn the Keepers from neutrality. What makes you think they'd do it for the Tribune?"

"In all the centuries since Earthfall no faction has ever controlled the entire planet. I'm not saying that they will turn completely. Hell, I don't even know if I believe Zaimur that they have been turning slowly for years. But there is another war coming, of that I have no doubt, and this time we will wind up the fathers that die in the fighting."

"So what does that all have to do with one shipment of Gravitum for one lazy ass Tribune?" Vellish questioned, the skin on his crooked nose wrinkling. "We'll need a hell of a lot more than that."

"Must be why there's been rumors of other Tribunary transports bein' robbed throughout the Cell recently," Julius considered.

"Couldn't tell you. Zaimur knows as little about that as we do," Talon clarified.

"But whoever's responsible for those attacks has somehow been able to avoid being powered down and tracked by the Tribune's security encryptions which we mistakenly thought were unbreachable. They've been taking the ships completely intact, and disappearing into thin air. Fortunately Zaimur only wants the cargo and doesn't care if we turn the transport into nothing but shrapnel."

"Sounds simple enough," Vellish said sarcastically. "What if we run into whoever these mystery pirates are while we're there?"

Talon opened his mouth, but wasn't immediately sure of what to say. He hadn't considered that possibility. "Well...then we'll just have to hope that they're on our side."

"I'd be more worried about the Tribune," Julius added sternly. "They're sure to beef up defenses eventually."

"Look," Talon sighed. He got to his feet and faced out over the tremendous hollow before continuing, "I won't force either of you. To be honest I'd rather you both say no and make this easy. I don't want to be the reason anyone joins me in death, but I don't have many people I trust. This may very well be a suicide mission for me, but I'll do whatever it takes to bring you back to Ceres alive." They all went quiet for a long moment, too long, and Talon couldn't help but fear the worst.

"You ever done anything like this before when you were with Zargo Morastus?" Vellish finally broke the silence and asked.

Talon began listing his accomplishments with neither pride nor disdain. "I've helped steal from all of the clan leaders in the asteroid belt. I've killed men for him that were born so close to the surface that I'd never have met them otherwise. I've commandeered ships with a handful of men, and I've escaped some all the same. But never of the Tribune, and never with so little to go on. I—" Talon began to gather another thought when two hands fell upon his shoulders. He turned around quickly to see Julius and Vellish wearing crooked smirks that told him all he needed to know.

"We're in, Tal." Julius said as he patted him on the arm.

"Hell, if I have to take another stint in the mines I'll kill myself anyway," Vellish added, his eyes glinting with hawkish enthusiasm Talon didn't even know they were capable of. "Let's blow those Tribune bastards back to the Spirit of the Earth, or whatever the fuck it is they believe in."

Talon was trying his best to hide his excitement, but he could feel the muscles above his mouth desperately trying to draw his upper lip into a smile. "I can't promise you'll never have to go back," he noted.

"We ain't ever had a choice before." Julius shoved him forward playfully, forcing Talon to give up on his attempts to remain stoic.

"I thought you guys would never say yes," Talon said, beaming. He lunged forward and wrapped them both in a heavy embrace. "Come on let's head down to the Dome. No better place in all of Ceres Prime to find mercs as mad we are."

"Hey, you're definitely the only madman here!" Vellish protested as Talon began to pull them toward the way down from the promontory. "We're just following along, right Julius?"

"O'course. Just two innocents trying to make an honest living."

"Keep it up." Talon tightened his arms around their necks. "I'll tell Morastus not to pay either of you."

"So serious all the time." Vellish ducked out of Talon's grip and began backing up in the other direction. "I'll meet up with you two later though. I'm gonna go talk to Ulson. We're gonna need a pilot and I know he used to run transports out of Pallus Major. I've heard there's no one better."

"He can wait." Talon stopped and protested, teasingly trying to grab Vellish back. "There are fights down in the Dome soon. Culver the Hammer. They say he's never lost. Could be perfect for us."

"Go on ahead. I've never had the stomach for those things. I'm sure you'll be able to find plenty of crazy fucks down there, but I'm gonna go get us a pilot." Vellish slipped away and hopped down a formation of bulbous rocks where Talon couldn't reach him.

"Suit yourself." Julius shooed him away jokingly and then put his arm around Talon's neck. "Screw 'em, Tal, his loss."

They headed back down to Dome 534 where the crowd was already building. Arena fights were a big part of Ceresian culture. The rich bet on them and sponsored the best, and the poor projected themselves onto warriors who also came from nothing. It was a necessary distraction from the lifetime of mining most of them endured.

The rules were simple. Fight until your opponent either surrendered or died. Most career fighters would surrender to live another day, but criminals thrown into one of the many arenas throughout the Ceresian Pact weren't giving a choice, and volunteers usually wound up dead before they had a choice.

It took a while for Talon and Julius to squeeze down to the front row, but Julius' size didn't hurt. The arena under Dome 534 was famous for its battles, even if it wasn't very opulent in nature. A cage surrounded the lip of a pit were the fighters would be unleashed. People without credit packed around the edge on their feet, while glassy, private boxes protruded from the surrounding rock walls above for those with it. Flickering HOLO-Screens projected around the cage for people who couldn't get a good view.

Talon leaned up against the cage excitedly as the fight moderator came walking out from tunnels beneath.

"My people!" the bearded man began floridly. He made a show of announcing, occupying the entire space of the arena as he spoke. "Today Dome 534 is happy to bring you a treat. He has traveled all the way from Pallus Major to take on your champion! But first I will whet your appetite. He will take on each and every one of your challengers as a warm up. You know him, you love him. The undefeated champion of Pallus Major, Culver the Hammer!"

The crowd went wild as from the darkness emerged a mountain of a man so built with muscle that it appeared to be a challenge for him to turn his head. He pumped his arms up and down like a conquering hero, taking in the applause as if it fueled him.

Julius looked to Talon. "You think he'd do it?"

"No, not him. But any volunteer mad enough to take him on might. If one of them survives that is," Talon responded.

The moderator turned to the other entrance into the arena. "His first challenger may be small, what but this woman lacks in size, she makes up in madness."

The whole world went quiet as Talon watched a woman emerge from the shadows. Her facial features were difficult to distinguish from so far away, but her green eyes were framed by dark hair, and glowed bright and fierce. The tight boiler suit she wore hugged the lithe curves of her toned figure, leaving little doubt that she was beautiful. He couldn't help but feel his heart break a little for a life he knew was about to come to a swift end.

CHAPTER TWENTY-ONE
THE TIGRESS OF CERES PRIME

Sage Volus struggled to regain her senses. Thick beads of sweat trickled down the loose strands of her tousled hair. She panted wildly from her knees, her hot breath bouncing off the rocky surface to warm the drying blood sticking to her lips.

The crowd grew more and more raucous as they anticipated her impending defeat. They rattled against the fence, saliva and drink spewing from their mouths like a mob of rabid animals. Their cheers, however, greeted her ears like a dull drone, barely discernible over her own hastened heartbeat. *Guess I haven't recovered as well as I thought,* she mused to herself as her fists ground into the uneven surface. She had only been in Ceres Prime for a little over a day, but finding a fight in one of the colonies underground arenas had proven all too easy. There was nothing so barbaric on New Terrene, but it was at least something she knew she couldn't lose.

A tall, brutish man approached her, his shirtless figure laced with dense muscles. He wore a wicked smirk, the kind that someone puts on when they know they've got their enemy on the ropes. The ground rumbled more vigorously with each nearing step. The crowd's enthusiasm augmented like a rising storm, but all Sage was worried about was settling her throbbing head so she didn't see two of everything. She had been in that position before, but she wasn't used to this lot of bare-handed brawling. *Just be patient.* She told herself. *Remember your training.*

Feigning defeat, she kept her head lowered. While doing that she unnoticeably re-positioned her limbs to be ready to pounce. Her artificial hand cracked the rock beneath her fist as she braced herself. There was no way to take her much larger opponent down with sheer strength—that she had already been assured of—but there was a reason she was an Executor of the Tribune. Her vision was still cloudy as she strained to keep her peripherals on the man's face, but it was enough. She waited until his brash expression made an effort to acknowledge the boisterous crowd. Then she shot forward like a bullet from a rifle, her shoulder burrowing into a set of crunching ribs.

They bowled over, slamming into the hard ground as Sage delivered a second paralyzing blow into the man's tender side. She rolled off quickly to avoid a rampant counterattack and took an aggressive grappling stance a few feet away. The brute roared as he forced himself back on his feet, charging her with a relentless flurry of un-aimed, but powerful attacks.

Sage reeled, using her attacker's own force to deflect the blows, but she wouldn't be able to withstand the barrage forever. Ducking under a swipe she rolled to the side, trying to ignore the scraping rock tearing across her back. Before she could evade it a powerful kick struck her in the stomach, lifting her off the ground and sending her sprawling into the craggy side of the arena. It was rare that she made a move too late, but she knew she had jumped into a fight far too quickly after the explosion.

Groping frantically as she wheezed, her artificial hand found a fragment of loose rock nestled in the corner. She could feel her opponent bearing down. Shifting from defense, she took up the weapon and jolted forward. There was an audible crack, the man's knee snapping brutally inward as Sage swung with all of her might. An insufferable scream of agony rang out. She then lashed upward in a wide arc, the rock smashing her opponent across the temple. The force exerted through the synthetic arm split the man's skull open like a sack of rotten fruits, causing him to crumble into a heap of tangled limbs.

At first the crowd released a collective gasp before thunderous cheers rained down from all around the small arena in Ceres Prime. Sage stood where she was. She paid them no heed as her eyes remained locked on the still-twitching corpse lain before her feet. The rock slipped from her fingers. She never enjoyed taking life senselessly, but she didn't care for the Ceresians. They were as the Tribune had told her—animals. Instead, what chilled her to her core was how little seeing the blood and brains trickle from the Ceresian's lacerated head affected her. *He was a Ceresian. He needed to die. He deserved to die*, she convinced herself before the arena moderator raised her arm in victory.

"My, my folks," a red-faced man with a thick beard announced to the hundreds of patrons packed against the raised, octagonal cage enclosing them. "The victor, by cause of death, is…" He whispered in Sage's ear, "what's your name again, girl?"

"S…Agatha Lavos," she responded wearily.

"Agatha Lavos! The Tigress of Ceres Prime!"

The crowd went wild as she was escorted through a tunnel carved into the rock wall of the ring. She had no idea what a Tigress was, probably some mythical creature from ancient Earth, but she liked the sound of it.

Once the door sealed behind them, the moderator's smile turned to a scowl. "Culver was undefeated. Gonna cost me a pretty penny killin' him like that."

Sage didn't respond. There was a pool of warm water in the center of the room, which had showers lining the rim and some benches beside them where the next fighters were waiting. None of them were women, and they took no care to hide their enamored stares as she walked by half naked and glistening with sweat. She dipped her hands in the water, washing the blood out from beneath her fingernails on one and out of creases in the metal plates of the other.

"I'll pay you two hundred Pico, but that's all I can do. They're going to kill me for this." The bearded man activated the HOLO-Screen on his wrist and began typing in some commands.

"I thought you said four?" Sage questioned coolly, not looking up from the basin. She didn't really care about the money, she had a part to play. She got the exposure she needed when she smashed a rock across Culver's skull.

"That arm of yours ain't like any I've ever seen. You may be a woman, but with that thing you might as well not be. Two-fifty, and that's all. But don't ever expect to fight in here again unless you cut that thing off!"

"Fine by me," she grumbled and walked over to her locker. She brought out her CP card and the moderator placed it in a slot on his bracer. Two-hundred and fifty Pico were transferred over before he handed it back and left to usher two more unlucky combatants into the arena.

"Didn't expect you to come walking back in, beautiful," a handsome man sitting nearby teased her as placed his hand on her side. "Don't listen to him, I like the arm."

She gripped his wrist with her artificial hand and growled, "You like it now?" She began squeezing so hard that she could sense the bones would crack if she applied any more pressure.

"Fuck!" He groaned and she let go. "Crazy bitch." He got up and hurried away, holding his wrist out in front of his shocked expression the whole way.

Sage smiled as all the men in the room stopped staring. She didn't like to be seen. No Executor did truthfully, but her more than most others. She grabbed her armor and weapons before stepping into the shower to wash and change into it. It was time to see what attention her victory would garner in the bar above.

CHAPTER TWENTY-TWO
BLUE AS THE ANCIENT SKY

Sage emerged from the lift leading up from the arena. She attempted to hide herself behind the tall bodies of guards standing on each corner of the platform, but there was no point in trying. The crowd surrounding the fence of the sunken arena immediately turned to greet her. Some shouted words of praise, but most of the men offered her drinks or a night in their company. She thought that changing into her armor would keep them at bay, but it only seemed to make them more ravenous. Not only was she a beautiful, female warrior who they had watched savage a brute twice her size, but living on Mars had made her tan, or at least tan compared to the milky skin of Ceresians

She ignored them all. She had a mission, and none of the ingrates begging for her lips were worth the time. Moving quickly to escape any conversation, she got lost in the sultry darkness of one of *Dome 534's* notorious dance floors. Colorful lights flashed and grooved with the pulsing music. The men were already so infatuated with the strippers flaunting their emaciated bodies in transparent cases hanging all around like ornaments that they hardly noticed her.

She was happy to escape all of the attention, but the crass behavior of the Ceresians was enough to make her sick. Sweat splashed on her from every direction as men and women danced in ways she could never have imagined. Slimy, bare legs wriggled with the music like a crowd of frantic worms. Tongues thrashed. Women moaned. And everybody seemed to be celebrating as if they had just won a war.

Sage was about to vomit when she reached a break in the noxious revelry. She wiped the sticky layer of sweat which had formed over her brow; whether it was hers or the Ceresian's she did not know. Then she headed toward the bar, only to find that there was a robot serving from behind the counter. Just hearing its cold, monotone voice taking orders didn't help the sick feeling in her gut, so she decided to find a seat at an empty table as far away from all of the clamor as possible.

When she pulled out the chair and went to sit, a sudden feeling of vertigo rushed to her head. She would have toppled over if the table hadn't been there to brace her. After the dizziness waned, it felt like a small creature was pounding on the inside of her skull with a hammer. She shuffled her hands along the arm of the chair until she was able to position herself and fall into it.

I am a knight in the darkness, a vessel of their wisdom. She began reciting the vows of an Executor in her head to keep calm. *I am the silent hand of the Tribune. I will not lose faith amongst the faithless. We are in eternal service to the Spirit of the Earth, which binds us. With the Tribune as our guide we will prove worthy of the home which breathed its life into us, life which we so selfishly brought to ruin. Extinguished will be the flames we have kindled. Light shall be the shadow we have bidden. The Earth will rise again.*

"Got somethin' on your mind, honey?" A large, dark-skinned man rested his big hands on her table. He wore a skintight, black suit with numbers demarking a certain unit over his chest. She hadn't been in Ceres Prime long, but she instantly recognized him to be a miner.

"I'm not looking for a drink so why don't you get lost?" She leaned on her still aching head and looked away. As she did that her hand slid inconspicuously down to her holster.

"Whoa!" The man's unexpectedly kind eyes widened as he took a step back. "Look, I ain't here for that. Since you don' seem too fond of wastin' time, I guess I'll cut right to it. The names Julius, and me and my business associate saw you down in the arena. Very impressive stuff. We got a job. A big one. And we need fighters to get it done."

Finally there was an offer that peaked her interest. "What kind of job? I'm not a miner if that's what you're after."

Julius released a resonant laugh. "Don't let the outfit fool you. I can take you to my associate, but I can't tell you here. Too many pryin' ears and such."

"You think I'm that easy? What is it you and your *friend* want? My armor, or what's underneath it?" She pulled up her pulse pistol and placed it on the table so that the barrel was casually facing in Julius' direction.

"You didn't grow up here did you?" He leaned over close enough to her so that anybody looking wouldn't be able to see the fact that she had drawn her weapon. "Why don' you put that thing away before we both find trouble."

"Trouble with who? There are no laws here. Are one of those bags of metal going to take me down?" She didn't need to see the robot guards in action to recognize their ineffectiveness. The Tribune had made sure she knew that. She also didn't realize her spiteful tone, which only must've helped Julius confirm his assumption.

"You must be really new here." He got even closer to her and whispered. "All I can tell you is the job involves Tribunary Freighters and a shit ton of Gravitum. Now I suggest you come before you really do get yourself into trouble."

She tried not to sound too eager, but her green eyes began to sparkle as she realized how lucky she was. "I'll come, but I'll have my eyes on you."

"Whatever helps." Julius sighed and began to lead her out of *Dome 534*.

She wasn't lying. Sage stayed right at his back with the hand at her side curled into half a fist. He guided her out of the latticed structure and through the tram station where stumbling drunkards waited and bantered over nothing. They moved up a winding pathway carved out of a cliff. The higher they got, the darker it was, and Sage was about ready to give up on the venture when they arrived at a flat clearing dug into the surface of a sharp promontory. A man in a navy-blue tunic sat with his feet dangling over the edge, staring off at the great cavity below filled with the flickering lights of metal shacks and the colorful dome.

The man turned his head, but it was too dark up there for her to make out any of his features. There were a few small lights set into the surface, but nothing too bright. "My father used to take me here when I was just a child," he reminisced. His voice was smooth and articulate, a breath of fresh air compared to the typical incoherence she found characterized most Ceresians. "Not many people come up here anymore. Our sad excuse for a park. Nothing as beautiful as the Conduits you grew up on I bet?"

It took her a moment to realize that it was a question. "I... How did you know where I'm from?" She stepped to the side so that Julius and the mysterious man were both in front of her. Her fingers wrapped quietly around the grip of her pistol.

"Well, for starters, it'll take a few months down here before your skin is pale enough for you to blend in. Since I already know you arrived recently, I'd have to imagine you're the beauty I've heard so many guards drooling over. They weren't lying," the man said as Julius walked over to sit behind him on an outcrop of rock facing her.

"I do miss seeing the sun," she replied, and she meant it.

"And now you're here fighting in the arena like some common brawler, though I can tell that there is nothing common about you. There was a time I took to those rocks. I bet they didn't care too much for a woman taking out their top combatant."

"No they didn't."

"I can't imagine you've come here to live as a fighter. So what brings you to this district?"

"Opportunity." She didn't want to reveal too much too soon. Agatha Lavos didn't seem like someone who trusted easily, and she wasn't keen on it either.

The man got up and approached her with a slight limp. "The name is Talon Rayne." She was pleasantly surprised by his face as he moved beyond the shadow. He was incredibly handsome, with a scruffy beard and short, unkempt hair. A burn mark scarred the skin over his right eyebrow, but it wasn't enough to draw her attention away from his eyes. As blue as the ancient sky of Earth she imagined, they held a certain weariness that made him appear as if he had a longer story to tell then his age indicated. When he got close enough he held out an open, gloved hand.

"Agatha Lavos." Sage made sure to peek over her shoulder before stepping forward. She instinctually went to clasp her hands together and bow, then remembered how the Arena supervisor had originally established their deal. It wasn't what she was used to on New Terrene, but she extended her human hand, struggling to avoid looking into Talon's eyes.

She had expected a stronger grip from looking at his muscular physique, but she was used to men treating her like she was fragile. She only then realized that she had been staring into his eyes since the moment he approached her, and that he had been doing the same to hers. Their hands remained locked, and she could feel their palms growing moist as they pressed together. It was like they were frozen in that moment. She felt her heart begin to race in such an unexpected fury that she quickly let go and looked to the ground. She stumbled slightly on her way backward, but quickly composed herself and hoped that he didn't notice.

"It is a pleasure to meet you, Agatha." Talon stared down at his empty hand with a look of astonishment.

"What is this job?" she shot back. She wasn't sure why she felt bad for lying to the stranger, but she wanted more than anything to move on.

"Straight to the point. Just like a true merchant," Julius chimed in as Talon sat down beside her.

"Oh come on, Julius. Don't be jealous. The mines aren't too bad," Talon said as he tried to hide the fact that he was eyeing her from head to toe out of the corner of his eye. She noticed.

"So you know everything about me?" she responded anxiously and moved to stand right in front of them.

"Just what you told the moderator down at the arena. I figure any servant of the Tribune wouldn't be allowed to leave, but the Conduits are supposed to be free of ownership. Or are we wrong?"

"My parents were smugglers, but I was too young to remember that. The Tribune killed them outside New Terrene when they were caught. I grew up with some extended family moving from Conduit to Conduit. It took almost everything my parents left me to repair my arm after a shipping accident...everything but my mom's armor and pistol. But I was never meant to be a merchant," she explained, carefully making sure to insert some emotion so it didn't seem like she was reciting from note cards.

"You were meant to fight, to take from those who took your parents from you." Talon took the words right out of her mouth. "I used to think the same way. Well, Agatha, I can't promise you much, but I can say you'll get to take down some of those Tribunal bastards."

"Nothing would..." She paused to gather her breath enough to allow her words to betray all that she stood for. "...make me happier."

"Perfect!" Talon slapped Julius across the back and smiled. "The Morastus clan will pay us handsomely. I can't tell you the numbers yet, but we'll be hitting a Tribunal freighter carrying a hell of a load of Gravitum."

Her eyes grew wide as goosebumps popped up along her skin. "So you're the ones causing all the reports of attacks on freighters?"

"We wish." Julius laughed.

"No. None of us has any idea what clan has been responsible for that, but the Morastus want in on the action," Talon clarified. "Anybody who could do what you did in the arena is either half insane or exactly what we need."

Julius spat over the edge. "Probably a little bit of both." He began to snicker.

Sage shot a look at him so scathing that he immediately fell silent and pretended to see something in the distance. She turned to Talon and said, "As long as the pay is good, I'm in." The Ceresian fascination with credits was foreign to her, but she had to make sure she sounded sincere.

"If we succeed, you'll never be hungry again," Talon promised her. "So are you in?" He extended his hand.

She didn't hesitate this time before taking it. "I'm in," she agreed, "just tell me what to do."

"For now, you just have to wait. We need to do some more recruiting. So in the meantime you'll be staying with Julius."

"And why is that?" Her eyebrows furrowed. She shot him a harsh glare. "You didn't buy me."

"Of course not. But the Morastus don't want anything about this mission leaking out. Judging by the way you're fiddling with that gun of yours leads me to believe you're just about as untrusting as I am." He nodded to her hand, which she didn't even realize was so close to her holster. "I may not think you'll tell anybody, but I've known Julius here my whole life and I'd trust him with my own, so I know it's the truth when I say you'll be safe with him. Plus I doubt somebody so new to this place probably has anywhere else to stay. So how about it? Deal?"

She gave in and looked at his face, into his eyes. He seemed genuine enough, and for some reason she hung on his words more than she knew she should. Even if he was lying, so was she. Unless he was an Executor of the Tribune as well, there was nothing for her to fear. Even if it was all some elaborate scheme to get her to bed, she wasn't afraid of having to fight off two untrained Ceresian's.

"That's fine with me." She feigned a grin as best she could. They might not have been the ones she was sent to find, but maybe by attacking they'd run into those who were responsible. The Tribune would be proud of her quick work, but that wasn't what she was thinking about as the meeting concluded and she followed Julius. Talon watched her as she walked away. She didn't have to look to make sure, but Talon was watching and she felt it…and for whatever reason it didn't repulse her.

CHAPTER TWENTY-THREE
SIMPLE, BEAUTIFUL THINGS

Talon sprung awake a few days later, reaching futilely for the gun that he no longer wore on his hip. He panted wildly as he struggled to regain a sense of his surroundings. Sweat matted his hair to his forehead, and he imagined he looked as if he had just been swimming in the reservoirs in the depths of Ceres Prime.

"Daddy, are you okay?" Elisha's tiny voice asked as she looked up at him. She was lying down beside him on his hammock, with her head resting on his heaving chest. His heart was racing.

"Yeah, sweetie." He pulled his shirt over his face to wipe his brow. "Just a scary dream." It wasn't a dream. The Blue Death was making it harder and harder to sleep. He'd been back on Ceres for a week already and had woken up in the same way almost every morning.

"What happened?" She rolled over onto her stomach and rubbed her puffy eyes.

"Oh, you know. The usual." He ran his hair through her hair, wondering if he had ever felt anything in the Circuit so soft. "A shadowy monster with fiery, red eyes came and tried to take you away from me."

Elisha pulled herself tight against his tunic as she stared up at him with her eyes nearly popping out of her sockets.

"Don't worry." He picked her up and hugged her so that he was able to whisper into her ear. "When I was through with it, the beast was as much ash as the surface of the Earth." He swung her over the side of the hammock with his legs and placed her down on his thighs.

"Oh…" She furrowed her brow and sulked. "That doesn't sound scary!"

"Trust me it was. I'd never seen anything like it, and for a while I thought I might lose you."

"Now I know you're lying!" Elisha hopped off of him and crossed her arms.

"And why is that?" Talon asked. He always forgot how shrewd she could be despite being so young. He liked to think that she got that from him.

"You would never lose me."

"Never," he said, not realizing how austerely it would come out. "Not even in a dream." Talon then got up off of the hammock, using the post as a support so that Elisha wouldn't notice his sore legs. It took a little bit of teeth grinding to get fully upright, but his affliction was always the most straining in the dawn. "So, how do you feel about spending the day together?"

She turned around, her smile stretching from one rosy cheek to the other. "You have no work today?"

"Never again!" He picked her up underneath her arms and began to spin. His arms grew weary quickly, but he didn't care. Holding her was worth however he might feel tomorrow, and he pulled her in tightly again so that her head was resting on his shoulder. "Me and you can travel to the far reaches of the Circuit together. See everything there is to see."

She pulled her head back to look at him, and her smile was quickly masked by skepticism. "You're lying."

"I wish I wasn't, but today you'll have me." He placed her down in front of their clothes locker which leaned against the wall. It was a crummy piece of furniture, half the metal rusted off, but it matched the shack's tarnished, corrugated-metal walls. There was little to fill the small room except for his tattered hammock, a faulty light, and another container pushed so far beneath the hammock that it was half plunged in shadow. It wasn't much, but it was home.

"What do you want to do?" he asked. "Head down to the bathing basins? Get some real, green lettuce?"

"No," she answered as she went to work on the locker. It took two hands and all of her strength to pull open the door. There were a few cloth tunics inside, some big enough for Talon and others for her, but they were all plainly colored. She reached in and grabbed one for her and one for her father and then turned to him. "Can we go to port and watch the ships?"

"If that's what you want, sure." He took the clothes from her tiny hand with a gentle smile. "Now get dressed and grab us some pills from the cabinet."

Elisha quickly followed his directions and when they were both ready, she eagerly grabbed him by the hand and pulled him out the door. She was always excited to watch the transports come and go to Ceres. Talon was the same way when he was younger, but it often troubled him with her. In his experience, he found that there wasn't much out there for the dreamer who wished to trace the worlds of the Circuit.

"Come on, Daddy!" She yanked him through the door, and he barely had time to turn around and lock it with his CP Card.

"'Bout time you two woke up!" Julius hollered from his seat around a fire pit as he held up a deck of cards. As usual, Ulson and Vellish were sitting with him with drinks in their hands. "Care for a game?"

"I…" Talon froze for a moment when he noticed Sage with them as well. He hadn't yet seen her outside of her armor up close, yet there she was with a drink in her hand. A loose-fitting tunic revealed her plunging neckline as it was drawn low around her slender shoulders. Her green eyes sparked from the flame, as magnificent as the Earth must have been in its final, dying breaths. His eyes moved along her body until they fell upon her synthetic arm. Outside of her suit, he expected it to look misplaced and clunky like all the other artificial limbs he had seen in his lifetime, but hers was exceptional. There was a grace to it that in certain light made the human body pale in comparison. "We're headed down to the spaceport," he stuttered, stumbling over his tongue.

"Gonna see the ships aye, Elisha?" Vellish asked as he took a healthy swig from his drink.

"Daddy promised!" Elisha looked up at him angrily as he had stopped moving.

"Yes…" He didn't mean to stare, but he couldn't manage to turn his gaze from her. His mouth went dry and his hands began to sweat. She finally turned her head and looked up at him. Their eyes met for a second, maybe less, before they both pretended that something else had caught their attention. "That I did."

Talon walked forward and nonchalantly took the Synthrol out of Ulson's hand just as he was about to take a sip. "Try not to drink too much. Can't have a drunken pilot." Talon stole a mouthful.

Ulson snatched it back with a smirk. "I can fly better drunk than half the pilots in the Circuit. You don' worry yourself, Tal." He opened his throat and drank the rest of the glass, the bitterness making his face clench.

"Never doubted you for a second." Talon patted Ulson on the back when he started to cough. "See you all later. Hopefully we'll find some more tonight." He nodded to Julius and Vellish, who waved back, and then to Sage, who didn't even bother to look up. Ever since they made eye contact, she had been staring incessantly into the fire. He tried to think of something to say to her before he left, but nothing came to mind. Instead, he was left wearing what he imagined was a ridiculous smile. At least he thought so, but right before Elisha jerked him away, he noticed the beginnings of the slightest smile imaginable tugging at the corner of her lips, and that was all the farewell he needed.

Talon and Elisha made their way down to the Underpass and took the busiest line to the major spaceport out of Ceres Prime. It didn't have a specific name, but most of the locals simply referred to it as the Buckle. Nobody had ever told Talon exactly why it was called that, but it seemed simple enough. Together with the Conduit station it connected to, the Buckle served to hold together all of the Ceresian colonies of the asteroid belt.

"Stay close to me." Talon grabbed onto Elisha's hand tightly as they squeezed off of the tram. The landing was crowded with people of all types, from wealthy Conduit merchants to the unfortunate souls dwelling in the depths of Ceres with their lanky bodies and ash-white skin. He noticed servants of a few different banking clans wearing their faction's respective armor. There was a Morastus guard nearby, putting far too much effort into not looking in Talon's direction and pretending he was busy. He had no doubt that Zaimur had men keeping tabs on him to make sure he wouldn't try to run away, but he didn't expect them to make it so easy to find out. Their lack of finesse was insulting to a profession he used to call his own.

Talon stopped in the middle of the landing and leaned over so that Elisha could hear. "Can you keep up?" He asked with a sly grin.

Elisha pursed her lips and nodded assertively.

Talon squeezed her hand a little tighter and began to guide her through the crowd at a quickened pace. It wasn't quite a jog, but they weaved through traffic and onto a wide avenue. There was no bigger hollow then the Buckle in all of Ceres, and it was mostly comprised of one meandering avenue, which pierced through clusters of rock formations that were carved up with metal structures. There was no uniformity to it, with many of the structures built along massive stalactites all the way up to the Buckle's lofty ceiling, giving it the appearance of an insect hive. These were the hollowed-out, vertical hangars where ships from all over Ceresian space came and went.

He looked over his shoulder to see Elisha struggling to keep pace, her tiny feet pattering along the ground in quick succession. Talon saw a long, transport vehicle speeding toward them and he scooped her up before hurrying across the avenue just in time to get in front of it. Then they headed down a narrow crevice carved into the root of a towering stalactite, and emerged onto the upper floor of a vertical hangar.

"Slow…" Elisha stopped to put her hands on her knees and pant. "Down."

Talon quickly turned around. He had almost forgotten that she was just a child. "Are you okay?" For his own reasons he was breathing just as heavily.

She gathered herself and proudly stood up as tall as she could without being on her heels. "What are we running from?"

"Nothing." Talon forced a smile. Moving quickly wasn't as easy as it used to be. "I just wanted to see how fast you were." He grabbed her hand and began to guide her through the fissure. After a dozen feet, it was so cramped that they had to shuffle through sideways.

"Try to be as quiet as possible," Talon whispered as he peered around both corners of the exit. "The Lakura Clan still doesn't know about this entrance." He squeezed through and quickly snuck behind a pile of metal crates. The upper level of the Buckle's hangars was usually reserved for storage, so there was little chance of them being caught once already inside.

"Lakura?" Elisha questioned softly as she knelt down as close to her father as she could.

"The lowest of the clans. Think they speak for all of us as they terrorize innocent Tribunal colonies and citizens." He didn't tell her that he also suspected that they might be involved in the attacks on the Tribunal Freighters. "Follow me."

Together they skulked around the curved walkway until there was a low enough break in the crates where Elisha would be able to get a good view.

"Here." He stopped and knelt with his hands resting over a low container. She mimicked him exactly, only there was a glimmer in her eyes as everything became visible.

Talon had seen the inside of the hangars a thousand times. He didn't imagine anyone could find it anything more than ordinary, but Elisha had a knack for seeing the beauty in all things. A small ship was rising up through the shaft, making the grated floor beneath them begin to tremble. Then it shot past them, its humming ion-engines leaving behind a dappled trail of blue light. Talon glanced over at Elisha to see her doe-eyed and staring as if it were the most amazing thing in the world. The sound of it began to reverberate down the hollowed rock-tower, playing like a tremendous string instrument. Then he looked up again to see it pass through a transparent hatch, which when it sealed shut released a second, plated hatch above. For a moment they could see the stars through the far-off opening. It wasn't long, but Ceres rarely offered glimpses of what lay beyond its rock-strewn surface.

"Amazing, right?" Talon put his arm around her as the plated shaft shut and both the ship and space disappeared.

"Have you ever been on one?" She extended over the container and tried to see the floor of the hangar where men and slow-moving robots were loading up another ship.

"Dozens. I can't even remember them all." Talon leaned forward as well and tilted his head to try and hear better. He couldn't quite make out what they were saying, but there was nothing he could see that would incriminate them in the attacks. *Seemed too simple*, he thought to himself as he rested his chin on his fist in frustration.

"I wish I had one of my own."

"So did I. So does everyone born in this rock," Talon chuckled and squeezed her tight against his chest. "I think you will one day. A beautiful ship, much more so than that piece of junk." He gestured to the vessel parked at the bottom of the hangar. "But where would you take it? That's the question."

She wrinkled her brow and then her face lit up. "I really wanna see a planet!"

"A planet? What could be better than Ceres?" Talon mused and leaned back on his elbows, looking straight up the tall chute.

"Maybe Saturn. I've heard traders talk about the rings. Have you ever seen them?"

"Only once. But to tell you the truth, I never got the chance to really look at them."

"Or Earth!"

"Why in the name of the Ancients would you want to see that wasteland?"

"I don't know. Everybody says it's a scary place, but I bet it's not." The room began to tremble again as the other ship powered on. Elisha extended her neck as far across the container as she could. Talon pulled her back a bit. Now that the men below were done preparing the vessel, he didn't want to risk them seeing her.

"I wouldn't know. My father went there during the Reclaimer Wars and never came back." Talon sighed and rested his head against hers. "That's all I know of the place besides what travelers tell me." Talon could hardly remember the day when his father left for battle. All he remembered was that he never back came. That was the thought which gripped his heart every night and squeezed...that he would do the same to her.

"I bet it's beautiful." Elisha's eyes were even wider when the second ship ascended right in front of them, blowing her hair back.

"One look at you and it would sprout green and lush all over again."

He could tell she didn't hear him as she stared in awe at the departing ship, but he didn't mind. He ran his fingers over her shoulder and looked up with her as the view to space opened up again. She wasn't lying. It was beautiful.

Chapter Twenty-Four
Faith Amongst the Faithless

A week had passed since Sage was recruited, and over that time she did her best to stay relatively secluded. She didn't stray from the residential district, spending most of each day within Julius' metal shack praying and trying to rest her body. All the aches and pains from the explosion had pretty much vanished, and even her head felt fine for most of every day. Julius was the only person she had spoken to, though she tried her best not to. Despite her protests he insisted that he would sleep on the floor so that she could have the hammock, but she did her best to avoid any other unnecessary conversations. He was Ceresian after all.

When she was finally alone that morning, she rolled out of the hammock and got on both knees. It was dark, only a sliver of light slipping through the cracks of the shack's rusty door, which barely clung to its hinges. There was no chance that anybody could see her.

"I am blessed with ground beneath me," she whispered delicately. Then she extended her arms out and let the tips of her fingers touch the floor. There was a soft scratching noise as her artificial hand grazed slowly across the surface.

"Our Homeworld has been blighted by darkness, but we are the light. Those beside me, those beneath me, and above me. Ours is a collective unconscious, bound to each other and to the soul of the Earth. We are, all of us, shards of that Spirit, never alone as the dark void closes in. This day is yet another test of my conviction, but though the Earth may be wreathed in flame and shadow, she remains within me. May those who have left to join this essence guide my daily endeavors. Redemption is near. May my faith—"

Just as she began mouthing the final stanza in the prayer the shack's door swung open. She rolled to the side, banging into the hammock, which began to swing as if she had fallen off.

Julius burst into the room, but as soon as he did he threw his hand over his them. "Shit! I didn't mean." He took a big step back and closed the door halfway so that he could speak to her behind it.

Only then did Sage look down and realize that she was completely naked. She grabbed the ratty tunic lying in a pile on the floor and threw it over her head.

"Did I make you fall, Agatha?" he asked sounding every bit as embarrassed as Sage was. "I ain't used to havin' anyone here."

"No." She quickly remembered that the fact that she was naked was the only thing that kept Julius from seeing what she was really up to. "Well, yes. But, it's…it's okay."

"I swear I didn't see nothing!"

She hoped to the Ancients that he hadn't. "I believe you. I needed to wake up anyway."

"Well if you're up, grab a pill from the cabinet and come outside. You can meet some of the boys we'll be goin' to battle with. Have a few drinks, play some cards." He peeked around the edge of the door, his usually dark cheeks glowing an even darker shade of red.

"I don't know…" She didn't know how to play so it wouldn't be hard for them to figure out her guise if she tried.

"It's a miner's game, I know. We'll teach you, come on. You been in here alone for too long. We gotta keep our minds fresh."

She thought about it for a moment. If he immediately assumed that she didn't know then it must not have been a game Conduit Merchants would know. It was worth the risk, a bunch of men drinking were sure to tell her something valuable about the Tribune. "Sure. I'll be right there."

Julius shut the door and Sage used the hammock to pull herself to her feet. *That was way to close,* she warned herself as she shook her head. Then she tidied up her tunic and pulled it down so it covered her thighs. She thought about putting on her armor, but decided against it. Then she opened Julius' cabinet and grabbed a pill out of a small dish.

Sage looked around to see if there was anything to wash it down with. Just like her home in the depths of New Terrene, there was no personal sources of water. Only the most privileged people living in the skyscrapers above the Labyrinth of the Night had such luxuries. She imagined it was the same on Ceres Prime, with drinkable water being such a valuable commodity throughout the Circuit and all. In fact even Julius' shack reminded her of her home. Of course her unit was better put together and far less rusty, but Julius had as little of his own as she did.

She spotted a quarter-full glass of murky water placed at the back of the counter. It was probably Julius' from earlier, but it would have to do. She was parched. Placing the pill on the center of her tongue, she took a swig, swishing it around in her mouth before swallowing. The water had a metallic taste, but it was tolerable.

As the pill tumbled down her throat she began to miss the Feed on New Terrene. She couldn't believe it was something that she could miss, but she was always fond of the routine. So much of her life was unpredictable. It was the only thing she could always count on every day other than her faith. As much as the taste of *Crud* could make her cringe, there was at least more to it than surviving on some pill. There was a flavor to ground her and a texture, even if it was lumpy.

Once she was ready Sage headed outside of the shack. Housing block 543 wasn't anything remarkable, but again it bore a slight resemblance to her home in the Labyrinth of the Night. Instead of being built up along two vertical sides of a gorge like it was there, the meager shantytown was carved into the angled surface of the gaping cavern. It extended up and down the rocky hill in either direction until the slopes were too great to manage. Crude metal pathways worked alongside natural bridges between clefts and small valleys to negotiate the uneven landscape. There was very little order, but there was something undeniably picturesque about it. She never knew where a shack was going to pop up, or where a pathway would carve through the crags to surprise her.

"There she is! Told you boys that she would come." Julius wore a toothy grin as he waved Sage over. He and two others were sitting around a fire-pit with bluish drinks set on the ground by their feet. Above them was a rock bridge stretching from one taller outcrop to another. Housing units were built up on either side, with thin robes draping between them strung with dozens of articles of wet clothing.

As Sage approached she could see them whispering to each other and trying not to be caught staring at her. Just by the smirks on their faces she could tell what they were talking about. She was used to the way men looked at her, no matter how much she detested it.

Vellish got to his feet. He wasn't very tall, and his long, crooked nose took away from his strong jaw line somewhat. "Wow, Talon wasn't lyin'," he admired before Julius nudged him in the leg. "Uh, name's Vellish. Nice to finally meet the Tigress of Ceres Prime."

Sage tried to ignore his initial comment. She stuck out her artificial hand and waited for him to shake it, hoping that she was acting properly.

"By the Ancients that's a hell of a fuckin' arm. Who made that thing; I ain't never seen anythin' like it." Vellish grasped her hand and took it upon himself to let his other hand grope inquisitively along the synthetic limb.

She pulled it away. "Nobody!" She snapped, scaring him back into his seat. "I mean… Sorry. I don't like to think about it."

"I didn't mean anythin' by it. Just amazin' is all." Vellish picked his drink up off the ground and took a long sip to try and hide his reddened face.

"You'll hafta excuse our friend Vellish here. He ain't always the most charmin' of fellows." Ulson stood up and extended his left hand so that Sage would be able to put her human arm forward instead. "Name's Ulson."

"Agatha Lavos." She grasped his hand and feigned a smile. "And if you must know my uncle made this for me. Spent his whole life trying to give me an arm after I lost it when I was young. I would tell you how he made it, but he died shortly after he finished." The false story rolled off her lips as surely as she had repeated it in her own head. The only truth to it was that a man had made it for her, but she could never forget that. "He was a great man."

Julius signaled to the empty chair set up for her and said, "Wish I could've met him. I could use one of those arms. Or two." He chuckled to himself before lifting his glass up to his lips.

Sage shot him an angry look. She didn't necessarily mean to, but as much as the arm was a gift, the true story of its conception was a horrid tale. She had spent years blocking out the memories, until they were merely a dull ache tugging at the fringes of her consciousness.

"So you're a merchant girl, right?" Vellish finally broke the awkward silence pervading after Julius' ostensibly innocent joke.

"Not always." Sage pulled her seat closer to the fire. It wasn't often she got to feel the heat of a real flame. With so much of the Circuit drowned in the cold, it felt good to sweat.

"Agatha's parents were smugglers out of the Vergent Cell. Died back in the Reclaimer Wars." Julius informed the others. She was surprised he had remembered anything from their scant conversations.

"Whose didn't in this rock?" Vellish held up his glass and nodded his head, the others mimicking him before they all simultaneously took a sip. "You're in good company then. Ain't nobody on Ceres who wouldn't love a chance to get a piece of those Tribune fucks."

Sage grit her teeth and offered him an amenable nod. *There is one person,* she thought to herself as she began to stare into the fire, mesmerized by its unpredictable boughs as they grasped at her heels with soft hisses.

"Alright are we gonna chitchat all day or are we gonna play? Talon ran me dry on Kalliope, I gotta make some back while he's gone!" Ulson chimed in, rubbing his hands together vigorously.

"He's right!" Julius responded and went to pick up the deck from beside his foot, but then he glanced at Sage and paused. "But first where are our manners? Agatha's got nothin' to drink."

Sage's eyes shot up from the fire when she heard hm. She had forgotten that on New Terrene Synthrol was outlawed amongst the general populace. She had brought countless smugglers to justice trying to run it through the Conduit into the city, but she had never tried it before.

"That's okay," Sage graciously declined before quickly thinking up a credible excuse. "My uncle never let me touch the stuff. Preferred I keep my wits about me."

"Nonsense!" Julius nearly fell off his chair in astonishment. "You're telling me you've never tried it? Not even once?"

"What's so surprising? It's a man's drink, you know!" Vellish said with a snicker before Sage's unamused glare made him reconsider. "Well, at least… most ladies I know don't very well like the taste."

Julius and Ulson couldn't help but smirk as Vellish once again tried to mask his embarrassment by taking an exaggerated sip of his drink.

"One day me and my wife will teach you manners, Vel." Ulson patted Vellish on the back, causing him to begin choking and his cheeks to get even redder.

"Fuck you both." Vellish coughed and sunk his face into his palms.

Julius ignored Vellish and turned his attention back to Sage. "Here. Try mine." He held out his drink.

"I don't know…" Sage looked at him with a furrowed brow. On one hand it seemed like something Ceresians partook in with people that the trusted. That could surely benefit her cause. On the other it was against the law of the Tribune.

"Just a sip. I promise you'll be fine."

There was something about the look in his eyes. She could tell that he wasn't lying to her; that for whatever reason he genuinely wanted to include her. And even though he was Ceresian, she felt she could trust him.

"I'll do it," she declared proudly. She was an Executor of the Tribune. She could do whatever needed to be done for the good it, even if the law stood in her way. "Just a sip."

Sage snatched the glass out of Julius' hand. As soon as she did the others leaned forward and began to watch her eagerly. Even Vellish stirred from his chastened state. She brought it to her nose, recoiling initially from the smell. It was pungent, singing the hairs in her nostrils and making her eyes water.

"Trick is to be quick about it," Julius advised her.

She breathed out of her nose so she couldn't smell it, opened her mouth and tossed a sizeable amount of the bluish liquid in. It sat in her mouth for a second, probably less, before the intolerably bitter taste forced her to spit it out. The fire roared and began to sizzle as the spray rained down over it, forcing Vellish to have to scamper off his chair in order to avoid being burned.

The three of them began laughing so hysterically that it seemed like it was the funniest thing they'd ever seen. Julius was in tears, and Vellish was standing next to his chair holding his gut, unable to bring himself to sit. Sage pursed her lips and tried to ignore them, but their reaction was making her so irritated that the glass she held with her synthetic hand shattered. She hadn't even realized she was squeezing, but the high-pitched sound of it quickly silenced everyone.

The men immediately looked up at her, a fear in their eyes that she had seen all too many times before. She stared at the empty space within her cupped palm, Synthrol trickling from out the spaces between each metal plate. Then something happened to her, something she hadn't felt in longer than she cared to recall. It started in the depths of her gut and worked its way up her throat, until from her mouth came a chuckle. It was far from boisterous, in fact it was barely audible, but it startled her so much that she covered her mouth. Then there was another and another after that, and before long she joined the others in honest laughter.

"I…" The sensation was so unfamiliar that she had to pause for a moment to gather her voice. "I didn't expect it to taste that dreadful."

"I swear I've ain't never seen anybody react that bad," a completely winded Julius huffed and puffed.

"Seriously." Vellish wiped his eyes and took a seat. "You almost burnt my legs off!"

"Serves you right for letting me drink that! What in the Ancients is wrong with all of you?" Sage stuck her tongue out as her whole face scrunched in disgust, the foul taste still lingering in her mouth.

"Better than being sober all day," Ulson tittered. "You get used to it after a while."

"I'll be dead long before I'm used to that," Sage attested before realizing how wrong she might be. She had said the same thing the first time she tasted Crud on New Terrene, and now she craved it more than anything. *Could I ever miss this?* She looked up at the three Ceresian's smiling faces, and then she gazed down at the fire and shook her head.

I am a knight in the darkness, a vessel of their wisdom. I am the silent hand of the Tribune. She began reciting the Executor vows in her head, but then something happened that stole her train of thought.

"'Bout time you two woke up!" Julius shouted. "Care for a game?"

Sage saw him approaching in her peripheries with a young girl walking behind him. She didn't dare look at him directly, but as Talon approached them, the handsome lines of his face were painted by the flame in vibrant shades of orange and red. Their eyes locked for a moment too short to count, but a moment that made it feel like her heart was plummeting through her stomach.

She quickly turned back to the fire. It took all of her concentration to keep her vision trained on the sweltering plumes as they licked at her supple flesh. Whatever conversation was going on between the four Ceresians was rendered muffled whispers.

I am a knight in the darkness, a vessel of their wisdom. I am the silent hand of the Tribune. I will not lose faith amongst the faithless.

She repeated the vows in her head, but by the end of them she could feel Talon standing over her. His shadow swayed with the wavering light, but there was no doubt he was there. It was too much to bear. Out of the corner of her eye she allowed herself a glimpse. His cheeks were red as the Earth's core and a laughable smile stretched from one ear to the other. Seeing the expression was enough to make one end of her lips curl upward. It happened before she could stop it, and by the time she was able to he was already gone.

"Alright, Agatha, you ready? Agatha?"

Sage didn't hear who was speaking to her until a card fell flat onto her lap and caught her attention.

"You ready?" Julius asked again. "I'll teach you as we go."

Her mouth opened to say she was ready, but when nothing came out she nodded instead.

I will not lose faith amongst the faithless.

Chapter Twenty-Five
Taking the Circuit for all it's Worth

Talon and Julius spent two more weeks scouring all of the districts and Domes of Ceres Prime for a group of mercenaries willing to take up the risk of attacking a Tribunary freighter. Most scoffed at them and claimed it was impossible, but the promise of wealth was irresistible for some, not to mention a chance to take on Tribunal soldiers. By the end of their quest they had twelve others in their squad, enough to fill a small transport, though none of them had any clue how many it would take.

It was the eve before their departure, and Talon stood beside Julius atop a small promontory overlooking their housing district. Elisha and her mother sat a short distance behind them in the shadow of an overhang, waiting for them to conclude their discussion.

"Tell me straight, Julius. You think the squad we have is good enough to get this done?" Talon asked, hoping for as earnest an answer as possible.

"Honestly Tal, I have no idea. We been through our share of shit, you more than I, but this…" Julius grabbed his friend by the shoulders and turned him so that the girls watching wouldn't be able to read their lips. "More I think about it, more it seems like suicide."

"Sounds perfect to me." Talon grinned complacently, masking his true outlook on the idea.

"We'll come back alive." Julius nodded sharply, more to provide himself with some assurance than anything else. "I won't let you go out like this. If and when you die, she'll be at your side,

Tal. I promise that."

"When…" Talon lamented. "I sure hope she isn't. I hope she's far away from here bathing in the sun somewhere with grass wriggling between her toes."

"Yeah, and I hope Earth'll be green and beautiful again," Julius jested. He lightly punched Talon in the chest.

Talon glanced over at Elisha whispering with her mother, a blithe smile prominent on her sweet face. "Maybe one day it will be…"

"You okay? You're startin' to sound like one of them!" Julius chuckled. "I'll always look after her, Tal. You know that. We may not be blood, but she's my daughter too."

"Then can I ask something of you?" He reached out and laid his hand on Julius' brawny chest. "Something I would never trust with any of the others?"

"Anythin'."

Talon took a deep breath. It was as difficult for him to ask as he knew it would be for Julius to hear. "Stay here with her. I can't go back, but there's still hope for you."

"Wha…" Julius mouthed, unable to get the full word out.

Talon pulled him closer. "If we fail, I don't think Zaimur will hold up his end of the bargain! I know it. He's not the man his father is. He'll sneer as the vile men of this rock fuck her until her eyes are black with envy."

Julius pushed Talon away and protested, "What about her mother?"

"If she isn't playing with needles, she's got some piece of shit buried half inside her. You think she'll do anything to keep Zaimur's hands off her? She'd probably take the credits and watch. No, I can't let Elisha follow that same path."

"But…" Julius' bulging eyes began to well up and his hands trembled. "You guys need me," he implored. "I… I don't want to be stuck in the mines my whole life. You don't understand."

"I know I don't, and I know we need you…that's what makes this so hard to ask." Talon gulped. "But she needs you too, and I know you love her as much as I do."

"Tal…"

"I'm dying, Julius. I feel it every damned day. Every time I wake up, I'm sore all over. Every time I run, my lungs are ready to burst out of my chest. But as long as I still have something left to give, I'm going to fight for her to have a better life."

"Then stay with her! I'll lead the men. You can have everythin' I earn, just don't leave me behind." Tears began to dribble down his cheeks in reedy streams.

"No. This is my mess." Talon reached out and wrapped his hand around his friend's neck before staring solemnly into his wet eyes. "This is the last thing I'll ever ask of you. Everything I own. Everything I make, I'll leave to you and her."

Julius wiped his tears away and let his forehead fall against Talon's. "Fuck...I'll do it for you." He stood up straight and sniveled. "But you need to make me a promise too."

Talon bit his lower lip. "Of course."

"When you *do* get back, we'll leave this place. We'll be pirates or smugglers out on the Vergent Cell living the rest of our lives the way we were always meant to."

"Taking the Circuit for all its worth?" Talon lunged forward and embraced Julius, squeezing as hard has he could manage around his friend's thick frame. "Thank you, Julius. I wouldn't trust her with anybody else." Then he backed away so that they were at arm's length. He wasn't used to seeing his hulking friend so somber.

Julius did his best to smile. "I know. You ain't givin' me much of a choice. But we'll see you soon anyway so it don't matter." He pulled him back in and crushed him with another hug.

"I hope so."

"Hope is for pussies." Julius patted him on the back and nudged him toward his daughter. "You ain't one."

Talon laughed to himself as Julius turned around and sat with his feet dangling off the edge. Talon had always known him to wear his emotions on his sleeve, but the giant man never liked showing when he was sad.

"You two lovers done over there?" Vera commented as she picked her teeth with her long fingernails.

"For now." Talon shot her a smirk and knelt down in front of his daughter who had been watching him keenly. "Hey sweetie."

"Don't leave, Daddy!" She burst into tears and buried herself in his chest, her tiny hands grabbing his wrists as if to hold him down.

He threw his arms around her and pulled her close, rubbing his face through her hair so the smell would rub off. "It won't be long."

Her watery blue eyes met his straight on as she said worriedly, "I heard Julius saying you could die one night. I don't want you to die."

Talon allowed himself to grin and ran his covered fingers through her hair. "Julius was only exaggerating. You know him. A week or two tops and I'll be back."

"You promise?" She sniveled and wiped her nose.

"Yeah," he lied. "Yeah I do. And you promise you'll be nice to him while I'm gone?"

"I'll try." Her lips curled into a sinister little grin.

Talon laughed and hugged her one more time.

"I love you, Daddy."

"I...I love you too." Talon did his best not to whimper. He tenderly placed his lips in the center of her forehead and then quickly got up to walk away before he started sobbing. Vera caught up with him and gave him a kiss on the cheek. She said something, but he didn't hear it. It was all he could do to hold the tears back, and when he was far enough away they began to flow unimpeded.

Never looking back, he traversed the series of bridges and lifts leading to his home, keeping his head down to avoid any conversation. When he reached his shack, he pushed through the rickety door and switched on the faulty lights. Then Talon knelt down below his hammock and pulled an old trunk forward. Wiping away the dusts, he placed his CP card into the slot at the top. There was an audible click as it unlocked and the lid slid backward to fold over the rear.

Inside laid a customized pulse rifle. There was an interchanging pattern of blue and gray coating each part of the weapon, with the serrated barrel striped in those colors. A few cases of clips were nestled against the side, and below it all was the composite-armor suit Talon had worn during his days serving the Morastus clan.

He reached under the hammock again, this time dragging out a helmet. The smooth, convex visor was covered in grime. He spat in his hand and rubbed it down until he could see his reflection in the glass. His eyelashes were matted with tears and his cheeks wet and dirty. He hated to see himself appear so weary, to see his veins coruscate out like blue webs over his temples.

He took a deep breath. "Too late to turn back now," he whispered to himself, and then he reached into the box and pulled out his rifle.

Chapter Twenty-Six
A Small Part of Her

Sage stood at attention. She was at the base of a tall hangar carved up through the core of a tremendous pillar of rock. The entire shaft was intended only for the personal use of the Morastus clan and its affairs. A group of guards in blue and gray were running a background check on the squad beside her. She wasn't nervous. She had faith in the Tribune's diligence.

She looked to her left and right. There were ten other mercenaries, including Vellish and Ulson. The others were little more than guns for hire, each of them in unique and relatively battered suits of armor. None appeared to be anything extravagant, but they were in the same precarious position as her. She guessed from their noticeable edginess that they probably wouldn't try to help stop her even if she had to escape, each of them with their own checkered past. The Morastus guards across from her, on the other hand, would.

Tinted visors gave them an air of mystery that attempted at being intimidating, but she knew she could hold them off with ease. Stationed amongst them were at least half a dozen robots armed with rifles. She found them to be the most threatening, and began to chart out an escape route with her eyes leading her as far away from their line of fire. She figured she had just as good a shot of getting out as she did of being killed if things went sour. Fifty, fifty odds, not bad considering how deep she had wound up undercover in only a few weeks.

An important looking man stepped away from the nearby engineering station. He approached them behind a host of guards and said, "I must say, Talon put together a clean squad."

She had heard his name was Zaimur Morastus from Julius.

His wonderfully combed hair fell to rest gently on the vibrant shoulders of his robe, bouncing with each of his haughty steps. A fearsome beast lurked at his side, its voracious, black eyes moving across the line of mercenaries as if all he saw was a meal.

Sage was so distracted by the animal that she barely noticed Zaimur walking directly toward her until he was only feet away. She didn't let it show, but she carefully positioned herself so that she would be able to deliver an incapacitating blow with her artificial arm if it came to that.

"One stunning woman." Zaimur licked his lips as he reached up and affectionately ran his fingers through her hair. Her immediate response was to break his arm in half, but she restrained herself. "You could make a much better living away from all this violence."

The beast began to sniff her legs. As it moved around her, baring the end of its white fangs, she knew it was far more of a danger to her then the pampered Morastus Prince.

"A shame to see such beauty go to waste," Zaimur concluded.

"Not wasted!" Talon responded brashly as he entered the hangar just before she could respond.

His sudden entrance was enough to earn her attention, and this time she didn't look away. His armor looked as though it had survived a thousand battles and he slung a specially designed pulse rifle over his shoulder with one hand. In the other arm, he carried a helmet the same as the Morastus guards. His smoldering blue eyes glared forward with a quiet confidence she had rarely seen in a soldier. He looked ready. "We won't fail you."

"And I hope you don't." Zaimur turned from Talon to give Sage one quick look. He reached out and let the back of his long, manicured fingers run down her cheek. Under any other circumstances she would have made sure her face was the last thing he'd ever touched, but again she restrained herself. "But it would be quite a shame to lose her."

"Look who finally decided to show up!" Vellish remarked with obvious sarcasm from the other end of the line. He gave Talon a friendly pat on the back and they embraced.

"Where's Julius at?" Ulson asked from adjacent to them. "The big man decide to sleep in?"

"He didn't tell you? I sent him on another mission," Talon

stated firmly as he greeted Ulson.

"You've gotta be fuckin' kiddin' me. Right as we leave? Don't tell me he chickened out!" Vellish stepped forward and shook his fist.

"Julius would've done anything to be here with us, but I needed him for something more vital. Without him all of this would be for nothing." Talon tried to explain, but Sage could infer from the tone of his voice that there was something he wasn't saying.

"Just saw him last night. You'd think he woulda told us." Vellish sighed and returned to his position.

"You'll see when we get back how crucial his role is. He isn't a fighter anyway, you both know that." Talon put a hand on each of their shoulders and offered a heartening nod. It was enough to make them both feel at ease. She didn't know much about Talon. All Julius revealed was that he was a miner, but judging by how much his reassurance comforted his friends, she knew there was something more to him than that.

"Fuckin' gentle giant." Vellish snickered under his breath.

"I assume you're all chatting about the big, dark-skinned man?" Zaimur reached them along his line of inspection. The dog began to sniff them one at a time, and only then did Zaimur get any closer to them. "Good. He's a hell of a miner." Finished with his assessment, he moved in front of the entire squad to address them. "The Morastus Clan values your service." He bowed his head and offered a haughty smile. "Now, all of you but Talon onto the transport."

The guards came forward to lead them up the ramp of the ship. It had a wide, rectangular back sitting under notched wings and one flat ion engine. Beneath it was a collection of long, sharp chambers that jutted out like the legs of an insect.

She watched Talon talking to Zaimur out of the corner of her eyes until she was ushered onto the vessel and they were out of view. There were two rows of seats and she took an empty one next to a tall mercenary with a scarred chin.

"Lucky bastard. They pay him a shit load more than us for workin' that fuckin' Mech," Vellish complained from across the aisle as he pulled the restraint down over his shoulders.

"He's smart. Hasn't got a death wish I suppose!" Ulson

shouted back from the cozy cockpit.

"You two girls gonna complain the whole time?" the mercenary with a scarred chin grunted.

The lot of them began to bicker as Sage sat quietly thinking. She had spent around two weeks living in Julius' shack. They didn't speak much, but he was kind to her. He offered water and implored her every night her to sleep on his hammock while he took the floor. He had seemed keen to join in their mission, and so whatever was keeping him behind had to be more important than any of the men whining around her cared to consider. There was even a part of her that wished she had said goodbye, Ceresian or not. Though it was only a very small part.

Everyone quieted down immediately when Talon entered the ship and the ramp sealed shut behind him with a snap-hiss. He moved to sit next to Vellish, directly across from her and laid his rifle flat over his thighs before pulling down his restraints. As he did, he quickly glanced over at her. Sage didn't even realize she had been staring, but he must have. She noticed his lips wriggle into some semblance of a smirk before he barked out. "Ulson! Take us up!"

Everyone howled in unison until the whining of the engines powering on drowned them out. Sage remained quiet. For the first time since she got to Ceres she began to doubt everything she was doing. *What if I don't discover anything about the attackers? Then I'd be helping the Ceresians.* The very people who stood against the Tribune and all that she was. And then it dawned on her. When they attacked the freighter, retainers of the Tribune were going to try and kill her. It wouldn't be the first time she would have to kill her own for the greater good...such was an Executor's duty... but never before as a supposed Ceresian.

Her mind raced so fast that it made her head hurt. She squeezed her eyes together to try and alleviate some of the pain, but when they reopened they fixed firmly on Talon, watching as he fiddled with his rifle. A sinking feeling pulled at her chest as if her heart was slowly drowning in water.

I am a knight in the darkness, a vessel of their wisdom. She took steady breaths as she recited the Executor Vows in her head, but the sensation refused to leave her.

CHAPTER TWENTY-SEVEN
FROM THE ASHES OF THE EARTH

Cassius Vale leaned over a large HOLO-Screen with the image of Tribune Joran Noscondra on it. "Cassius. I hope you have been able to make progress since we last saw each other?" Joran asked calmly but with a stern glare.

"A pleasure to see you as well, Joran," Cassius quipped, but the Tribune was clearly not amused as his features tightened. "No time to waste I see. I've recoded the protocol. Your technicians should be able to adjust the system manually on any ships you desire. It won't be a permanent solution, but whoever has been staging these raids won't be able to crack the encryption on those ships at least. Should they try again, the protocol will work as expected, and you'll have them dead in space."

"That is excellent news! Send your changes to the enclave and it will be distributed to trusted engineers throughout the Circuit. With that in place alongside operations on our end, hopefully we will catch those damned Ceresians in the act!"

"Glad to be of service, though you have hardly upheld your end."

"What are you talking about?" Joran's eyebrows wrinkled.

"Random searches of my colony were not a part of the agreement. They claimed to have been sent by Nora, but I know Benjar was behind it. I must say, the soldiers were less than courteous, not nearly representative of the infallible Tribune."

"Inspections are to be expected." Joran's words didn't match his face. Cassius could tell by his irritated expression that Benjar had left him completely in the dark. "The Vales have long presided over Titan, but you are a member of the Tribune. Remember that."

"I know who I serve!" Cassius growled and slammed his

hands on the end of the console. "This was no ordinary inspection, Joran. I don't know what Benjar thinks I'm up to, but I don't need him causing more unrest amongst my people. A Gravitum leak is no small hazard."

"Cassius..." Joran sighed and looked off to the side. "Because you fulfilled your end of the bargain, I will speak with him."

"At least there is one member of your Holy Council who gives way to reason," Cassius slighted, readjusting his collar.

"I will keep you apprised. In the meantime continue searching for a more permanent solution. As always, may the Spirit of the Earth guide your steps."

The transmission cut out before Cassius could respond, but the conversation brought a smile to his lips. The changes would be meaningless in helping to stop the true culprits. He shut down the communications array and left the room with a hop in his step

It was deafeningly loud outside with the Plasmatic Drill working tirelessly to carve through the crust of Titan. Cassius had brought back the mining bots from his last trip to Ennomos. They had already been re-outfitted for Gravitum recovery and were sent down with ADIM. He was anxiously awaiting their return, rocking back and forth from his heel to his sole. This was everything. The key to the future of humanity he imagined was at stake. He hadn't felt such exuberance in so long that it was almost too much to bear.

Just as he was about to go and distract himself with lesser business, he noticed the reddish glow of ADIM's eyes as the android clambered up the side of the bottomless pit. Cassius hurried around the rail to get a better view. His heart was either beating unfathomably fast or had stopped completely. Beads of sweat rolled down his forehead and back, his eyes darting in frantic search for the luminous blue of Gravitum.

"Creator!" ADIM projected as loud as his vocal systems could. His arm rotated so that he could begin running sideways up the walls of the circular fissure. He sprung up onto one of the drill's legs, twirling around it to build momentum until he launched himself toward Cassius and landed dexterously a few feet away on the same level.

"ADIM, is it there? Are we free of our shackles?" Cassius stuttered, unable to contain his excitement.

"The others are behind this unit." ADIM stepped forward and, unable to display the emotion he thought was proper, grabbed his Creator's hand. "The core, like Mars, is without Gravitum. This unit has failed."

"So Titan is not destined for more either. It is the damned Universe that has failed me, not you!" Cassius' smile quickly faded as slammed his fists down against the railing. ADIM grabbed his arms to calm him. Cassius gazed hopelessly at the mining bots scurrying out of the endless chasm empty-handedly. The drill was like a beating heart, expanding and contracting and hissing and wining, but it offered nothing. A tear rolled down from Cassius' eye as he continued staring, deeply wounded, but not surprised. He turned his cheek so that ADIM would not see.

"This unit did not think you truly believed there would be any here."

Cassius wiped his eyes and turned back to ADIM. "I didn't..." he grumbled quietly, "but I hoped, blindly! So many lives could have been spared if only..."

"The weak will perish in the flames, and from the ashes of Earth humanity will rise to claim their mantle," ADIM recounted.

"I said that didn't I?" Cassius turned to face ADIM, his wet eyes reflecting the red of his creations.

"On the four-hundred and eighty-fourth day of my existence."

"Oh, ADIM." He placed his hand on the android's shoulder, his lips trembling. "Titan has failed us, as it has continually failed my family. Are we ready to do what must be done, then?"

"The will of the Creator is what must be done. This unit was forged to be ready."

"Well then." Cassius took a step back to observe his disappointment. He averted his gaze and shook his head. "We must leave this futile experiment behind." He switched on the HOLO-Screen along his bracer and keyed the commands to slowly power down the drill.

"Is it finally time to test the new weapon on a physical subject?" ADIM's eyes began to spin rapidly.

"Yes. All of our preparation will now come to light." Cassius stopped to take one last moment to breathe it in. There was some solace in knowing that now that there was no other alternative. Then, as if suddenly reinvigorated, he set off toward the upper level in a decidedly spry manner. "Come, ADIM. You must help me complete all the preparations on the Conduit before you head back to Ennomos."

"The Creator will not accompany this unit?"

Cassius placed his hand on ADIM's shoulder as they walked. "How I would love to see it, but unfortunately I must remain here to greet my Tribunal guests when they soon arrive."

"This unit understands," ADIM responded, surprising Cassius with his answer. He was rarely so easily convinced to part with him for any long period of time. "If you are too near the weapon unprotected or its blast, it is probable that you would contract the Blue Death. This unit would not risk your health."

"It is appreciated, ADIM. We will be reunited soon after, and all the Circuit will envy what we possess."

They reached the hangar where the *White Hand* was safely docked without any interruption. Once they got aboard, Cassius powered it on began to guide it up through Edeoria: Shaft 23.

It was darker then when they had arrived roughly a month before, and far quieter. As they rose up the shaft, it didn't take long for Cassius to recognize what the Drill and all his other ventures had cost. The displaced people were either severely emaciated or dead. More guards were positioned around the levels to keep a starving population at bay. Rations had to be traded to fund his project, and he imagined all the shafts of Edeoria were suffering. They would blame him first, and then the New Earth Tribunal. And when they rose up and the Tribune sent their ilk to seize his colony, he would make them watch with a smile on his face as his plans came to fruition.

CHAPTER TWENTY-EIGHT
SPLINTERS THROUGH SPACE

"Tal, we're closin' in on the coordinates fast!" Ulson shouted back from the cockpit as he slid his hands across the HOLO-Screen projected on the viewport. Zaimur had scouts feeding them intel and the map showed them closing in on a red blip.

Talon unfastened his restraint and hurried to the front to get a view of where they were headed. "Pull behind that asteroid," he said, signaling to a lone fragment of floating rock that appeared no bigger than a thimble from their vantage. Then he returned to his seat and strapped himself back in. His index finger began rhythmically tapping the chambers of his rifle. When he noticed Sage was watching he stopped and brought the weapon to rest on his lap. As nervous as he was, he couldn't afford to let any of them see it.

"You ready?" he said to her, but she didn't seem to hear him. She had hardly moved since they left, falling into a sort of ruminating stare, as if she were trapped in a trance. There was no excitement or anxiety, just numbness. Talon figured he knew what was wrong. "Was the man in the arena your first?"

"My first?" She hesitated to make eye contact, pretending that she was trying to listen in on the other quiet conversations throughout the vessel.

"Kill. Was he the first man you've killed?" Talon repeated.

"No." There was a coldness to her response, a sort of apathy that only comes from those who have seen more than their fair share of carnage. At that moment he knew she wasn't born with the hollow stare she wielded. Whether out of self-preservation, or to keep her mind at bay, life had taught it to her.

"First man with a rock to the head?" he joked, leaning forward with his rifle as a crutch and lifting his eyebrow.

"Yes, " she muttered. Her mouth creased into a feeble smile. Her hand quickly rose to her lips as her eyes lifted to look at him. She hid it well, but there was so much emotion swelling in her cavernous, green eyes that the hairs on the back of his neck stood on end. Before he could respond Ulson shouted back again.

"I got a readin' on the freighter! The metal in the asteroid should keep us hidden for long enough. You guys ready back there?" Their ship banked a grayish mass of crags and craters passing across the viewport.

Everybody answered right away with a grunt or a slap on the side of their guns, everybody except for Talon and Sage. He stared into her eyes and she didn't look away. "We're ready," he said, as if speaking directly to her. "Helmets on gentlemen! Let's make this quick."

Each member of the squad hoisted their helmets and placed them over their heads. They went on with a snap-hiss, the tops of their armor latching on and connecting to an air supply located on their backs. Talon gave Sage a nod before he pulled his own over his head, his vision tinted as the visor came down over his eyes. She pressed a button on her bracer and from the upper part of her back, plates of metal rose up like a conveyer belt. When they were all in place, a bowed, amber visor slid down from the piece above her brow, connecting to the plates which rose to fit around her jaw. *Who is this girl?* Talon wondered as he gawked, never having seen a suit like it in all of his life.

"Ready to send you boys down, Tal. On your signal." Ulson pulled up the HOLO-Screen again.

Talon took a few deep breaths and firmly gripped his gun. Then he reached up and held down a button on his chest. All of their comm systems were set to the same frequency. "Send us out."

Ulson keyed a few commands and all of their seats rotated vertically. Their restraints shifted as the floor opened, sliding them down the back of the ship and into a small, narrow chamber. It was large enough to fit no more than a single man lying on his back, and Talon leaned up to catch one more glimpse of Sage's white armor before a transparent roof sealed over him.

"Remember, once we get in to stay together," Talon began

giving his orders over the comm system. "Alpha squad, you're on me. We'll be shot in first and head to the command deck. Beta squad you're on Chavos. When Ulson banks around, you'll be sent toward the back of the freighter. Secure the engineering quarters and the cargo deck." Talon received a chorus of "yes sirs," though he heard no female voice amongst them.

"Don't worry about breaking anything," he continued. "We don't want the ship, just the Cargo. We'll disable the freighter and any resistance, and that'll be the end of it. Beta you get that cargo hatch open for Ulson and we'll load up and get out. Easy as taking you fools in a game of cards."

"Remind me when we get back to take you up on that offer," Vellish mused.

"Will do. Everybody stay off them comms unless it's urgent. We'll take these bastards for all they're worth."

Talon let go of the switch and held his rifle at his chest. The chamber was rumbling intensely as Ulson swung the ship around the asteroid. His finger began to tap the gun as his pulse quickened. He could hear the roar of the engines even through his suit. He closed his eyes and pictured Elisha's face, smiling as she ran toward his open arms.

I will see you again, he promised, and then metal cuffs rose up to strap around his limbs and helmet so that he couldn't move.

"Alpha squad. Have a good trip." Ulson's voice filled his ears before his vessel was shot forward like a missile.

The pressure was almost too much to bear. Talon screamed as his eyes snapped open, looking through the glass to see only blackness and stars rushing by in blinding fashion. It wasn't his first time using the splinter tactic of raiding ships that the Ceresian Pact had grown fond of, but he forgot how much it hurt. It had taken decades to perfect the strategy enough to keep the impact from severely injuring or killing the passengers, but that didn't keep Talon from doubting the Splinter Chambers every time he crawled into one.

He clenched his teeth and squeezed his eyes, the pressure almost too much to bear. And then when he felt like his skull was going to explode, the jagged front of the chamber sliced into the hull of the freighter. A coupling of the restraints, advanced recoil technologies and the use of magnets and Gravitum kept his body from breaking as it came to a sudden and bone-chattering stop.

"Alpha squad engaged. Coming around the Freighter. Firing Beta Squad," Ulson updated them.

The restraints lifted off Talon and the front of the chamber opened like prongs. He stretched out his limbs. He was sore all over, with lines of burning pain shooting along his elbows and knees. As the Blue Death was slowly taking him he knew the pain would linger for days, but he would live. The surface within the chamber suddenly lurched forward, launching him through a narrow gash and into the freighter.

CHAPTER TWENTY-NINE
A KNIGHT IN THE DARKNESS

"Beta Squad engaged," Ulson said over the Comm system as Sage was thrust forward into the freighter. Her feet landed against the wall and she pushed off, falling into a tight roll and coming to a low, battle-ready crouch with her eye aimed straight down the barrel of her pistol. The interior was flashing with emergency red lights to the tune of a wailing alarm. Around her were only the five other members of her squad, all of them scrambling to their feet after clumsy entrances. It may not have been the prettiest strategy of boarding a vessel, but it was efficient. She would give the Ceresians that.

The mercenary with the scar on his chin, named Chavos, pressed a switch to slide his visor up into his helmet once he got his bearings. She and the rest followed his lead as Talon commanded, "Talon's keeping them occupied. Let's do this quick. You three." He pointed to Sage and two others with whom she wasn't familiar. "Head down to engineering and disable all systems. We'll take the cargo bay."

Sage's group nodded in unison and one of the mercenaries took the lead and began to head down the corridor with his rifle at the ready. They moved slowly in a staggered line formation, with Sage taking up the rear position.

"Did you study the schematics?" one of the mercenaries asked as the leader peaked around a corner. It was empty.

"I think it's this way." The leader waved them on when suddenly a group of Tribunal soldiers cut around the far end of the hall and opened fire. A bullet burst through his head, splattering his brains on the inside of his helmet.

"Fuck!" the surviving mercenary shouted as Sage pulled them

back around the corner.

"Give me cover fire!" she ordered.

Without questioning her, he poked his rifle around the corner and fired. Bullet trails danced and smoke leaked out as the walls were peppered with a spray of projectiles. Sage dove over the leader's carcass, rolling safely to the other side of the opening and sliding down the wall so that her legs were cocked. She glanced at the reflection in the corpse's half open visor. There were four Tribunal soldiers pressing forward in two rows through a misty haze. The two in front were crouched with the other standing at their backs.

Sage held up a fist to the mercenary to get him to stop firing. He looked back at her with a baffled glare, but he obliged. All of the gunfire stopped, leaving only the alarm and the hiss of leaking pipes. She listened for their footsteps, waiting until they were at the right distance.

"Beta squad!" Talon's anxious voice rang over the comm system. "We're receiving heavy resistance at the command deck!" He paused. "Beta, take out the defense systems! Auto turrets up here have already taken out two of us!"

"En route," the mercenary beside her whispered as the footsteps grew nearer.

"My group is in a standoff at the cargo bay entrance. We should hold!" Chavos updated his position.

"They were ready for us. Use whatever means necessary! We'll take this son of a bitch down with us if we have to!" Talon cut out to a chorus of screams and gunfire.

His words urged her artificial finger to wrap around the trigger of her pistol. Then she paused for the first time since boarding the ship.

What am I doing? she thought to herself as she peeked around the corner. They were soldiers of the Tribune, serving the same faith as she did. She should have been helping them, but the Executor order was far too clandestine for any normal Tribunal soldiers to know who she was. To them she was no different than any of the other mercenaries, but she reminded herself that she was the extended hand of a just and righteous Tribune. Talon and his mercenaries were not responsible for the attacks. She couldn't let them be blamed for it. Then the Tribune would still be in danger from the real culprits. All she could hope to do was make it out alive in order to continue her assigned mission.

For the good of the Tribune, she thought as she slowly exhaled and then she went to work.

She nodded to the other mercenary and he fired blindly to draw attention. Just as the soldiers unloaded their clips eon him she snapped around the corner, firing four succinct shots. The bullets stopped flowing and she rushed forward into the haze. The soldiers lay in a clean heap in the ground.

"Clear!" she hollered back as she kneeled and set her sights down the corridor.

"By the fuckin' Ancients!" the mercenary marveled as he saw the four bodies, each of them with a hole in the center of their foreheads leaking a thin stream of blood.

"You heard him, let's move! It's this way!" Sage urged the mercenary on and moved at a faster pace. She was no stranger to the layout of a tribunal freighter. Talon was right. No transport should have as many defenders as they faced. The Tribune was baiting whoever had been raiding their ships to attack again, and they had fallen right in the middle of their ploy. Only Talon and the rest of them weren't who they were looking for.

Sage slid leg first around the next corner, the whiz of bullets over her head tossing her hair back. The two soldiers were dead before they could locate her and she sprinted forward over the bodies, challenging the other mercenary to keep up. The door to the engineering bay was just ahead. A turret sprang down from the ceiling in front of it. She threw herself into the wall, the bullets zipping passed her and cutting the mercenary in half. As it turned toward her she fired at the base of it, sending out a shower of sparks as the disabled gun slumped down.

Turrets by engineering. This ship has been outfitted to hold, she realized as she looked back to see the bloodbath. The entrance to the engineering bay was shut, and the expanse of frosted translucency beside it was too opaque to see through. She hurried to the retinal scanner at the side of it. Emergency procedures had locked it with only ranking members of the ship able to override, but an Executor could bypass such systems. She placed her eye in the scanner.

The door slid open and she crouched at the side of it. A soldier peeked out for a second before she fired a round through his skull.

"Raiders!" men inside shouted as she snapped the pulse rifle from the falling body. They fired at the open door, but she was already moving down the corridor outside. She squeezed her artificial hand into a fist and with a roar slammed it through the thick, bullet-proof glass. Then she pulled the rifle up to her shoulder and blasted through the break. Shrieks rang out as she ditched the rifle, rolled back to the door, pressing through with her pistol and taking out all resistance inside with ease.

"Any progress back there?" Talon shouted over the comm.

Before answering Sage ran over and tossed a body off of a console before sitting down. Even as an Executor she couldn't disable the Vale Protocol so that they could take control of the ship. She was, however, able to power down all of the automated defenses and cameras. Then she switched off the primary lighting systems, so that only the reserve illumination would paint the whole ship in a dull red. The darkness would make it harder for both sides, and hopefully keep Talon and the rest of them alive long enough for her to help.

"Automated defenses deactivated! Hold on up there. I'll try to give you a gravity boost," Sage announced over the comm system. She didn't hesitate before leaving the engineering bay and heading in another direction.

"Sounds good." Talon wheezed heavily. "We're pushing into the command deck." There was a barrage of loud blasts followed by bloodcurdling screams. "They've surrounded us with a Mech! Fuck, it came out of nowhere!"

"Just hold tight!" Sage didn't bother to be cautious. They were on the defensive and nobody would expect her to come charging. The Gravitum Generator was toward the back of the ship, across from the reactor on the lower level.

After a short sprint she could hear the echoes of Chavos and his group battling a ways down. She stopped and peered around a corner, where she saw her destination as expected. There was a set of stairs leading down, with two guards on either side of it. Before they noticed her she sent a single bullet through their temples. *Too easy. I'll have to let Benjar know.*

She moved swiftly, suspecting that there would be no guards down by the reactor. Nobody would be stupid enough to engage in a firefight where only a single stray bullet could send the thing into a meltdown.

She reached the bottom, where an elliptical catwalk was suspended around a smoldering, red sphere surrounded by an array of violently, rotating blades. There were only engineers on the floor below, monitoring the reactor, and they wouldn't hear her over the racket. She hopped over the rail, hanging down until one of them passed beneath her. Then she dropped, knocking him unconscious with an elbow to the head.

First making sure that none of the others noticed, she passed through the shadow toward a chamber sealed by a thick door. She came to the retinal scanner and keyed the override. Then she closed her visor and made sure her suit was completely sealed. She had been told that the suit could withstand direct exposure to Gravitum and keep her from contracting the Blue Death, but she had never tested it. The heavy door slowly rose, revealing the pulsating blue of the Gravitum generator, and she stepped in. It was a necessary risk.

Chapter Thirty
Cornered in the Void

Talon threw his back against the wall and switched on his comm system. "We're receiving heavy resistance at the command deck!" He popped around the corner and took out one of the auto-turrets on the ceiling. "Beta take out the defense system! Auto turrets up here have already taken out two men!"

There were four of them left including Talon, Vellish, and two other mercenaries who stood on either side of the wide entrance into the command deck. They were locked in a stalemate. The turrets were protected by a constant spray of fire from the soldiers inside. The chaos had already left half a dozen bodies from both sides lying throughout the opening. Blood sprayed up from them to form a congealing red mist as they were battered by bullets. Smoke and sparks poured out of the walls to mix with it, making it difficult to see.

"Vellish! You have any smoke left?" Talon lifted his visor and shouted across the hall.

"Got one!" he responded as he fired around the corner.

"Toss it right at the other side of the entrance. As soon as it's thick, move in and use the consoles for cover. Everyone pick a spot where the turrets can't get you."

Talon waited a moment to gage his destination and let the others do the same. "Okay, everybody ready?" he asked, to which they both nodded. "Toss it!"

A cylindrical grenade with a band of white light around the top rolled across the floor. "Fall back!" one of the men inside barked as the device clanked to a halt, thinking it was an explosive. There was a deafening *bang* and a flash of white light as a thick veil of smoke began to leak out. His ears ringing from the blast,

Talon gave the orders as the veil of smoke rendered everything unseen. "Go, go go!"

They swept in, firing blindly through the shroud. Talon heard a yelp as the mercenary behind him took a shot through the chest. He dove, a bullet glancing off of his right arm, and slammed against a console.

Only a flesh wound, he thought to himself gratefully as he noticed the gash cut into his armor, a thin line of blood dripping out. There wasn't much time to analyze it. Sparks spewed over his head as bullets rained down on his position. He scrambled to pull in his legs, firing blindly over the console until he was safely in cover. Then he glanced over to see that Vellish and the one other surviving mercenary had also made it, and had taken out one of the remaining turrets on their way.

"Any progress back there?" Talon shouted over the comm. He peeked over the console and took out one of the soldiers before a flurry of bullets zipped overhead and forced him back down with his hands over his ears.

After around half a minute in cover, holding back the Tribunal soldiers as best as they could, the lights throughout the command deck suddenly went off, leaving only the flashing red of the alarms.

"Automated defenses off! Hold on up there, I'll try and give you a gravity lift!" Sage announced over the comm system. The news reinvigorated Talon, who, in concert with the other mercenaries, immediately sprung from his cover shooting. They pressed forward, cutting the defenders to pieces and turning the tables on the few Tribunal survivors who had to drop to shield themselves on the lower level of the command deck. The soldiers hadn't expected to lose their advantage so swiftly. Their new position was perilous. Against the backdrop of the ship's expansive translucency they were illuminated by the stars.

"Not sure what that is, but anything sounds good right about now," Talon panted over the comm as he took one of them out with a burst of fire. "We're pushing through the command deck." Just as he said it, the floor shook and a powerful volley took the mercenary beside Vellish's head off. Talon ducked quickly, looking through the bottoms of chairs and consoles to see a Mech stomping through the entrance. The hulking mass of metal tore across the deck with a chain gun on its arm, clipping Vellish's leg as he clambered for cover.

"They've surrounded us with a Mech," Talon screamed. "Fuck, it came out of nowhere!"

"Just hold tight!" Sage's optimistic voice came through.

Talon looked behind him to see the soldiers at the viewport coming out of hiding. He rolled onto his back and unloaded on them until he had to switch out his clip.

"Move down there Vellish!" he shouted across the room. Vellish was on the ground holding his bleeding leg, but was able to turn and fire down at the level below, killing the men trying to sneak up behind him. He crawled over the edge and Talon made sure there were none left before he followed.

Talon peered over the edge quickly. They were only about six feet below the main deck. The Mech fired in his direction, stray bullets slamming into the glass viewport in such tight succession that it was ready to shatter. Protective panels slid down as Talon's ears popped and his body was pulled backward. The entrance behind the Mech sealed shut as it stomped forward, each of its massive limbs causing the whole room to shudder. Vellish pulled himself to his feet and sent a few rounds into the Mech to draw its fire.

"We can't hold out against this!" Vellish groaned. His wounded leg gave out and he fell down.

Come on Sage, Talon thought to himself. He glanced up again at his impending doom, the metal goliath painted in ominous red light every time the alarm wailed. A host of soldiers were arrayed in a line on either side of it, slowly pushing forward until there would be nowhere left to run.

"Talon...Talon are you there?" Sage's voice pleaded over the comm system.

"We're here." He coughed. His lungs were filled with smoke. "Whatever you're gonna do, do it!"

He had the sudden urge to close his eyes as the Mech got closer. It wasn't the way he had expected to die. But then, just before the machine could reach his cover, the gravity of the room shifted. Talon felt himself being slowly pulled upward.

Gravity lift, Talon realized her earlier meaning and couldn't help but smirk. "Hold on Vellish!" he yelled and grabbed onto the grated floor. Vellish did the same and they watched as the Mech and the soldiers floated up into the air, looking around frantically with no idea about what was happening to them.

"System will override in thirty seconds. Hold on!" Sage's voice urged into his ear.

The Tribunal soldiers thrashed around, trying to swim through the air as they dangled. Talon kept his eye on the Mech and as soon as it tapped against the tall ceiling, the gravity rapidly returned to normal. Everything fell to the floor, the Mech landing with a loud crash. Talon caught his rifle as it plummeted and quickly turned to fire. The bewildered soldiers dropped in succession as he ran up the stairs. Struggling to come to its feet, the Mech stretched out its arm and fired, forcing Talon to sprawl behind a console out of the way.

A deafening torrent of bullets tore through the equipment, burrowing toward him. And then, just as he thought the Mech was going to tear him to pieces, the shooting stopped. He peered around the corner. The entrance to the command deck was open, and as he came further around he saw her.

Sage was standing atop the colossal Mech, her artificial hand reaching through its chest and into the pilot's chamber. The whole thing twitched a few times until she pulled her arm out covered in blood. Its heavy limbs collapsed to the ground, almost throwing Talon off balance as he stared at her.

Who is this woman?

"They knew we were coming!" she snarled as she slid down the Mech's chassis. She landed nimbly on two feet, as if she didn't even realize how remarkable the move was.

"I know," Talon panted as his eyes widened over Sage's handiwork. "You realize you—"

"We need Ulson to get here now!" Sage heard one of the fallen soldiers reach for his gun and shot him through the chest.

Talon stammered for words as Sage ran down to help Vellish up to the command deck. Unable to take his eyes off of the Mech, he held down the button on his chest. "Chavos, what's your status?"

"We just took the cargo bay!" Chavos responded immediately. Talon could hear what sounded like tarps being peeled over.

"There's nothing! It's all empty! All the Gravitum is gone. Fu—" Chavos was cut off by static and the whole ship lurched to the side.

"Holy shit, Tal!" Ulson spoke somberly over the comm. "The whole Cargo bay just went up in flames."

Talon leaned against the Mech's leg, his heart sinking. "The Tribune knew..." He looked to Sage, his eyes glazed over as though all hope was lost. "They knew."

It only seemed to fill her face with fervor. She stopped in front of him with her arm around Vellish and switched on her comm. "Ulson, I know it's crazy, but stay on the back of the ship. We're gonna come through the cargo bay and float to you."

"It's only sparks and bodies now," Ulson informed them. "You should be able to make it through."

Talon looked into her eyes and nodded firmly. He threw his arm around Vellish to assist her and they headed toward the door as fast as they could.

"Wait. There are more ships coming."

"Is it the other raiders?" Sage questioned before he could finish.

"No. Tribunal! I'll try to—" Ulson cut out to static before they could hear his screams. He looked to Sage, but all her vigor appeared to be sapped as well. It was then that he knew. Ulson was shot down and they were trapped. The Tribune had them and there was no way off. All they could do was wait.

CHAPTER THIRTY-ONE
CONDUIT'S END

Cassius was in the center of one of the merchant bays within the Conduit Station over Titan. He took a seat on a bench in the aisle positioned under the outstretched bough of a planted tree. His eyes shifted from side to side, observing every inch of the century old marvel of the ancients engineering. Metal and glass danced throughout the space to weaving an structure half-veiling the starry expanse of space.

His eyes came to rest on a leaf dangling just in front of his face. He reached out and took it between his fingers, spinning it slowly so that he could see the many veins running up its underside. It began to twist under the pressure until the center vein tore through the side and it fell, dithering down from the branch through the stale air.

He sighed and looked up again. The great, arcing hall was bustling. Soldiers both of the NET and Titan specifically were interspersed throughout the crowd of travelers, wanderers, beggars and merchants. Those who recognized Cassius offered him nods of acknowledgement, though there were a few deferential bows sprinkled in.

He watched them all, soldiers and civilians alike, and studied their ignorant faces, knowing that soon most of them would die. There was even a peculiar looking man sitting on a nearby bench and trying too hard not to pay attention to him. They would all be the unfortunate victims of a war that had not yet come to pass, a necessary expense. *For the greater good,* Cassius reminded himself.

"Creator," an NET soldier addressed him suddenly. He came to a stop just in front of Cassius and stood at attention so faultlessly that it was obvious he was trying too hard. "The last charge has been set." He said, lowering his voice an octave.

"Good. My business has been concluded as well." Cassius snuck a glance over his shoulder at the unusual man sitting close by. "Let's head to the hangar and be done with this place for the last time. Too many prying eyes about." He whispered before patting the soldier on the back, his hand slipping through the hologram of armor to fall flat against ADIM's cold, metal back.

They made their way toward the hangar bay as quickly as possible. Merchants peddled their wares, no robots, but all sorts of other luxuries. Cassius had no trouble ignoring them, and the few that got too close were swiftly pushed back onto their rears by the disguised ADIM.

When they reached the entrance of the White Hand's reserved hangar, the engineer in charge stood tall in the entrance, his back straight and his head up.

"Was everything to your satisfaction, Ex-Tribune Vale?" He asked sincerely, not to make eye contact as was customary.

It seems not all of their servants have been trained to scorn me, Cassius mused to himself. "The station is running impeccably!" he praised. "Keep up the good work."

The engineer fell to his knee and brushed his fingers against the floor. "Thank you, Your Eminence. We will try."

Cassius sneered and walked passed him. "Save that for the real Tribunes, boy." He grumbled as he and ADIM stepped up the ramp of the *White Hand*.

Once a loud hiss signaled they were completely sealed inside, ADIM deactivated the projection which had shrouded him in the image of an NET soldier. They stopped by the *Shadow Chariot* which was holding few crates of food Cassius had purchased earlier.

"Creator, by the very nature of our purpose here he, and all others aboard this station, have in fact failed their duties. Why be false with him?" ADIM questioned, the tiny red blips around his eyes spinning rapidly.

"Mercy, perhaps, if I'm capable of such a thing. No reason to break a man's soul just before his inevitable end," Cassius sighed. He flipped the latch on the *Shadow Chariot* so the cockpit swung open.

ADIM turned his head without moving his body and looked at Cassius. His eyes stopped rotating. "By this unit's approximation of the extent of damage from the explosives, everyone in this sector will die at minimum."

"Yes, and now I've been made to look upon their faces before I do what I must do. I will feel every death." He put his hand on ADIM's shoulder and looked at him, a glint forming in his grayish eyes as they narrowed. "And my resolve has never been stronger."

ADIM hopped up into the *Shadow Chariot* with ease. "They must be punished for their weakness."

As ADIM prepped the ship, Cassius watched him with a proud smile. "I will see you soon, ADIM. I know you don't need it, but good luck on your end."

ADIM's head snapped toward Cassius, his glowing red eyes coming to a complete halt. "Goodbye, Creator."

Cassius turned away and headed to the command deck. He took his seat in the captain's chair, powered on the *White Hand* and guided it out of the hangar.

"Captain, the *Shadow Chariot* has been deployed and is enroute to Ennomos," Gaia announced over the ships speakers.

Cassius didn't respond. He gazed out of the viewport and breathed in the view. The jointed rings of the Conduit receded, casting a large shadow over the top of Titan's thick atmosphere. All of it was bathed in the shadow of Saturn, and just over the sickle-like ring in the distance, he could make out the web of city lights across the surface of Enceladus. Though smaller than Titan, the moon was the site of the NET's primary base in the area. It was where the newest Tribune, Nora Gressler, called home.

He let the *White Hand* drift in space over the Conduit as the sight of it led him to remember the day he first met her. That fateful day more than seven years ago…

———— •≒≡≣◆D⊕◐≣≡⊹• ————

Cassius was walking down a long, luminous hallway connecting the main Tribunal Complex on the Earth's moon to the hangar where his ship was located. He was younger then, but the most noticeable difference, besides a few less gray hairs, was that he wasn't shrouded by his usual aura of grimness. There was a lightness to his stride.

He stopped to gaze out of a translucency. Beyond the craterous landscape of the grey world, the Earth rose up to take up his entire view. The planet's blackened atmosphere was hardly anything to look at. Even as sunlight was beginning to camber around the top edge like a blade of flame, the world remained dark and gloomy...rotting.

"Beautiful isn't it?" Tribune Benjar Vakari said reverently as he stepped into the corridor from an adjacent room.

Cassius was about to respond when a low beep sounded from a pouch attached to his belt. He reached in and pulled out his spherical, HOLO-Recorder, which was blinking. *Caleb*, he thought, recognizing immediately that the light meant his son was trying to contact him. *From so nearby the Earth they w*ould've been able to set up a live-feed with each other, but that would reveal his position. As far as Caleb knew, he was millions of miles away on Mars. He didn't want to ruin the surprise.

"Do you think the Ancients ever thought that there would be more people living on Earth's moon than on the planet it orbits?" Cassius said pensively to his fellow Tribune, Benjar Vakari, as he placed the device back into his pouch.

Benjar didn't answer at first. Cassius turned around to look at him. The Tribune approached with a striking woman at his side, her short black hair framing the soft cambers of her neck. Despite her pleasing face, she had the unmistakable demeanor of a soldier, and wore the armor of a Tribune's Hand. It was Nora Gressler, before the weather of time and lofty status had claimed her beauty.

"What do you think...what's your name?" Cassius turned to the woman standing in Benjar's shadow. He didn't know much about her, only that Benjar had recently chosen her to serve as his personal Hand. Cassius didn't think much of it. Benjar had always enjoyed his women.

"Nora, Your Eminence," she responded firmly as she knelt down and touched the floor.

"The Ancients foresaw much," Benjar said plainly before Cassius could respond to her. There was no real animosity in his voice, though there was hardly a real interest in conversation either. At the time he and Cassius had the decency to tolerate each other because they had to for the good of the New Earth Tribunal.

Cassius smiled toward in Nora's direction. She nodded meekly in response before taking a step backward to stand quietly at attention.

"Who could have foreseen this?" Cassius turned back to the view and asked whoever was listening. "I can't imagine that it was ever blue and green. What a sight that must have been."

Benjar shot him a stern glare. "And it is a sight we shall see once more, if we stay on the proper path."

"My son doesn't think so." Cassius placed his hand against the glass and squinted at Earth. He could barely make out the landmass where his son's research lab was supposedly located.

"Yes well, he shall soon see what a fool's errand he is on. One man cannot save Earth. Her Spirit begs a grander act of penance."

"But what if he can?" Cassius cut Benjar off excitedly, not interested in hearing what the Tribune had said a thousand times before. "What if science can fix our world as simply it has given us new ones?"

Benjar had to reach up to place his hand on the center of Cassius' tall back. He then used it to usher him along down the corridor. "Such are the thoughts which ruined Earth in the first place. Gravitum is the curse of our curiosity. One element to give us so much, but to take away so much more. Men spent centuries trying to alter the landscapes of Mars and Titan before the Tribune stepped in. Wasted years. Some things are not meant to change until the universe wills it."

"And some things need more time to grow." Cassius sighed and continued to walk down the hallway. "It seems there are some things we will never agree upon."

"As I have learned," Benjar grumbled as they proceeded into the lofty, private hangar of the moon complex. There were only a few ships inside, mostly small transports, but to the far side, the *White Hand* was glistening like roughly cut pearl.

"Well, I must be off," Cassius said as he veered toward his ship.

"Is Caleb expecting you so soon?"

"No. I figured I'd surprise him on my birthday and see his work first hand." He paused and took a deep breath. "I haven't returned to Earth since the war." The words slipped out of his mouth with a sour note. As much glory as the Earth Reclaimer Wars had brought him, Cassius had few fond memories of the conflict.

"The planet is forever in your debt, but you will find it has not changed much, despite your son's intervention," Benjar said with a hint of sarcasm.

"Ahh, Benjar." Cassius smiled warmly and placed his palm upon his fellow Tribune's shoulder. "One day I will make a believer out of you."

"And I you." Benjar put on his patented, complacent grin before he clasped his hands together and bowed. "May the Spirit of the Earth guide your steps."

"It always does," Cassius replied and returned the gesture.

He swiftly turned around to board his ship when out of nowhere a group of engineers burst into the hangar. The few Tribunal guards posted around the space were roused by the commotion and began to form a defensive line in front their masters.

"Your Eminences!" the head engineer shouted frantically. When he reached them he was so winded he could barely speak. Though he still found the energy to kneel down and touch the floor before them.

"Out with it!" Nora stepped in front of the Tribunes with her rifle pistol and ordered.

"There is..." he gathered his breath. "Intense seismic activity on Earth. A new rupture appears to be opening from the core... I...I don't know."

"When?" Cassius whirled around and stormed down the ramp onto his ship with fire in his eyes.

"Right now. We couldn't pick it up in time, but it's off the charts!"

Cassius seized him by the collar of his uniform. "Where? Show me!"

The engineer was quaking in fear as he activated the HOLO-Screen on his wrist and pulled up a projection of Earth. It was rendered as a matrix of blue lines composing a sphere, and there was a substantial blob of red light growing beneath the surface of one of the continents.

"It can't be." Cassius' eyes widened in horror. His fingers

slipped off of the Engineer and he stumbled backwards as if he were shot in the chest.

"What's the matter, Cassius?" Benjar asked, without appearing overly concerned.

"Caleb…it's right under him." Cassius could hardly mouth the words as he began running toward his ship.

"Your Eminence!" the head engineer cried out after him. "It's too dangerous!"

Cassius bounded through the cargo bay of the *White Hand* and headed around the corridors toward the command deck.

"Ready the engines and set a course for Earth," he screamed into his bracer.

"Beginning preparations, Cassius," the virtual intelligence Gaia responded through the ship's speaker system.

When he reached the command deck, Cassius leapt over the back of his seat and took his position. The ground began to rumble as the twin ion engines powered on. The hangar doors outside remained closed, blocking him in as he impatiently rolled his fingers across the armrest.

"Cassius. Step down. I can't let you do this," the voice of Benjar Vakari demanded calmly from behind him.

"I'll blast through it if I have to. Get out!" Cassius squeezed his hand into a fist and continued staring at the sealed exit.

"And have everyone inside sucked out into space?"

Cassius got to his feet, pulled out his pistol and wheeled around. There were three Tribunal guards standing behind Benjar with their weapons at the ready. Nora was just in front of him, alertly holding her pistol at her side. The head engineer stood directly beside him with his eyes trained on the projection of Earth.

Cassius knew the engineer was the one with the codes to open the hangar and he took aim directly at his chest. "Open it," he commanded sternly, his lips and hands quivering equal amounts.

The engineer went to key some commands on his HOLO-Screen but was stopped by Benjar. "No!" the Tribune barked. "The risk is too great."

"Do it." Cassius' voice barely rose above a whisper as he kept aiming at the engineer, but the ferocity in it was enough to make the man freeze in pure dread. "Open it." Cassius shot at his feet and the three Tribunal guards instantly stepped in front of Benjar and armed themselves. Nora took aim at him.

"He will do no such thing. Cassius, you are not thinking clearly." Benjar took a step forward through his guards. "You are a member of the New Earth Tribunal."

"It is my son!" Cassius roared, shifting his aim to Benjar, when all of a sudden a bullet from Nora's gun slammed into the side of his pistol and smacked it out of his hands. He stood still, staring into his empty hands. He could hardly make out any of the muddle of noises surrounding him, until the engineer spoke up.

"Your Eminences," the man began meekly. "Scanners are picking up a ship escaping from the site of the seismic activity."

"There are survivors?" Cassius snapped out of it. He rushed past the group of anxious guards. "Show me!" He grasped the engineer's wrist to get a closer look at the projection, seeing a tiny, red blip flying away from the Earth toward the moon. "Tell them to head here. Open the hangar doors! Quickly!" Cassius ran to the viewport and leaned over the rail.

The engineer looked to Benjar who shot back a reluctant nod before he went back to staring at Cassius, a narrow grin pasted onto his face. After a few moments, everybody in the hangar evacuated and it began to pressurize. Then the two sides of the doors slid open like a mouth filled with serrated teeth, and the Earth became visible, painted in the yellowish radiance of the sun.

Everybody waited quietly, the guards with their fingers on their triggers. The engineer was ready to break into tears as he glanced down at the bullet hole in front of his feet. Cassius' hands squeezed the railing, watching anxiously as the trail of ion-engines traced across the blackness toward their location.

Minutes went by. All in silence. Then, finally the small ship darted over the gray landscape of the Moon. It was coming in low, and once it was close enough Cassius could tell that one of the wings was severely damaged. It was barely able to reach the surface of the hangar, skidding along the floor until it came to a sudden, deafening halt against the opposite wall within a shower of sparks.

Cassius didn't hesitate for a second. He bounded out of the command deck before anybody could stop him, quickly traversing the halls of his ship. Then he exited out into the larger hangar of the Tribunal Complex.

The crashed transport was small, with just enough room for a pilot and a small load. As he approached he saw the pilot through the translucency get up and head to the back. Then the cargo doors slid open, and the pilot tumbled out, covered in blood from head to toe and gripping his leg in clear agony.

"There are more inside," he groaned. "I don't know if they made it."

Cassius ignored him. His eyes were fixed on the open transport. There were two bodies inside, he was sure of that. Once he got closer he saw that they were side by side with one's arm thrown over the other. A thick piece of metal structure was piercing it, severing the limb before it plunged through the chest of the other body.

His heart raced. He immediately recognized the body on top with her long, wavy auburn hair. "Sage," he mouthed as he noticed her chest was still expanding and contracting. She was alive, though if not tended to immediately she would likely bleed out through her ravaged arm. The face of the other was blocked by her.

Cassius moved forward slowly. He almost didn't want to know. There was so much blood that it was impossible to tell whether or not it was even his son's clothing. After countless battles and brushes with death, that moment of uncertainty was the most frightened he had ever been. He reached in and brushed Sage's hair back. The face that was revealed to him stung him like a knife through his heart.

"Caleb," he whimpered, his eyes freezing in horror over the sight. "Caleb!" He pulled the body out, dragged it to the ground and began pushing down on his son's chest. Then he attempted to kiss air into his lungs, but all he tasted was blood. "Caleb come on!" He repeated the same process over and over, pushing down harder and blowing harder each time. "Breathe!" he wailed, tears raining down his cheeks as he fell into his sons chest. "Breathe…"

"I tried to help him. He went back for this." The pilot struggled to pull something out from his belt, but before he could, Cassius turned around, roaring with a rage as feral as an unchained beast's, and struck him across the head. A small glass cylinder with a wiry plant floating inside rolled out from the pilot's belt as he flipped over. Cassius was too incensed to notice.

Tribunal guards raced over to pull Cassius away but he fought them off, driving blow after blow forward into the poor pilot's face until he was spitting up his own bloody teeth. It took all six of the soldiers to peel Cassius away, but he had already beaten the pilot to the precipice of death.

"Your Eminence, You must calm down!" Nora Gressler hurried over to tend to the groaning pilot.

Cassius was sitting upright on both knees, staring at his bloodied knuckles as the guards backed away. The whole room was spinning so much that he felt like he was going to vomit. He didn't even notice at the time that Benjar picked up the plant and tucked it beneath his robes.

"Caleb," Cassius whispered as he began crawling over to the corpse. He ran his hands through his son's short hair and lifted his limp head to his chest, cradling it as he sobbed. Then he went to grab Caleb's hand only to find a small, spherical device held firmly in the dead finger's grip. When he saw it, Cassius broke down completely. He couldn't even speak. He was shattered.

Nearly eight years later Cassius held out that same device in the center of his palm. He had made it for Caleb, one of two small HOLO-Recorders able to transmit messages across the Circuit, or even initiate Holo-communications if they were close enough to each other. He had watched the message that never reached him for his birthday nearly a thousand times since that day. It was all he had left to remember Caleb in his final moments of life.

Tears pooled in the corners of his eyes as he looked back up toward Enceladus, where Nora Gressler made home. *I will see you soon, my stunning replacement,* he thought. Then he grit his teeth. His period of rumination was over. War had taught him well the sacrifice that had to be made. He was ready.

CHAPTER THIRTY-TWO
MAKE SURE HE SEES YOU FIRST

ADIM was in a half-hibernating state as the *Shadow Chariot* raced through space. He was a little more than a day out of Titan when the ship's scanner picked up an unidentified object nearby.

He stirred promptly, studying the analysis which lit up a screen across the viewport. It showed a small spacefaring vessel, one that likely wouldn't be able to make it anywhere once it followed him to Ennomos. Cassius had taught him all the different types of NET ships, so he knew right away what was following him.

Creator, This unit is being followed by a small ship, Executor Class. ADIM transmitted the message to Cassius. He subtly began to alter the direction his ship was going so that whoever was tracking him wouldn't notice. *This unit has modified course. He cannot be allowed to track the Shadow Chariot's trajectory toward Ennomos.*

Not soon after his Creator responded, a hint of excitement touching his voice. *Finally. I had a feeling I saw one tracking us all the way back from the Conduit! It appears she is not as coy as I believed."*

She? ADIM questioned.

Tribune Nora Gressler. It appears Benjar has her entirely on his leash now.

Shall this unit destroy the Executor?

Not yet. Head in your new bearing for an hour as if you haven't noticed him. Then I want you to do something that will contradict everything I've ever asked of you.

Yes, Creator?

Disable the ship's engines, then board it personally in order to dispose of him. Make sure he sees you first.

ADIM's eyes again began to rotate wildly. *This unit will be discovered. He's an Executor. It is as you said, the Tribune is always watching through the eyes of the knights in the darkness.*

I'm betting on it. Cassius' tone grew firm. *It is time for you to reveal your existence to the Circuit.*

For all of his existence he had remained in the shadows, so the order led him to pause in a manner he wasn't used to. He never had a strong need to interact with any other humans, but he was curious to see how they lived. By understanding his Creator's people more extensively, he began to think that he could better help bring the change they sought.

As his ship continued to cruise, his thinking shifted. He shuffled through all of the possible outcomes, not used to uncertainty. *What if they fear me?* he wondered as he was pulled out into space, though he wasn't truly sure what that would mean for him. But the will of his creator was all that drove him, and it had never led him astray.

This unit shall not fail.

ADIM did as directed, waiting precisely an hour before he took complete command of the *Shadow Chariot's* systems and abruptly twisted it around. He zoomed through the blackness until he got visual on the Executor ship. He held off on his missiles and instead opened fire with his forward guns, knowing that a direct shot would blow the Executor to dust and he would fail Cassius.

The enemy pilot was more talented than expected. His ship shot up in a tight spiral out of the way before snaking around to fire one of his missiles. ADIM waited until the last second to release flares and evade, causing the heat-seeking projectile to zip right over the *Shadow Chariot's* narrow wing. He saw it explode in a dazzling flare of orange and blue in the reflection of his viewport.

The ability to use missiles gave ADIM's opponent a distinct advantage. He had to kill the Executor in a more personal manner, forcing him to reconsider his tactics. He maintained a straight line, allowing the Executor to come around and trail him. Another missile locked on and he waited until it was close before releasing flares to draw it off of him. Then he unlatched the circuits binding him to the ship and began processing the exact speeds of both ships.

*12 seconds...11 seconds...*He counted down to when he'd make his move.

Another missile shot out. ADIM powered down the *Shadow*

Chariot, lifted open the cockpit hatch and let himself be yanked out by the change in pressure. While soaring he made sure to target the missile and shoot it down before it could hit his ship. Then ADIM activated his magnetic chassis and his body was sucked down onto the top of the Executor vessel. Focused on the *Shadow Chariot*, the Executor had no chance to get out of the way.

He crawled over the translucency, looking down at the armored man sitting at the controls inside. The ship sped up and began to do a series of barrel rolls, the Executor desperately trying to fling him off, but it didn't affect ADIM in the slightest. He climbed down over the front of the vessel, just far enough so that the man was looking right at him. He saw brown eyes open wide and the man's mouth hang in a puzzled stare.

This Unit has been seen, Creator. ADIM transmitted to Cassius. *Shall I dispose of the Executor?*

However you see fit, Cassius replied almost instantly, a noticeable level of satisfaction in his tone.

Without hesitating, ADIM reared up and smashed through the translucency. He grasped the Executor by the neck and heaved him out, holding the body in the air as he stood atop the empty ship. The helmetless man grabbed at his neck frantically, his mouth trying to scream, but nothing came out. His eyes began to bulge as he thrashed around and tried to pry off ADIM's powerful grip.

ADIM watched for a few seconds as space rapidly sucked the air from the Executor's lungs and left him swollen and dead.. He knew humans couldn't survive in space, but he had never seen it.

The human dies instantly, but this Unit does not, he considered. Just like on Earth, he was able to survive where humans could not. He could follow the will of the Creator to any place.

Satisfied with the revelation, ADIM tossed the body to the side like a weightless sack of meat. Then he targeted the *Shadow Chariot* caught in inertia almost directly below. He moved into position and calculated the angle before pushing off toward it.

Using just a slight boost by shooting off one of his personal missiles he was able to grab hold of the hull of the *Shadow Chariot* and climb back into it. The cockpit sealed tight behind him, Cassius' formidable engineering skills keeping it in tact through the entirety of the affair.

The Executor is dead, Creator. ADIM informed Cassius.

Well done. Reduce his ship to scraps and proceed to Ennomos. That's all the Tribune needs to see. I have business I must attend to now. Message me when you reach the weapon. Farewell.

The cold silence of Cassius switching off his comm returned as ADIM brought his ship about. He expected it, but it was jarring nonetheless. The entire Tribune would know of his existence now, and he wished he could share that pivotal moment with his Creator. But he understood. Time was of the essence, and he had helped Cassius plan for far too long to let curiosity stand in the way.

He stored all of his questions in his memory before turning the *Shadow Chariot's* engines up to full thrust and re-setting course for Ennomos.

CHAPTER THIRTY-THREE
THE BLUE DEATH!

The freighter holding Sage, Talon, and Vellish was being escorted away from Ceresian space so that they could be dealt with. They were in the brig of the ship, stripped of their weapons. A plasma shield kept them detained in a small cell. Its orangey shimmer only visible like a translucent film at certain angles, but it was hot enough to peel the skin from their bones should they try to escape.

"I didn't see it ending like this," Talon ruminated. He was sitting against the wall of their small, empty cell next to Sage. He made sure to keep his voice down since Vellish was sleeping off the pain of his wound across the room. They had dressed it as best they could with the clothes beneath their armor, but he had already lost a lot of blood.

Sage turned to him, reached out to place a reassuring hand on his thigh, and then decided against it. "It's not over," she assured him.

Talon's laugh turned into a series of guttural coughs. She had noticed since the battle that his strength began to wane. At first she looked into his solemn, drawn back eyes and thought he was merely giving up, but there was more to it. As much as he tried to hide it, he barely had the strength to lift his arms.

"Please, Sage." He smiled meekly in her direction. "You saved my life once today, I don't need you risking anything else. A pretty girl like you they might make use of, but me? Do you know what the Tribune does to Ceresians who dare attack them?"

Cut off their arms? Sage thought to herself, remembering what she had done when she caught the bomber in New Terrene. "Better than most," she sighed, letting her head fall back against the wall and gazed across their cell. Even her synthetic arm could do nothing against a Plasma shield. Not that it mattered. She had seen a New Earth Cruiser through the freighter's translucency before they were captured, which meant that at least a Hand was present. Somebody with clearance enough to know what she was. When the Tribune discovered the truth, she would be spared and most likely rewarded. *Then why do I care?*

"I've heard stories of how they torture their heretics." Talon pointed to his forehead. "Rather them put a bullet right here and make it quick."

"I'll ask them to," Sage joked, though it didn't take her long to realize that it might come to that. Talon attempted to laugh but all that came through was a fatigued grin. Before she even realized it, her face returned a similar expression.

"I just hoped I'd get to see her one last time." He looked like he was about to cry, his eyes were shiny as glass and his lower lip trembled.

Sage furrowed her brow at the statement. Her human palm began to sweat. *Her?* She thought.

"My daughter," Talon quickly clarified, noticing her obvious unease. "You probably saw her around. Cute girl, eye's like mine. She's six now, and she's all I have." His hands curled into quivering fists. He was struggling to keep his composure.

Sage breathed a sigh of relief. *Of course, the little girl.* She remembered seeing her out of the corner of her eye while playing cards on Ceres. Her relief quickly turned to heartache as it dawned on her what that meant for him. "Talon…" she whispered gently as she unconsciously threaded her hand through his fingers, both of them taking a deep, startled gasp as she did. She stared down at their intertwined fingers, completely unsure of what she was doing. *I will not lose faith amongst the faithless,* she recited to herself almost out of instinct, but she didn't let go. "…I really would like to see her again one day. To really meet her."

She felt Talon squeeze a little tighter as he replied, "You and me both. I'd love to see her grow into a woman." He looked directly at her, a tear rolling down his cheek. "A woman like you, maybe. But that was never in the cards for me."

Sage opened her mouth to tell him, to let him know who she

was and that she could convince the Tribune to spare his life. But just as her mouth opened she noticed something peculiar about his uncovered hands. As pale as his Ceresian skin was, the veins running down the top of them showed a little too vibrantly. Most people wouldn't recognize it, but she had seen a number of those afflicted. The blue in them was unnatural, and it would explain why he was so physically sore even though he appeared in good shape. It was still in the early stages of development, but at that moment she knew why he had taken this foolish mission.

"The Blue Death…" she mouthed somberly, lifting up their conjoined hands to get a closer look at his.

"Wha…" Talon pulled back his hand and shot her an exasperated look. Or was it relieved? "How did you know?"

"Your hands. The veins always start to grow brighter around the extremities before it spreads." She shifted her body to sit in front of him and went to grab both of his hands to get a better look. He was hesitant at first, but before long he allowed her to take them. "How long?"

"Little over half a year. Didn't notice anything wrong for a few months." He began breathing heavier as soon as the words left his lips. She could see the layer of sweat building over his brow, and could tell he had probably never opened up about it to anybody. Maybe not even Julius.

"I was working the mines on Kalliope," Talon continued. "It was a typical day down there, until Zargo Morastus, Zaimur's father, arrived for an inspection. They never told us exactly what happened, but we all suspect. An assassin was gunning for the old Patriarch and tampered with the Gravity Generator. I was meeting with Zargo on my time off, not for business, just talking about old times together, when I used to carry a gun for him. That was when it happened. The generator overloaded and the blast nearly sent the whole complex to hell. Me and him were the closest to the Gravitum leak, and both of us paid for it dearly. The disease has crippled him faster, old man that he is, but I won't be far behind." He bit his lower lip to keep it from quivering.

"I'm so sorry," she said. *That's it?* She scolded herself, but she didn't know what else to say. At least she knew that she had meant it, and truthfully she knew she shouldn't care. He was Ceresian.

"It's ironic really. I stopped fighting for Zargo because I didn't want Elisha to lose her father, but in the end I couldn't escape my fate. We were just sharing a drink, reminiscing before he left to return to Ceres. Maybe we deserved it for all that we'd done...I don't know. When you know there's such little time left, none of that matters anymore...only her."

His tears began to roll out and as he went to wipe his eyes, Sage threw herself forward and embraced him. All of a sudden it happened and she couldn't stop it, nor urge herself to pull away. *What am I doing?* she thought.

"You will see her again. I promise," she whispered directly into his ear. Her hands rubbed the back of his bloody tunic, sliding up to run through his short hair and pull his head close. Their damp foreheads gently came together and Talon grabbed her shoulders to hold her back so he could look into her eyes.

"You can't promise that." He brushed her hair back over her ear, their enamored gazes locked together as if forcefully bound.

"I made a promise once..." The face of a young, handsome man flashed through her mind, making her wince. She ignored it and held firm. "And I broke it. I...I won't break a promise again."

Talon tenderly placed his hands on either side of her head. "Agatha...Who are you?" He smiled through his tears and leaned in toward her when suddenly there was a loud discharge of energy. Their heads snapped around to see a cohort of soldiers with their guns trained on the detention cell.

"On your feet Ceresian scum!" the leader of the group grumbled as he walked in. His green armor was far more decorated than the others, with the gold Tribunal Emblem on his shoulder denoting that he was one of the four Hands. The collection of long, scabrous scars running down from his shaved head helped her identify which one. *Hand Yavortha*, she thought darkly, Tribune Benjar Vakari's personal assistant, and a man whose rank outweighed even hers. Benjar gave him a long leash so she had never actually seen him in action, but she had heard stories of his cruel and often uncompromising tendencies.

"Come on now!" Yavortha kicked Vellish in the gut to wake him, causing him to hunch over and began coughing up drops of blood. This left Yavortha with little choice but to hoist him up by the back and drag him out.

Sage helped Talon to his feet before soldiers seized them and bound their hands behind their backs. They held each other's stares as they were forced out of the room. "We'll be okay," she whispered to him, but she could tell by his look and dragging soles that he didn't believe it.

"Time for your trial," Yavortha snickered as he lugged a half-conscious Vellish along.

Sage knew he was just making a harsh joke. There were no trials for those who stood against the Tribune in battle. She would be safe once her identity was discovered, but the others had nothing to offer. They were as good as dead. Unless…

The Blue Death! Her eyes widened with newfound hope. *The Keepers of the Circuit!* Her heart began to race. That was how she would keep Talon alive.

CHAPTER THRTY-FOUR
FROM THE FIRST WIRE

The *Shadow Chariot* touched down gracefully in the long hangar of Cassius Vale's secret base on Ennomos. ADIM powered down the ship and hopped over the edge. Then he unlatched the cargo from the back and carried a container of food with each hand.

Creator, This Unit has arrived on Ennomos. He messaged Cassius, and stood in place waiting for an answer. When it didn't come right away he headed toward the lift, his eyes beginning to spin.

The hangar was empty of any being but for him. The mining bots had all been transported to the drill on Titan, and there were only six fully-repaired Tribunary freighters sitting quietly in a row. When he reached the end of the space, ADIM placed his hand against the retinal, opening the door into the lift. ADIM had to turn sideways to enter with the container in his arms, and once he was inside it descended deep into Ennomos.

Once it came to a stop, he moved down a short corridor to a reinforced door. A small HOLO-Screen was projected at the side of it, displaying what was inside.

There were almost fifty men and woman sitting on the floor and against the walls of a mostly empty chamber. Only a narrow trough of water ran around the edges with a few of the people trying to scoop out handfuls.

ADIM placed his hand over this retinal scanner and again the door began to open. Once it rose into the ceiling, he moved through.

The people inside appeared clean, their NET service suits not tattered or covered in grime, but the smell of sweat was foul in the air. They were emaciated, some of them shivering simply from leaning against the cold metal wall. All of their eyes we were drawn back into darkened sockets. It took them a few moments to notice that somebody was present, but as soon as they realized their sunken stares listlessly shifted to face him. When they realized it was ADIM they cowered against the walls.

"Help us..." one of the brave ones groaned while most of them trembled in fear.

ADIM placed the container down in the center of the room. He entered a code in a pad on the center, causing the lid to pop off and slide to the side. In it were smaller containers filled with enough ration bars and other nutrients to last them for a month if used prudently. "You all must eat."

None of them budged. Even as their hawkish eyes widened and they began to salivate, none of them moved so much as an inch. It was why Cassius wouldn't let ADIM detain any military personal. Engineers and ship-aids were never quick to act rashly, and as predicted they didn't turn on each other. They were starving and terrified, but they remained docile in the shadow of ADIM.

"Why are you doing this to us?" another one of them grated.

"The Creator does not wish any of you to die. You must eat." ADIM responded coldly as he backed out of the room.

"Who are you?"

Ignoring the question, ADIM left and sealed the door behind him. Then he paused. Cassius had always told him to keep his identity hidden, but that was before the Executor gazed upon him. He wondered, as he observed the HOLO-Screen to see them timidly approach the open container, if they too were supposed to know what he was.

Forgive my delay, ADIM. Cassius' voice suddenly spoke to him. *Preparations on my end have kept me busy."*

The humans have been fed.

Good.

ADIM cut him off, his eyes beginning to revolve. *This unit sensed heightened anxiety upon entering the room. On the freighter they had reason to be frightened, but even as this unit offers them nutrients, they still are.*

Of course they are. They are weak. Meager tools of the Tribune.

ADIM continued to watch them. Only a few were brave enough to look into the container, and even they trembled as they brought out what was inside and analyzed every angle of it.

This unit will be discovered by the Circuit soon. Will all humans be frightened?

There was a pause before Cassius answered. *Humans are always afraid of what they do not understand. Those of the Tribune especially will be. It will take them time to see what a magnificent work of art you truly are.* Cassius stopped again, as if he knew ADIM's eyes had begun to churn more vigorously than before. *But they will.*

Are you afraid? There was never any emotion in ADIM's voice, but he hesitated before annunciating each word, as if to indicate doubt.

Of course not! I've known you from the first wire I laid down on the table. As I knew my own son. We will make them see, ADIM. Together we will make them strong.

ADIM's eyes slowed down and he didn't respond right away, a sign that he was pleased with Cassius' response. He continued on down the hall and entered the glass vestibule. There was a loud beep, and then a web of lights lowered down the room.

"Purification complete" The voice of Gaia spoke and then the door into the laboratory came unhinged.

It was a generously sized room with equipment and HOLO-Screens arranged all over in no real order. Everything switched on upon their entry, but nothing was brighter than the glowing blue chamber at the other end of the room. There was thick, metal lattice structure surrounding a sphere of roiling blue so resplendent that it was like staring at a newly birthed sun. It had the appearance of a Gravity Generator, but its purpose was far less innocent.

This unit has reached the Gravitum Bomb. ADIM said as he stepped over the circuits feeding it. His eyes began to rotate at a new speed, indicating a level of anticipation.

Simulations can only tell us so much. It is time we see how capable this new device really is. Key the loading sequence.

As ADIM got closer, his sensors picked up the intense level of heat emanating from it. He moved in front of a HOLO-Screen and typed in a few commands. Once he was done, a ceiling shaft directly above the weapon began to open. It fed into the main hangar. The floor below the blue sphere began to rise, lifting it up through the opening so that the laboratory went almost entirely dark.

The sequence is initiated. Where shall this unit bring the weapon?

Switch on the map. Cassius said.

ADIM keyed a few more commands into the HOLO-Screen. A diagrammatic projection of the Circuit lit up behind him.

The target is 22 Kalliope. Cassius continued. *An M-type with an orbital period of 1,814 days.*

ADIM used his hands to navigate the image, expanding the region of the main asteroid belt in the Ignescent Cell. He paused and shuffled across the image until he stopped at the hologram of the small asteroid Cassius described.

It is a mining facility owned by the Morastus Clan. A member of the Ceresian Pact. This unit does not comprehend. Isn't the Tribune our enemy?

All people are our enemies for now. The Earth Reclaimer War was a battle for control of our homeland, and though the Tribune may have won, the Circuit itself remains changed. Now they try to bleed the Ceresian's out slowly over time. I'd wager they are willing to wait centuries, but our little attack will shatter what fragile peace remains to tie the Circuit together. They will blame the Tribune for your attack, and we join our greatest threats into war.

It never took long for ADIM to grasp the entirety of his Creator's machinations. His spinning eyes began to slow down as he responded. *And as they terminate each other, we shall show them the way.*

Precisely.

ADIM continued to rotate the image of Kalliope, studying its outer defenses, which were decidedly limited.

The mine is still operational. There will be humans present. Shall this unit attempt to transport any survivors to safety first?

This time Cassius didn't say anything for a while. There was a deep breath on his end before he gave his orders. *Fitting more than one small person aboard the Shadow Chariot would prove impossible. It isn't necessary. The attack should appear to be a flagrant assault on a profitable, but unimportant colony by the Tribune. Like they're trying to send a message. Let us hope that our new weapon will aid any miners there to a swift end.*

ADIM spun Kalliope one last time before he shut off the projection. *Yes, Creator.* He said, his red eyes the only thing remaining to shine through the darkness.

CHAPTER THIRTY-FIVE
EXECUTER

An armed escort led by Hand Yavortha guided Talon, Sage and Vellish through the ravaged cargo bay of the freighter. All of the flames had been extinguished, leaving behind a mess of ruptured circuits and sharps of blackened, splaying metal. They exited into a more massive hangar, big enough to fit at least ten more of the freighters. There were smaller ships throughout, attack vessels Talon assumed, and hundreds of engineers and soldiers were working diligently on every one. The floors and walls were all smooth and shiny—a glistening light, silver with streams of blue light running across them in a wide grid.

A New Earth Cruiser. Talon marveled inwardly. He tried not to be too obvious as he gawked around the hangar.

He glanced over at Sage to see if she realized where they were and she returned a panicked nod. It was indeed one of the legendary New Earth Cruisers. The enormous frigates could give the Solar-Arcs of the Circuit a run for their money in size, and there were only four of them in existence, a flagship for each member of the Tribune. Unrivaled in both defense and firepower, they were completed toward the end of the Earth Reclaimer War, or rather they ended the war.

They moved into the cruiser's generous corridors, which had a trapezoidal shape. The top plane above was fitted with a strip of cool, blue light that accentuated the surreal feeling that seized Talon's entire person. Everything was burnished and sleek. The walls were similar to the inside of the hangar while the floors had a white, almost pearlescent luster to them. It was quite a contrast from the unsightly Tribunary Freighter with its grated floors and often exposed circuitry.

"Much nicer than the hell you come from, huh?" Hand Yavortha scoffed. "Up this way." He tugged a barely standing Vellish into a lift branching off of the corridor.

Talon realized he had been ogling the cruiser, much like his daughter every time she saw a new ship. It was indeed spectacular, but he didn't want his enemies knowing he thought that. He dropped his gaze, swallowed any witty response, and followed Yavortha onto the lift.

They were carried up the tall elevator shaft and Talon had a feeling he knew what awaited them on the top. His pulse raced uncontrollably. He had known he was going to die for a long time, but as the moment neared he knew he wasn't ready. The hairs all over his body stood on end. He tried to picture Elisha's face, but it only filled him with anger.

He peeked to his left and right.

Seven soldiers, he counted. He could make his move; smash the guard holding his wrists against the fast moving wall and then use it to rip apart his bindings. Though the process would probably tear open his hands and make wielding a gun more difficult than it already was for his increasingly weakened arms. He'd then have to take out at least three before the others reacted so that the odds were even.

It wasn't an impossible task, but as much as his heart willed him to try, he couldn't. It was his life to throw away, but not Sage's or Vellish's. Losing Ulson was already enough to have on his conscience. As the lift came to a gradual halt, he straightened his back and decided that he'd have to face what awaited them with courage.

The wide, semicircular doors slid open and the din of a busy command deck greeted them. But it was unlike any command deck Talon had ever seen. A raised platform of polished black tile ran down the center, reflecting the stars and vastness of space through the gently curved translucency spanning over the far half of the oblong room. Down either side of it were terraces outfitted with almost a hundred stations, filled with HOLO-Screens and other navigation equipment. The translucency itself was beautiful and trellised with a thick structure that bowed perfectly with the glass.

Tribunal Honor-guards were arrayed down the edges, each of their ornate chest plates stamped with the emblem of the Tribune.

They all also had one-sided green capes draped over their left arms. Down at the end of the platform was a tall seat with the back rising into a face of five offset plates of metal that could almost be said to resemble the open palm of a hand. A Tribune sat in it, the folds of a silken, green cloak tumbling down over his shoulders and most of his arms. He wasn't wearing a crown, but he might as well have been. A spectacularly molded silver chestplate wrapped around his black, fitted tunic to granting him an undeniably regal appearance. It was the grand throne of a ship worthy of a king.

"The *Ascendant* is quite a vessel isn't she?" The Tribune said as he spread his arms wide and rose to his feet, all while wearing a rapacious grin.

Talon and the other prisoners were forced to their knees and waited in silence as the resonating footsteps of the Tribune grew nearer. Vellish was hardly conscious, but a guard behind him was keeping him from collapsing. Sage hung her head so that her dark hair fell over her face.

The Tribune himself wasn't as impressive looking once he got close…a short man with a prim beard hugging a smug grin only made intimidating by the host of guns at his beck and call. His eyes and lips were accentuated by black and gold-tinted makeup, which Talon thought only made him look ridiculous.

"You may be wondering why I brought you all the way up here." The Tribune stopped and leaned over to address them. "I am Tribune Benjar Vakari and I trust you appreciate my more than gracious treatment of heretics so far. It is my hope that you may see what majesty you attempt to defile. What beauty!" He slowly spun around to flaunt his spectacular cruiser.

"It's a little too pretty for me," Talon murmured under his breath.

"Don't address the Tribune!" Yavortha snarled and kicked him in the gut. He reeled over trying to grasp his stomach as the wind was knocked out of him, but his hands were bound. He squinted over to see if Sage was looking, but through the strands of her hair he could see that her eyes were closed.

"Now, now Yavortha. That is no way to treat our guests." Tribune Vakari briskly paced back and forth before stopping to look directly at Talon. "What an attempt! I haven't had the luxury of watching the Splinter Tactic fail for decades. When will you foolish Ceresians learn?" He grabbed Talon by the cheeks and snickered.

Talon straightened his back and wheezed, "Didn't stop us from taking your other ships." If they were going to die, he figured he would at least draw the ire of the Tribune in hopes of lessening the torture inflicted on the others.

"Oh stop. I know your motley crew wasn't responsible for that." Benjar quickly turned to Sage and knelt down in front of her. She didn't budge. Then he reached out and with one finger below her chin lifted her head. Every part of her face seemed to tremble as her eyes opened to face him. "There is no need to hide," he whispered to her as he ran his hand across her cheek. Then he gently kissed the corner of her lip.

Talon's stomach churned as he watched Benjar take advantage of her. He was about to launch himself at the man and beat in his skull when the Tribune suddenly got to his feet to speak.

"Thank you for delivering these dissidents to us, Sage." He offered a haughty nod in Yavortha's direction. "Remove her cuffs."

Sage? Talon thought, confused by the unfamiliar name. The nauseous feeling was quickly replaced by a stinging in his chest. His arms began to wobble and he felt all the air sucked from his lungs again. *It can't be.*

Yavortha let her loose and she slowly rose. Talon hoped for a moment that she'd use the opportunity to snap the Tribune's neck in two with her artificial arm, but she only stood there, staring down at her empty palms in silence.

"Excellent work! I should never have doubted you." Benjar embraced her and offered another kiss. She didn't move. She merely wore a sullen expression that made Talon wonder what he was missing. "Now, as a reward I will allow you to finish what you started. Return her pistol, Yavortha."

Hand Yavortha reached behind his belt and pulled out her gun. Talon watched in awe as it was placed in her open palms and he could no longer deny it.

It was her! he thought, seething. He had only just met her, but never in his whole life had he felt so betrayed. The air felt like it was sucked right out of his lungs.

"Redemption is near," Benjar quoted. "It is time we return

their vagrant souls to the unifying spirit." He closed her hand around the handle of the pistol and turned her around. She didn't look at Talon or Vellish. There was no pride in her blank stare as there should be after springing a successful trap. She looked lost.

"Go on. Take the lively one first." Benjar gestured to Talon.

"I can't..." she whimpered, her voice cracking.

"What?" Benjar's expression darkened.

"I can't." She swallowed a dry throat. "He has... he has the blue death."

Talon wished she would have just shot him in the head. Her eyes met his for the shortest moment and it was more torturous than anything else the Tribune could muster. Everything he had told her was just a way for her to feel less guilty—to keep him alive so that his blood wouldn't be on her hands.

"How..." he mouthed, but it was no use.

"Does he now?" The Tribune looked Talon over curiously.

"Yes I promise!" She grabbed Benjar's arm.

The Tribune rubbed the chin beneath his arrogant grin before he flicked her hands off of him. "Then perhaps he is of further use to us. The Keepers are always looking for new recruits and we are so close to having them on our side. A noble gesture, Sage, but an attack on the Tribune must be punished! Put the injured one out of his misery." He turned her toward Vellish and lifted her arm. "Make the diseased one watch."

Talon roared and sprung at Benjar with all of his might, but at that instant Yavortha's fist crashed across his jaw and sent him sprawling onto all fours where he was restrained by other soldiers.

Sage froze. She couldn't bring herself to look at Talon, but she didn't move the gun. Tribune Vakari placed his hands around her hips like a vice. With his help her pistol was aimed at Vellish, the soldiers holding him up so the barrel was only inches away from his forehead.

Benjar glanced down at Talon and his lips curled into an even more sinister smile, if that was possible. "Has another fallen under your spell? How precious." He walked over and seized Talon's face, forcing him to look right at Vellish. "Kill him."

Sage's hand began to tremble.

"Agatha..." Talon mouthed through his throbbing jaw.

Vellish puffed out his chest and lifted his head. "It's okay, Tal. At least I'll go down like a true Ceresian." He growled and spat at her feet. Talon could tell it took all he had to get those words though his bloody lips. "Do it you traitorous bitch."

"Go on," Benjar urged her. "Remember who you are."

"I am a knight in the darkness; a vessel of their wisdom." She began to mouth the words as if they were some sort of prayer. Her eyes glared hollowly just over the crown of Vellish's head.

"Agatha Don——" Talon shouted, but it was too late. The clang of her pistol rang out as she squeezed the trigger. Blood sprayed out and Vellish crumbled to the ground with a gaping hole in the center of his forehead.

Talon's whole body shook in rage as his friend's head turned toward him with his eyes stuck open. He wanted to reach out but then another blow struck him in the side of the head, knocking him unconscious.

CHAPTER THIRTY-SIX
CRIPPLED FAITH

Sage stared at a silver plate covered in the greenest pieces of lettuce she had ever seen. A silky, olive colored blanket was draped over her shoulders, covering her naked body.

She languidly twirled a fork in her fingers, watching as tiny droplets of water tumbled along the veins of one of the shreds of lettuce as it wound around the prongs. Her reflection in the handle of the utensil stared back at her, and it almost slipped through her fingers as she looked away. Her long, wavy red hair was back, but she felt more lost than ever.

"I dare say that I have never seen a woman so beautiful in all the Circuit," Benjar Vakari admired as he entered the dining room of his personal quarters aboard the *Ascendant*.

Sage quickly pulled the blanket tight around her so that it concealed her breasts and looked up. The whole space was wrapped in one extensive HOLO-Screen, displaying a living image of what Sage assumed was ancient Earth. Tall blades of green grass swayed with the wind as puffy white clouds drifted across a preposterously blue sky. Tremendous mountains rose in the distance to cut through them, painted a pale mauve color by the looming vapor. And the sun. It glimmered like a radiant jewel, casting its light upon all that was visible. It was a remarkable scene, but at that moment she couldn't bring herself to imagine anything like it ever existing on the frigid wasteland Earth had become.

"Come now, eat. You must be hungry after living amongst those wretches." He fiddled with the sash around the waste of his half open robe.

She lifted the lettuce stuck to the end of her fork up in front of her mouth. She was starving for anything besides pills, but the sick feeling in her stomach made it almost impossible to swallow. She took a small bite and forced it down, and then instantly knew why it was considered a delicacy.

"Good, see? I had it brought up special for you." He moved around the table toward her.

After the first bite she began to quickly shovel it into her mouth and wash it down with the tall glass of crystalline water placed beside the plate. Each piece washed away the foul taste in her mouth and helped to settle her stomach.

"We need you to stay strong." He knelt at her side and began to stare at the artificial hand resting on her bare thigh. She froze as he grabbed the blanket around her and began to peel it back to reveal the rest of her arm. She dropped the fork and pulled it down out of reflex. When he tried again she found herself unable to resist. Half of her lithe figure was revealed as she covered her showing breast with her natural hand.

"Remarkable..." he whispered as he pulled the arm closer to his face and began to analyze all its facets. He was careful to leave his free hand on her thigh, his fingers running around the soft curve.

Her lower lip began to tremble. She looked up and stared into the light above the table, trying her best to ignore the tingling sensation, which began to seize her whole body.

"I never truly took the time to admire his work. You feel nothing?" He got a look at it from every angle, playing with the fingers and trying to see what was behind every plate. She shook her head as she watched out of the corner of her eye. All she could feel were his fingers running down her leg. The tiny pinch which she used to feel in her shoulder whenever she moved the arm was gone.

"And you can move it all with your mind?"

Suddenly Sage remembered Talon's face; his glassy, blue eyes staring at her with that shattered gaze. She reached over and pushed his hand away from her leg, then threw the blanket back over her shoulder and picked up her fork to continue eating. "All with my mind," she replied coldly.

"Amazing," Benjar remarked, his tone clearly dissatisfied by her denial. He leaned on the table to get to his feet, then ambled around to the other end of the long table where a similar meal was arrayed. There he sat down, elegantly unfolding a napkin and laying it over his lap before picking up his fork. His pearly, white teeth tore through a chunk of lettuce, water running over his loudly smacking gums that made it appear like he either wasn't enjoying the taste or he was ravenously hungry. "Onto the next mission I suppose." He continued crunching without looking up.

"Wha.. what," she stumbled over her words. "What happened to Talon?" It took all of her courage to ask.

"Talon?" Benjar began to chortle, spewing out tiny bits of his meal before he took a long sip of water to wash it all down. "Who in the name of Earth is Talon?"

"The man…" She chose her words carefully. "The Ceresian with the Blue Death."

"Him?" Benjar looked up at her with a wrinkled brow. "He was sent off with a transport to become a Keeper of the Circuit. Those self-righteous bastards… better if we could have just killed him here for what he did. No matter. The Spirit is just, afflicting him so. What bother is he to you?"

She didn't say anything; she didn't even feel her expression change but she could see by the way Benjar reacted that he knew. Of all the Tribunes, he was the most attuned to her feelings. As if he could see right through her.

"I see. The incomparable Sage Volus as taken with a merce-nary from Ceres as he is with her!" Benjar began to laugh so hard that he almost choked. "So that explains your apathy last night in my bed! You always have had a peculiar taste in men. What was his name?"

"Stop it…" she whimpered, her artificial hand squeezing the table so hard that it began to dent.

"Caleb. That's right. Caleb Va—"

"Stop it!" She screamed, cutting him off before he could finish the name. Her arm slid across the table, slapping the plate into the wall and disturbing the tranquil scene of Earth projected. She fell into her hands, sobbing as an uncontrollable storm of thoughts and visions raced through her consciousness. There was fire and ash, blood and water, and her head began to pound as if the concussion had never relinquished.

A hand fell upon her shoulder and she snapped up, grasping the forearm and wrenching Benjar to his knees. Her whole body quaked as she realized who it was. His smug grin was wiped away. There was fear in his face; fear like she had never seen in it before. Two soldiers appeared in the doorway, their rifles trained on her head and moving closer.

"Sage…" the Tribune whimpered. "Sage let go. Let go now or they are going to kill you."

She didn't say or do anything. She just continued to stare over his shoulder as a blur of images flashed before her eyes. Fire and blood and death all at once.

"My dear, you must release me!"

Sage blinked and looked around as if waking up from a nightmare. The barrel of one of the soldier's guns pressed against the back of her head. Her breathing beginning to slow down, she looked down at her numb, artificial arm and realized what she was doing. Her eyes widened in horror as she let go and pulled the blanket up, which had fallen down from her shoulders.

"How dare you assault me!" Benjar growled as the back of his hand struck Sage across her tear-stained cheek. "You are an Executor of the New Earth Tribunal!" He grabbed her by the jaw and pulled her face close. "You don't fall for some Ceresian! For a heretic!" He pushed her away forcefully and stepped back, taking a few long breaths to calm himself and fix his clothing.

"Do you know why we exist, Sage?" he then said calmly.

Sage sniveled and nodded her head. The soldier behind her backed away a bit, but she could still feel his weapon rustling through the ends of her hair.

"Before we came along humanity was lost. Yes there was the Circuit, but that was merely a means of survival. Left to themselves humanity would crumble. You have seen it; seen the way those piti-ful Ceresians revel and drink and fuck without a second thought. We exist to provide order in the name of the unifying Spirit. As Earth once provided for the Ancients, we must be the scaffold that holds our species together! We are a homeless people. This ship. These cities. They are all an illusion to hold us together until the Earth is ready to receive us again. Until we are worthy." He brought himself to stand tall in front of her, drowning her in his shadow so that she quickly forgot the frightened man he had just been.

"But will we ever truly be worthy?" Sage asked meekly. She couldn't believe those words of doubt actually slipped through her lips.

"Of course we will!" Benjar's brown eyes sparkled with fervor. "But there are some amongst us who I fear have had their faith crippled."

"Me?" she asked.

"Not you." He grasped her shoulders and squeezed passionately. "I have never doubted your faith. But I need you now, Sage. I need you to help Cassius Vale remember his oaths. The Tribune needs you. Before it is too late."

"Cassius?" Sage leaned forward anxiously. "Is he okay?"

"I know your history with him." Benjar glanced at her artificial arm. "I have reason to believe he was behind the attacks on our freighters, before this Talon character."

He would never do such a thing "That can't be. Why would he ever do that?"

"I don't know, but I fear he is losing his grip on sanity. He needs your help, Sage. Whatever he is planning, he needs your help to remember his faith. Edeoria is suffering from neglect. His people starve and are forced from their homes for whatever projects he is concocting. Soon we will be left with no choice but to take action."

"No!" She slid off of the chair to her knees and begged. "Please don't hurt him. I can help him."

"It is because he once sat on the council that I am sending you to him first. Use your shared past. Find out what he's up to and try to dissuade him. Cassius has always been an obstinate man, but this...well if our suspicions are true then it would be tragic... truly devastating."

Sage shook her head defiantly. Cassius was the closest thing she had left to family. "No. It can't be him! Cassius is loyal, I know it."

"Then go to him, my dear. A ship has been prepped for you. Go to him and rescue his soul." Benjar lifted her to his feet and signaled the guard to stand down. "And prove you worth to the Spirit."

"I will," she decided without thinking twice. There was a time when they were close and if he would open up to anybody she hoped it would be her. *I will save him*, she thought to herself, remembering all that he had done for her in a sudden epiphany. *I have too.*

"Good!" Benjar kneeled down and picked up the plate she had knocked over. "And we'll put all of this behind us." Then he wrapped his arm around her shoulder, and with a complacent smile on his face began to walk her toward the exit. "May the Spirit of the Earth guide your steps."

Chapter Thirty-Seven
The Ship of the Dead

Boarding a Solar-Ark locked onto the Circuit was an intricate affair. Moving at nearly a tenth the speed of light, the enormous ships never even slowed down, let alone came to a complete stop. They passed through the Conduit Stations like gushing water through perfectly sized pipes. The Ancients designed them before the Earth fell, developing a complicated system of magnetics and Gravitum Generators capable of disbursing or receiving cargo containers to and from the Conduit in a fraction of a second. It took some time after the fall of Earth for humans themselves to figure out how to survive the transfer without fail, but by the 2nd century of the Kepler Circuit it had become an ordinary routine.

Talon was locked into his seat on a shipping container in the Conduit above New Terrene. Every inch of his body was strapped in by nano-fiber fastenings able to adapt to the incredible force of the transfer. A circle of rolling blue light shone brightly from above and beneath him, giving his whole body the impression of weightlessness. He somewhat enjoyed the feeling. It took an edge off of the insufferable soreness creeping through every one of his muscles.

"Three," a computerized, female voice spoke over a speaker.

He had never boarded a Solar-Ark before. All of the others seated around the cylindrical container looked terrified, their teeth chattering. Talon was calm. It was his one chance since the incident aboard the *New Earth Cruiser* to be distracted by something other than debilitating thoughts of how Sage betrayed him—of how he led Ulson and Vellish to their doom.

"Two."

To some degree he hoped that the transfer would kill him.

That would be the least I deserve, he thought. It seemed like a nice way to die—quick and painless. Though all options sounded preferable to spending the rest of his abridged life deteriorating aboard a ship until he was a helpless cripple.

"One."

There was a deafening clap. He wanted to keep his eyes open to watch, but it was impossible. His frame was wreathed in such crushing pressure that he thought all of his bones were ready to snap. His face felt as though it were being peeled back over his skull, which in turn felt like it was going to crush his brain. The Splinter Chamber he rode into battle was nothing in comparison. The sudden and excruciating pain was unbearable.

Then, as if nothing out of the ordinary had occurred, there was silence. He was sitting in the same position, struggling to regain his breath. His head was pounding. His stomach was curdling and the soreness had returned all over, but he was alive.

The straps came off of him and when he tried to stand a powerful sense of vertigo seized him. He fell forward onto his knees and vomited, which didn't help make the bright lines of pain running along his ribs feel any better. When he was done he looked around to see that the dozen or so others all had the same reaction.

"I remember my first time!" the silhouette of a man chuckled. He descended from a lift through the ceiling in the center of the room. "There is no shame in it." He placed his hand on one of the other cursed men who continued violently heaving. "Let it all out. We'll clean it. You will be safe here." The silhouetted man had a gentle voice, one that made it hard to doubt the earnestness in his words.

"Welcome to the Solar-Ark *Amerigo!*" he continued. "Named after one of the last empires of the Earth, this vessel has sailed the Circuit since its fall. I am Tarsis Yoler and it will be my great honor to be the first to walk you through the halls the Ancients built for us."

When Talon was able to center his vision he saw something that he did not expect. The man's eyes were blue as glass and the veins on his temples shone with a cobalt radiance as bright as an ion engine. He was thin and bearded, with messy, brown hair that intentionally made it impossible to tell how close he was to death.

He stood erect, attached to a suit that appeared like it could be the skeleton of a Mining Mech if they had one. There was a body-shaped core wrapped around his torso and extending to a brace beneath his chin. Bulky, artificial limbs stemmed from it, latching onto his arms and legs like some form of metal parasite. He took a few steps back, the suit hissing every time the joints bent.

The others around the room scrambled to their feet to join him on the lift. Their symptoms were far less noticeable, but Talon had no difficulty recognizing them. They were all around the same stage as he; all dying, and damned to spend the rest of their cursed lives aboard the *Amerigo*.

"No need to gawk," Tarsis addressed Talon. "There are many accommodations here that serve to elongate life."

He hadn't even realized he had been staring. The suit was like nothing he had ever seen throughout the Ceresian colonies. He tried to stop looking, but as he approached the lift his eyes were drawn back to get a closer look at Tarsis' face. It wasn't wrinkled, but his eyes were drawn back into dark patches. His skin was sallow and he appeared exhausted despite the content demeanor he was trying to project.

"How long have you had it?" Talon asked as he noticed how extensive the exoskeletal suit was.

"Oh, probably more than three years by now," Tarsis responded pensively as the lift started to rise. "You'd be happy to look as good as I do after so long! Outside of this ship it'd be impossible. First we get Nano-Suits, and when they're not enough we get these…" He bent his arm, the mechanical attachment whining as he did, and looked at his hand where five tiny slivers of jointed metal ran over each of his fingers. "Still moving though. We all must move. Otherwise we might as well be dead."

The lift stopped and Tarsis moved out. Each of his steps was noisy and accentuated. Not very different from the Mechs Julius operated on Kalliope, though small enough not to make the ground rumble.

They entered into a corridor so wide that it made the *Ascendant's* seem narrow, though the interior was far less pristine. It had an old world look to it. Everything was exposed—all of the circuitry, pipes and lighting systems. They proceeded along a grated floor with more visible systems beneath it. Everything made a noise. The soft purr of running liquid was audible and parts all over beeped and whistled like aged pistons.

It was a long walk through the complex network of corridors filling what Talon imagined was more than a mile long ship. They passed dozens of other people who served aboard it. Most of them wore black Nano-suits with highlights of glowing blue, but some wore the same mechanical suit as Tarsis. There were areas of translucency where the view into space was so expansive that Talon felt like he was going to be sucked out. He could get glimpses of the golden solar sail as it wrapped out from the front of the Ark. The ships were always moving so fast that he had never before realized how stunning the shimmering surface looked against a backdrop of stars, or how tremendous it was.

They followed Tarsis around a corner and made their way down a set of wide stairs, emerging into what appeared to be a great hall. The interior of the long space was empty except for a single man standing in the center facing away from them. Talon couldn't tell what the man was looking at until they were all the way down.

So this is how they plan to keep me alive. The rumors are true! Talon marveled. *'A hall of living graves to extend your doom.'* He had overheard a merchant saying that.

Lining both walls were hundreds of transparent chambers with a dormant human being occupying nearly half of them. They were stripped down to their underwear, with tubes stuck into their arms, legs and chest. He could tell by the varying brightness of their bluish veins that each of them had the Blue Death.

"Thank you, Tarsis. I can take them from here," the man standing at attention in the room's center said with his smooth, basso voice. He then turned around with the supreme refinement of a military man. His appearance matched his deportment. A clean beard hugged his powerful jaw and his hair was neatly combed. He wore an elegant black and gold tunic, with a cape that fell over only his left arm. It was obviously the garb of a captain, but more notable to Talon was that he definitely did not have the Blue Death.

"My pleasure, Captain Varns." Tarsis' suit hissed as he raised his hand to a salute. "Shall I resume my duties?"

Captain Varns sent Tarsis off with a nod and folded his arms neatly behind his back. "We are the Keepers of the Circuit. As are you now." He didn't order them to, but Talon and the others naturally formed a line in front of him. He had a commanding presence. "I don't know why you are here, or why fate took a shit on your lives. What I do know is that you are here, standing before me. I am the captain of this ship, Elrigo Varns. This position has been passed down through my family since the fall of the Earth." He began moving down the line one person at a time, sizing them up. When he came to Talon he stopped to get a closer look at the dried scrapes on his face and the tattered rags the Tribune had dressed him in.

Varns resumed his speech while continuing to scan Talon. "I would say it is a pleasure to make all of your acquaintances, but it is no real pleasure at all. If you are the damned then I am your shepherd." His scrutinizing gaze lingered on Talon for a few moments longer before he grunted and moved on. "I don't know what any of you have heard about our order, but let me put it simply: We serve the continued perseverance of humanity. We are aligned to no faction but that of our species. My duty and yours, is to keep this ship running along the Circuit and provide for all of her peoples no matter what their creed. That is it. We will serve here, and we will die here."

Talon meant to hold back his laughter but it came through softly. Captain Varns stormed over to him and glared into his eyes. His cheeks went red. "It is funny isn't it? There is always one who doubts the importance of our role!" Varns snapped.

"I don't doubt it," Talon countered. All of the awe was beginning to wear off of him as he remembered in detail the situation which had brought him aboard the *Amerigo*. "But favoring the Tribune seems to counter your, what did you call it… *Simple* outline."

"Another Ceresian who thinks he knows something." The term rolled off his tongue with salt. "Tell me. Do you monitor our shipments or just believe what those always judicious bankers tell you? The Tribune may control Earth, but we keep you and your ilk alive despite how they may feel about you!" He wheeled around, snobbishly tossing his cape over his arm before he snickered. "It doesn't matter anymore. Resist all you want, but you are a Keeper of the Circuit now and until the end." When he turned around again he shot Talon a venomous grin. "So, are you finished?"

Talon stuttered a bit before deciding not to say anything. The captain was right. He had no idea if anything that Zaimur Morastus or any others had said about them being low on Gravitum was true. People had suffered low gravity in the deeper regions of the asteroid colonies for centuries before the Tribune was even a thought. But for whatever reason, even as he stayed quiet he couldn't shake the feeling that the Keepers were slowly losing their impartiality. Captain Varns was doing nothing to alter his assumption.

"Good." Captain Varns continued and walked toward the chambers on the wall. "These are your lives." He patted the glass above one of the dormant humans. The person within didn't respond, though Talon thought he could see the sealed eyelids shudder a bit.

Talon and the other new recruits slowly huddled around the Captain at the chamber before he continued. "You will get Nano-suits that will amplify your muscles enough to help you move until the disease progresses too far. They have been worn by countless Keepers before you, and will be worn by countless ones after you're all dead. When that is not sufficient you will be provided with one of the outfits you saw my friend Tarsis wearing. Then you will die. It is a sad truth, but it is a certain one. There is no cure for the Blue Death. We can, however, extend your lives." There was no grief in his voice. It was evident that he had given the speech so many times in his life that he had grown numb to the actual meaning behind the words."

"What is it?" one of the recruits spoke up nervously.

"These are Cryo-Chambers. The Ancients once dreamed they could help on long trips to other stars. A fool's errand. Today they work tirelessly to slow the pervasion of the disease. Using these chambers can give you a year, sometimes more, of extra time. It isn't much, but unfortunately I am not the Keeper of life and death.

"You will each spend weeks at a time inside your own, on rotation, servicing this vessel until you are of no further use to the Circuit. You will perform your duties admirably, and you will learn every nook and cranny the *Amerigo* has to offer, this I promise you. For now, your superiors will instruct you of your shifts. For those first going under ice, we will be passing over Titan soon, so expect to see a few more new faces when you awaken."

Talon ignored the rest of what he was saying. Instead he stood staring at the inactive man lying within the chamber. He appeared peaceful with his eyes closed gently, but the sight of it sent a shiver up Talon's spine. That was where he would die; a frozen casket slowly ushering him toward the end.

I will get out of here. He made a silent vow to himself as his fingers ran over the cold glass. *Even if I have to kill them all to do so... I will see her again.*

CHAPTER THIRTY-EIGHT
TRUTH BEHIND HER EYES

Sage rubbed her dry eyes in order to try and keep herself awake. Then she shuffled through the HOLO-Screen projected from the console of the small ship Tribune Benjar Vakari had provided to her. The readings showed that she wasn't far from Saturn, which was good considering there wasn't enough fuel in it to get anywhere else. She switched off auto-pilot and took control.

Not long after, the planet Saturn crept ever closer.

She had seen it once, nearly a decade before, but she had forgotten how beautiful a sight it was. The planet's tilted discs wrapped it like crescent blades of ice and dust. Their soft pallet of blues, oranges and browns flawlessly complemented the toiling atmosphere of the gas-giant. Dancing around all of that was an archipelago of smaller bodies, one of which was the pale orange orb of Titan where she was headed. Nearby was the smaller moon known as Enceladus, where Tribune Nora Gressler's citadel was located. Those were the two main colonies hovering around Saturn, and floating closets to Titan was a Conduit Station. She could see the stream of smaller transport routes trickling between it and the two moons.

Once she was close enough to the orange globe of Titan she keyed a few commands and sent a transmission to Cassius Vale's compound. "Cassius. It's... it's Sage." She did her best to sound composed. "I don't know what's going on, but I must see you. I promise I am coming alone."

Her ship plunged through the thick atmosphere of the moon. It rattled and shook so violently that the restraints were pulled tightly against her armor. When it emerged into the frozen world below Cassius responded.

"Sage! What a pleasant surprise. I will open the hangar for you immediately. You know where to go."

She didn't expect him to be so compliant, especially if he was guilty, but there was no reason to argue over it. Pulling on the yolk, she turned and headed toward Edeoria. The ship shot over the ridge of its crater and she banked around, smoothly slipping into a hangar built into the wall of the crag.

The *White Hand* was already parked inside and she set her own ship down beside it. Once her ship was powered down she switched off the airlock and the translucency spanning over her head popped open. She unlatched her restraints and hopped over the side to see Cassius already approaching with a candid smile on his face.

"Sage, my dear," Cassius said as he spread his arms wide to embrace her. "I wasn't expecting your visit."

"I wish it were under better circumstances," Sage said gravely, returning a timid hug.

"Last I saw you, you were bedridden on New Terrene. I'm glad to see your injuries have all healed." He put his arm around her back and led her toward the exit.

What does he mean 'saw me?' Sage pondered. She imagined that word must have spread to him from the acting Tribunes as to what had occurred on Mars. She decided to ignore his remark. "It has been too many years, Cassius."

"Years?" His brow wrinkled as he looked at her with a confused expression. "It was only a few months ago that I helped you with that bomb. You saved many lives that day."

There he goes again, she thought, worried that Benjar was right about him losing his mind. "Helped me?" she asked. Then she tried her best to think back to the explosion on Mars. It still remained only a haze of distorted figures and shouting voices.

Cassius frowned and put an affectionate hand on her shoulder. "You don't remember do you? We must have less time than I thought."

"What are you talking about?"

"It... nothing. I will tell you everything soon enough."

"I didn't come here to exchange secrets!" She shook his hand off of her. "The Tribune is accusing you of crimes I know you wouldn't commit. You must—"

"No secrets. Come with me. I must show you something." His face was stern, overflowing with conviction. He led her down one of the branching corridors, and she could do nothing but follow.

It didn't take long for her to realize that the whole compound had been stripped bare. When she had visited almost a decade before it was flush with hand-crafted artifacts and beautifications collected by generations of the Vale family. As they got deeper inside it became even more stark and lifeless. She began to seriously wonder if what Benjar had said about Cassius was true. It didn't appear that anybody was living there; there wasn't even a single servant to aid him—complete and utter solitude.

"I don't remember it being so empty in here," Sage said matter-of-factly as they strolled side by side. She was hoping there would be at least a suitable reason.

"I found many of my parent's assets to be superfluous. It all reminded me too much of him… I enjoy the quiet." Cassius' robust voice echoed throughout the vacant halls.

"But so alone…" Sage mouthed, realizing she understood exactly what he was talking about.

"All Executors are alone. It is the vow we take. 'I am the silent hand of the Tribune.' Bullshit!" he snapped. "They never tell you how empty it makes you."

"But you rose beyond it! You became a Tribune. You achieved more than most men do in an entire lifetime!" she argued, the tone of her voice growing more urgent without her realizing.

Cassius burst into laughter and leaned toward her with malice in his eyes. "I was merely a figurehead placed there in honor of the war we won… I won. That's it. And after leaving all of it behind I have only a single regret, Sage, only one."

Sage looked at him curiously, her head half-tilted to the side. "What is that?"

"You." They stopped and he turned, his fervent gaze boring through her. "That I let them do this to you… What happened to the beautiful, affectionate, young girl my son fell in love with? I look at you now. I look into your eyes and see the same coldness which seized me. I could have stopped it, but I fear it may be too late."

"It was my choice," Sage said defensively as she looked away and continued to walk. They were entering the only hall she had seen with anything in it. There were rows of holographic busts lining the walls—detailed effigies of all the Vales whom had come before.

"Maybe it was, but I rebuilt you after that unfortunate day. I could have showed you the path of freedom! If only I wasn't so focused on the spineless Tribunes trying to depose me!" His face flushed with anger and he was forced to take a deep breath in order to calm down. "Do you even remember his face? Or is just a blur along with everything else that came before they took you in and made you numb?"

Cassius looked left at one of the busts and then Sage joined him. She stared for a short while at the young man before she recognized him. *It can't be*, she thought. Her throat went dry and her jaw dropped open. Her chest felt like it was being squeezed, her heart very nearly coming to a stop.

"Ca... Ca," she whimpered. The corners of her green eyes began to well. "Caleb." The name managed to escape her trembling lips as she stumbled forward, barely catching her balance on the pedestal projecting his face.

"It seems like an age ago doesn't it? Every life you take for them will make him more and more the stranger—your mind taken by the specters of the men you kill until he is gone. That blithe smile he always wore will be lost like ashes to the winds of Earth." Cassius placed his hand on her shoulder as tenderly as he could manage. "And then you will be no more than a mindless machine to them. A tool, as I was."

Caleb... Just repeating his name in her mind overwhelmed her so much that she dropped to her knees. She wasn't hysterical, but streams of silent tears ran down from her cavernous eyes. "Why are you showing me this...?" Her voice came out so frailly that Cassius had to kneel to hear her. "I haven't forgotten him..."

He placed his quaking hands over her wet cheeks. "Not yet. Not entirely. But I don't want for you what I have become. When I look at it; when I look at his face it fills me with enough rage to raze the Circuit to cinders." His voice was cracking. "It makes me want to go and kill something so that somebody else will understand... so that anybody else could know what I lost!"

Sage had always known Cassius as a serious man, but it was only then as he bellowed that she saw him for what he was. It gave her goosebumps. The hatred in his dark eyes emanated like a black hole ready to devour her and everything around her. She didn't want to admit it, but she was terrified.

"It was you, wasn't it?" she questioned weakly as her fingers fell to caress the handle of her pistol. "Benjar was right…"

"You always were bright." Cassius turned his back to her and leaned against the wall. "I think that's why he loved you so much. Not just a pretty face. You were worth conversing with."

Her index finger threaded through the trigger of her gun, but when Cassius glowered over his shoulder at her she pulled it away. As much as it frightened her, she recognized the hollowness. She saw it in her own eyes every time she looked at her reflection, but it didn't matter. She was an Executor of the Tribune. She had to do what was required of her.

"I must arrest you, Cassius," she whimpered. "I can't allow you to do any more harm to the people of the Circuit."

"I know, and I will not try to stop you." He whirled around, unfastened his holster and tossed it onto her lap with his gun inside. "But first allow me to show you something. Let me show you the truth." He extended his hand in order to help her to her feet.

She hesitated. She wanted to trust him, but despite how well she may have known him she had heard the legends of Cassius Vale and his cunning. As genuine as he seemed, she couldn't help but imagine that he was inviting her to her death.

"Please. I would never defile the legacy of my son." He extended his hand again after taking notice of her skepticism. "I promise."

She looked up toward the image of Caleb's face. *I believe him,* she thought as the static, hologram looked back at her. Then, placing aside her doubt, she attached his pistol to her belt and reached up to grasp his outstretched hand. Somehow she knew Cassius would never break a promise made in the name of his son.

One thing was still bugging her, however. "Why though? Why raid harmless transports?"

"Harmless?" Cassius appeared shocked by her question. "Gravitum, my dear. It is the key to all of this." Once they were both standing upright he went to wipe her cheeks but she instinctually pulled away.

"All of what?"

Cassius began to lead her back in the same direction from which they had arrived with an air of excitement about him.

"This!" he exclaimed. "The Circuit. Our survival. The war for our Homeworld. The element has been sought on all the worlds we know, but even after half a millennium beyond it, we remain bound to the Earth."

"The Spirit binds us. One day our homeworld will receive us with gracious arms."

"No, no. The ramblings of the Tribune are no more than a means of control. Tell me. Do you really believe in your heart that we are all connected by some power inherent to that wasteland?"

Sage grit her teeth, biting off the words. She took no pleasure in having her faith belittled, but chose to keep the conversation civil. "You don't think we'll ever return?"

"Through faith?" He sounded like he was about ready to burst into laughter. "You'll have better luck trying to turn water into alcohol. Perhaps we could fix Earth one day. My son believed that we could through science, and he is dead now for it. I believe with all my heart that he was right, but not without centuries of dedicated work, maybe more. I have no doubt that one day we could make the surface of Mars green and habitable, but there is no Spirit unifying us. The Tribune appeases its people with lies; a lie which I was once foolish enough to hope for. But faith is a powerful ally."

"How can you say all of that after serving alongside them for so long?" Sage argued, clearly irritated.

"How could I not? There was a time when we needed such order to pull us out of an age of darkness. But the value of the Tribune has outlasted its welcome. Is our perseverance really so in question anymore? I do not blame them for their methods, but it took the death of my only son for me to realize how much their dogmatic reign is holding us back." He stopped in front of an unmarked, serrated metal door. "I wish only to release the shackles both they and Earth have placed on us so that we may reach beyond our wildest contemplations!"

Cassius activated the HOLO-Screen on his bracer and pushed a few buttons. Then a console flipped out of the wall beside it and he placed his eye in front of a retinal scanner. The door slowly began to rise into the ceiling.

An ominous feeling ran through Sage as the opening grew. It was a tight space illuminated only by a tiny light above. "What if it is just you, Cassius, who wants to leave the Circuit behind? What if you're wrong?" she responded to him.

"Then at least... at least I will have opened some new eyes along the way." Cassius stepped forward onto an elevator and waited patiently for her to join him.

Everything in her body told her not to go in, but she couldn't help it. What he had said may have been heretical, but she couldn't deny that he had peaked her curiosity.

Why kill me now? she assured herself before stepping in. After all that Cassius had done for her it seemed like a valid question.

The door slammed shut behind her and the elevator began to descend quickly. A ringing sound started up in her head as if a bomb had gone off nearby, growing louder and louder the deeper they got. Again her heart began racing, her fingers impulsively falling toward the handle of her pistol.

"Don't be afraid." Cassius gently placed his palm over her artificial hand and guided it away from her weapon. "I would never harm you."

The lift came to a sudden halt and opened up. Sage gratefully stepped out into what appeared to be a brightly lit laboratory. The ringing was getting even louder. She moved forward and immediately noticed the array of HOLO-Screens set up on either side of the passage. Each of them showed the same thing, and it was exactly what she saw through her own two eyes. As she looked around the room the view followed her vision. She came to the center of them and turned to Cassius, and he appeared all around her, like there were cameras in her eyes.

"What is this?" she stammered as she began spinning, all of the screens racing to keep up with what she envisioned until she went dizzy.

"I must apologize," Cassius said contritely. "I did lie about one thing. I was expecting your visit."

When Sage's hand grasped her pistol that time, it wasn't out of reflex. "How are you doing this!" she shouted as she lifted her firearm to aim at him. With her other hand she was holding her ear to try and keep the ringing at bay.

"I am doing nothing. I have merely hacked onto an already existing system." He displayed his empty palms to her as if he were surrendering.

"What system? What are you talking about?" She carefully moved toward him without shifting her aim.

"There's the killer they made you," Cassius remarked. In the HOLO-Screens she realized that he could see her sight directed at the center of his forehead. "I'm talking about the Tribune! The true reason behind my visit to the Arbiter's Enclave on New Terrene."

Her frustration was building. Her natural hand began to tremble. Beads of sweat were dripping down her forehead and her whole expression darkened to the point where Cassius actually appeared worried that she might shoot.

"While there I was able to obtain the encryption in order to show you this. Did you wonder how your masters knew about the raid on that freighter without you having to contact them? Have you ever thought why the worm Benjar feels the need to enter you; to feel the supple touch of your skin when he could have any woman he so desires?"

She shook her ringing head repeatedly, reciting the vows of an Executor under her breath as if it would calm her. She wasn't even looking at him anymore, but her artificial grip held the gun steady on him. She couldn't help but see that on the many surrounding HOLO-Screens.

"After seeing through your eyes for so long and hearing your beautiful voice, it is no wonder he craves you. But now that I have seen it I won't let him or others poison you anymore." He remained cautious, but he began to slowly stride toward her with his palms held open. "I won't let them taint what my son loved. Not anymore."

"I led Tal...impossible. This is all you!" Sage struggled to speak. Her eyes darted from screen to screen, her pistol still raised.

"Why, you ask? You said it in your vows. A body must feel where its hand is going; it must see what its fingers graze against in order to explore the darker corners of our worlds. The Executors are the extent of their gaze... eyes with a gun, that is all you are to them." As he spoke Cassius took a few, hardly noticeable shuffles forward. He continued, "Even when I was a Tribune, it was all I remained to them too. A puppet with a legend they could exploit. I only found out this truth after I took my oath, but they used my son's life to keep me loyal. Now they don't have that luxury." He cradled her to the ground so that she was sitting.

"No...lies..." She could hardly speak, but somehow he understood what she was trying to ask him. "I am a knight in the darkness..."

"The implant they gave you does more than augment your ability to fight. It latches onto your mind. It is why your memory is fading and unclear; why Caleb remains no more than a blank face in your mind. It dulls all pain, not just physical, and after too long takes away all that makes you human."

She panted wildly, trying her best to hold back from vomiting. "You are a liar!"

He was so close now that he could almost reach out and rub his hand through her hair. Instead, he stared into her petrified eyes, knowing she wouldn't shoot.

"But you are not completely lost yet as I am," he continued. "I found a way to remove it without them killing you! I can make your eyes your own again." He turned his head so that she could see the long, jagged scar running up the back of his head from his neck. "You are a servant, Sage, but I won't allow it any longer." He reached out toward her artificial hand, its cold, metal fingers still wrapped around the handle of her gun. "Remember who fixed you before. It's my fault they got their hands on you, but please, let me help you now again."

She gazed back into Cassius' eyes and in them saw those of his son. She had given her whole life to Caleb Vale before he was prematurely taken from her. She even gave her arm to try and save him—an arm given back to her by the man standing in front of her promising his help. But that was before this, before he turned his back on the Tribune she had come to love. She shook her head as she stepped forward until the barrel of the gun hovered right in front of Cassius' head.

"I didn't want to forget him, Cassius," she whimpered. "I just wanted the pain to go away."

"I know." He stopped moving and raised his arms. Once they were behind his head he snuck a finger into his ear and went to press on a device within it. She quickly noticed and lurched forward with her gun to get him to pull his hand away. He remained wary of the pistol, but he was able to shoot a glance over her shoulder at something. "And it never does..."

"But betraying the Tribune... staging robberies...what are you planning, Cassius,? It's not too late to turn back!" she appealed, realizing then that she didn't have it in her to shoot. Not him.

I will not lose faith amongst the faithless. Her head pounded with the vows of an Executor on top of the incessant ringing. She struggled to keep them at bay while her foggy eyes scanned the room one more time to see all of the screens with her own vision projected on them. In them Cassius was staring down at her, with a zeal in his eyes that she had never seen before.

Then, suddenly, before he had a chance to respond she felt an incapacitating pressure against the back of her head. The side of her gun reflected a pair of red eyes before it was ripped out of her hand. Then she collapsed, Cassius lunging forward to catch her before she slammed against the ground.

He held her head up and whispered in her ear. "I will save you, my dear." Then her world faded to blackness.

CHAPTER THIRTY-NINE
CRUEL GAMES OF FATE

Cassius Vale leaned against the rail of his glass-enclosed terrace, gazing out over the many tops of Edeoria's shaft districts that filled the vast Ksa crater. He wore the stern glare of a man who was ready to plunge as far into the filth as necessary. His violet tunic was ironed and pulled neatly over the polished, carbon-fiber underlay beneath. His belt was perfectly aligned, the black and red pistol he rarely let out of his sight holstered at the very center of his hip. In his right hand he rolled his small, spherical HOLO-Recorder over his knuckles, fixated.

Dozens of Tribunal ships were shooting through the atmosphere like a swarm of angry bees. For the second time in his life he watched as attack ships and transports bore down on him with enough troops to occupy the colony his family had presided over since the foundation of the Circuit. Then his entire view was doused in shadow. The thick atmosphere parted ways and through them descended a *New Earth Cruiser*. Its massive engines roared with blinding, blue light that cast it as an oblong silhouette larger than any of the clouds. When they dulled it remained hovering about halfway up the height of the Edeoria Hub Tower.

He could read the name printed on the side of its plated hull, *Calypso*—flagship of the Tribune Nora Gressler. It showed him its broadside and the open hangar, which was releasing the flood of ships to invade his complex.

The cruiser itself had the appearance of a shotgun, with what could be imagined as the handle serving to house the two primary engines with the rest of them located at the stern. Sapphire colored illumination shone through the breaks in the vessels' dense armored-plating, forming a band of light around the center

like a belt. The weapon systems facing him on the side were auxiliary, but a tremendous railgun ran along the top from beneath
a semi-translucent command deck that peered over all the layers
of thick cladding.

Cassius switched on the device in his hand. He waited until
the entire head of his son materialized before pausing the recording. Then he spoke to it with a glimmer in his eyes. "You asked
me once, Caleb, what it was like to fight in a war. What it was like
to kill. You never were one for fighting," he chuckled to himself.
The whine of approaching ships grew nearer. "But you were always strong in your own way. The truth is, every kill chips away a
piece of you until you don't even blink as you pull the trigger. I'm
glad you never had to, but now I must kill again. I hope you can
understand why. Yours is the only forgiveness I will ever need. I
love you, son, with what little remains of me. I love you."

He took a long look at Caleb's face as the terrace grew dim-
mer beneath the ships crowding around outside the translucency.
He didn't shed tears as he switched off the hologram and placed
it into a pouch on his belt. There was too much at stake for him
to lose his composure. Instead, taking long, graceful strides, he
slowly backed out of the terrace and made his way into his bed-
room. There was nothing inside except for a lonely bed sitting in
the corner with crimson sheets.

He pressed on the com-link hooked into his ear and addressed
ADIM loudly enough so that he could hear himself speak over the
almost deafening rumble of engines, "ADIM. Proceed as planned.
Use any means necessary."

"This unit is primed, Creator. Will move to penetrate Kalliope defenses now," ADIM responded without a moment's delay.

"Good-" Cassius paused as the blast of the Tribunary forces
breaching the hangar made the floor shudder. "Good luck, ADIM."

"This unit does not require luck. With the will of the Creator
guiding it, the odds of failure are minimal."

"Noted." Cassius closed his eyes and allowed himself one last
grin. The glass of the terrace outside shattered. "ADIM you may
not be a human, but I care for you all the same. You understand
that I hope?"

"This unit understands. A man can feel love for whomever

he chooses. One day, when we're done, there will be other humans worthy of your will."

"Perhaps. But until then I have you. Goodbye ADIM."

"Goodbye, Creator."

Just as he switched the communications off, soldiers in green-hued Tribunal armor flooded into his room. An emergency seal fell down over the translucency in order to preserve the balance of warm, breathable air, but it was too late to keep the invaders out. There had to be at least twenty of them staring down the sights of their rifles at him.

"On your knees, traitor!" a group of voices shouted through their visors.

"Disarm him!" The leader of the squad signaled his men. Cassius recognized the armor as that of a Hand. *Belloth again*, he thought.

"I will not fight," Cassius proclaimed calmly just before the butt of a rifle slammed across the side of his face. Hands grabbed him from all over, keeping him upright until they could rip off his belt. When they were done they rolled him onto his stomach and wrenched his arms back to bind his wrists. "I see civility is lost on the Tribune these days!" he snarled and spit out a glob of blood.

One of the soldiers delivered the Hand Cassius' belt and he rustled through all of the pouches. When he found the HOLO-Sphere he carefully observed it before declaring it harmless and placing it back in. Then he fastened the belt around his waist and positioned Cassius' pistol opposite his own.

"Bring him up!" the Hand ordered, and Cassius was promptly lifted onto both knees. "Check the room." The soldiers began probing every corner, though there was little to search.

"Clear!" they pronounced one after the other and then turned to aim their rifles at Cassius again.

"Send her up," the Hand said and then removed his helmet.

"Hand Belloth. I was wondering when I would get to see you again," Cassius said as his red-stained lips formed a haughty grin.

"Shut your mouth!" the soldier standing behind Cassius shouted and kicked him in his bound wrists.

He lurched in pain, but he didn't allow his smiling face to shift.

"I told you I'd be watching." Belloth sheathed his pistol and approached Cassius with a hard grimace. "I can't wait to wipe that fuckin' smile off of your face!" His fist crashed into Cassius' cheek so forcefully that it would have knocked him over had the soldiers not been there to keep him upright.

More blood began oozing through Cassius' teeth. "Fate plays such cruel games." He thrust his head forward with a growl, causing Belloth to reel away nervously before the other soldiers ripped him back down. "I had hoped Benjar would come, but I suppose Nora will have to do," he snickered beneath his heavy breaths, noticing the fear in the Hand's eyes.

"I knew you were scum. Betray the Tribune after all it has done for you!" Belloth wound his arm back for another punch.

"Stand down, Belloth!" an authoritative and matronly voice ordered, arresting Belloth's blow just before it made contact. "I will deal with him myself."

Tribune Nora Gressler stood in the doorway, an elegant, form-fitting, turquoise dress blooming around her feet. Her hair was pulled up into a rigid bun. Strong lines of golden makeup swept out from the corners of her eyes, but no amount of cosmetics could mask the wrinkles forming all over her face.

Two rows of her own personal honor-guard entered on either side of her, dressed in white and emerald armor with the emblem of the Tribune printed on their chests and a green cape draped over their left arms.

"Nora Gressler! The lovely Hand chosen to fill my shoes. What a pleasure. I was just telling your own Hand here how much I had been hoping Benjar would come himself rather than send out his newest pet. What a reunion that would have been!" Cassius quipped, earning a glower that made her look even less appealing.

"Save your insults, Cassius. Do not try and deflect your lack of significance onto me!" Nora snapped before she and her host of honor-guards arrayed themselves in front of him. The ordinary soldiers receded to the back of the room without having to be asked.

"My lack of significance?" Cassius sneered. "Don't be naïve. Those old bastards would do anything for another pawn. Time has lessened your beauty, however. How long before they banish you to some forsaken colony like they did me?"

"Forsaken? Edeoria was the jewel of this Cell before we gave you control over it! The underground farms fail! Your people are displaced and dying!" She wagged her long, slender finger in his direction. "No, Cassius, it is you who has forsaken this place! And for what?"

"Jewel" Cassius laughed, ignoring the rest of what she said. "They really did well in finding you after my exile."

"A self-made exile!" she retorted. "After all that happened they gave you a colony to live out the rest of your pitiful life. It was you who chose never to return."

Cassius shook his head and sighed. "There is no reason to argue with you. You occupy my colony. You storm my home. What is it that you accuse me of doing?"

Nora mustered her most regal stride and came face to face with him. She looked him over angrily before pulling a com-link out of his ear and handing it to Belloth. "Next time take that off first," she commanded her Hand in a threatening manner. "I won't have him calling for help."

"Forgive me, Your Eminence." Belloth fell to his knee, bowed his head subserviently, and ran his fingers along the floor. Then he placed the com-link in the same pouch where he had already put Cassius' HOLO-Sphere.

"You know what you've done," she stated indubitably with her back turned to him.

"Well of course I know everything I have done!" Cassius jested, his response causing her to clench her hands into two quaking fists. "I hope you don't think I've simply lost my mind. I'm merely wondering what it is that Benjar has come up with to get you here so swiftly."

She wheeled around with ice in her glare. "Besides neglecting your own people to the point of near genocide you mean? He has reason to believe you were behind the attacks on our freighters and that you have fashioned some sort of twisted robot capable of unearthly deeds, such as the cold-blooded murder of an Executor!"

He could tell he was getting to her. Her cheeks grew red even through the layer of makeup covering them, and her nose creased with very visible lines of frustration. "All of it then...and what hard proof do you have of any of this to take up arms against me without questioning the order first?"

"Besides that the abomination came from your ship? The arm, Cassius!" she screamed, stamping forward with such force that her bun grew disheveled. "We witnessed the last moment of that Executor's life as your *creation* sent him adrift into space. It was forged of the same technology which constructed the arm on the other Executor you are now holding captive in this complex. I had my suspicions of Benjar's accusations, but that was before Sage arrived here. Or did you forget that we'd see and hear everything you said to her before you took her underground and cut us out."

"No, I counted on it. In fact I wish you could have seen as I set her free. She is quite alive if you must know. As for ADIM, well I won't deny my most treasured work. Unfortunately you will not have the chance to meet him. He is far away from here."

"You gave that creature a name?" She turned her appalled expression toward Belloth. "Hand Belloth, have him show you to where he is holding Executor Sage Volus. Then he will be taken to my ship and detained on Enceladus until we can decide what to do with him."

"Yes, Your Eminence." Belloth nodded and made a signal with his hand. Seven of the regular soldiers formed around him. One grabbed Cassius by his bindings and began shoving him along. He didn't fight it. The barrels of two rifles pressed tightly against his back as he was forced to lead them.

"Don't let your guard down, Belloth. His legend precedes him." Nora glowered at Cassius. He shot a smug grin back in her direction.

Belloth nodded again before Cassius led them out of the room. "You heard her. Guns on him," he ordered as they moved down the Hall of Holographic Busts.

"It's not far up this way," Cassius said loudly as he turned right at the first corner.

"Just shut your mouth and lead!" Belloth pushed him. "You're a shame to anyone who's ever wanted to be an Executor."

"A shame enough, I hope, to dissuade them from that horrid path." He stretched out his neck so that the ugly scar cutting up the back of it was impossible to miss.

Belloth ignored what he saw. "Is this it?" he questioned as

they stopped in front of a blank, metal door."

"Yes."

"How does it open?"

"I need my hands."

"Are you sure?" Belloth came around in front of him and gave him a stern glare. Cassius nodded and with a sigh Belloth signaled to one of the soldiers to unfasten the cuffs for a moment. He then lifted his pistol and pressed it against Cassius' forehead. "Try anything and I'll paint the walls with your brain."

"Charming." Cassius flashed a weak smile and he stretched out his sore wrists. Then he powered the HOLO-Screen on his bracer on and keyed the commands, which made the retinal scanner appear next to the door. "See? Easy." Without resisting it he placed his arms behind his back to be re-cuffed.

"Open it," Belloth growled and lowered his gun.

Cassius leaned over and placed his eye against the scanner, causing the door to rise up. "There you go." He took a step back so that the soldiers could pass him onto the lift.

"Oh no." Belloth shoved him on the elevator. "You're coming with us."

All of them squeezed shoulder to shoulder into the dim space. It was a tight fit. Cassius could still feel guns against his back. Before long the lift began to descend and when it came to a gradual halt he felt the barrels press even harder.

"Move."

Cassius stepped into the dark laboratory. The only illumination was provided by three red lights on the other end of the space giving off a menacing glow.

"What kind of hell is this place?" Belloth mouthed as they delved in.

There were rows of consoles and strange machinery arranged on either side of them in no real order. Once they were close enough Cassius was able to see the surgical table placed carefully in the center of it all. Even though it was obscure he could make out the curves of the beautiful woman lying unconscious on it in her underwear. Closer still and he knew the others would notice the bloody bandage wound around her head with her auburn hair sticking out from the top.

"There she is!" Belloth motioned two of his men to go and check on her while he remained by Cassius' side with his gun drawn. "What the fuck did you do to her?"

"Set her free." Cassius offered his most sanctimonious reply.

"She's got a pulse!" one of the soldiers shouted back.

"Can she be moved?" Belloth asked sharply without averting his gaze from her.

"Not by any of you." Just as the words slipped through Cassius' lips, eight succinct shots greeted his waiting ears. They were soft and silenced, no louder than a sudden gasp of wind. The seven soldiers around the room keeled over with precise bullet-holes in the center of the foreheads. Hand Belloth himself had been hit in the throat and lay on his back in a state of shock, blood bubbling over the wound as he struggled to speak. His arm grasped desperately to turn on his radio before Cassius gently placed his foot over it to hold it down.

"You should have stayed far away from here," he whispered callously as he watched the life flee the Hand's face. Cassius waited there, holding him down with his foot until the twitching stopped and his eyes glazed over. Then the ominous red lights began to close in around him, until three human-like profiles became visible as the sources.

"Is the Creator's will fulfilled?" they asked in unison, with emotionless voices almost precisely like ADIM's. They moved closer until their dark-metal frames were visible with rifts of smoldering red showing through plates of armor. Their faces were blank, only with red eyes that were surrounded by rings of smaller lights.

"Yes." Cassius spun around to admire their work. Then, without having to ask, one of the androids came behind him and cut the cuffs off him with a thin laser-shot.

Rubbing his bruised wrists Cassius knelt down and unfastened his belt from around Belloth's corpse. "A shame." He shook his head as he pulled it around his waist and made sure that the HOLO-Sphere was safe within the small satchel attached to it. Next he reclaimed his weapon, and when all his possessions were securely on his person he walked over to an array of HOLO-Screens and began quickly shifting through commands.

Cassius glanced over his shoulder when he heard the three androids coming up behind him. *ADIM will understand*, he assured himself before addressing them solemnly, "Are the other three in position?"

"Yes. Awaiting the Creator's command," they responded simultaneously.

When he looked back the main screen was prompting him to enter a password. He closed his eyes and took a deep breath. The lab had to be terminated. He had spent more years then he cared to remember working in its depths. He had constructed ADIM there, the whole room was his metal womb. But risking all of his work was no longer an option.

It took all of his resolve but one by one he entered the code until it was all there: 2AL3B82LE. Once it was done the screen was replaced with the image of a red blip approaching what appeared to be a projection of Titan and the Conduit Station above it. A series of numbers shuffled over the screen until they locked at eleven minutes and seven seconds, and began to count down.

"Come, my creations." Cassius whirled around and made his way toward the lift. "There isn't much time."

Despite his words he didn't hurry across the lab, instead taking his time to reminiscence at every piece of machinery inside. They were bathed in shadow, but he saw the table where ADIM once lay before he brought him to life. There were three more on either side of it now; one for each of the six androids he had finally powered on before Nora and her fleet arrived.

He stopped when he reached Sage and unfastened her from the surgical table. The androids tried to help him but he shooed them away before cradling her between both of his arms. Her artificial limb made her heavier than he had expected, but he carried her to the lift where he joined them.

The door slowly shut behind them. He stared into the dark lab until it was completely sealed and the floor began to rise.

Finally…

CHAPTER FORTY
FLAMES OVER TITAN

The three androids in front of Cassius stormed forward as the lift's door opened. There were soldiers waiting outside in a panic, but they were instantly cut down by a clatter of bullets into a tangle of thrashing limbs. Cassius carried Sage through the doors and stepped over a cluster of bodies. Two of the androids sprinted toward his personal quarters and the other went in the opposite direction toward the hangar. There were three more scattered throughout his compound, and he could tell by the echoing gunfire and screams that they had already made contact as expected.

With Sage in his arms he couldn't move fast, but he didn't have to. By the time he turned into the Hall of Holographic Busts it was already lined with bodies killed at the hands of his androids. There were soldiers scattered like bloody rags over the floor and against the walls. Even the water troughs running down the edges of the hall were stained red.

Cassius looked down at Sage's placid face to see her eyelids twitching. He knew from experience that the dreams and memories directly after surgery would be exhausting.

"You'll be safe here for now," he whispered gently in her ear before he kissed her on the forehead and placed her down against the pedestal of his son's holographic effigy. Then, after shooting one last ardent look into Caleb's artificial eyes, he opened the door to his chambers.

Two of the androids were already waiting for him inside when he stepped in, the door slamming shut behind him. Tribune Nora Gressler was on her knees in front of them both. She shielded her face as the guns on their wrists were held rigidly before her head. More than a dozen Tribunal Honor-guards were littered throughout. Not a single one of them was moving or even moaning in agony. They were some of the finest soldiers the Tribune had to offer and Cassius' creations mowed them down like children zapping insects with magnifying glasses. The further in he moved the more scarce the sounds of fighting and death from deeper into the complex grew.

"What have you done?" the trembling Nora whimpered. Her face and dress were doused in her soldier's blood.

"Only what I must," Cassius responded sternly. He stepped up in between the two androids holding the Tribune at gunpoint. "You should have brought Mechs of your own." He patted them on their cold, metal backs. They didn't avert their precise aim even the slightest from the impact.

"Even Benjar didn't know what you truly are…" She gazed up at him, her weathered face gripped by a look of absolute terror.

"And what am I?" he said calmly before grasping her by the jaw and hollering, "What am I!"

"A monster!" She squeezed the words out through her lips with disdain.

Cassius tossed her forward onto her stomach. "There are no monsters… only different perspectives." He walked over to the entrance onto the terrace, which was sealed by an emergency panel in order to conserve breathable air.

"Do you really hate people so much, Cassius?" She flipped her shaking body over to face him, but was immediately halted by the androids that wrapped around to her front. "That you would turn to these abominations?"

"I may not—" Cassius was caught off-guard by a sudden burst of distant shots succeeded by a bloodcurdling scream. When it was quiet again he continued, "I may not care for people, but I love humanity. I love what we stand for; what we've accomplished; our limitless potential to expand and invent. I will not sit idly by as the Tribune holds us back!"

He pressed an imbedded switch beside the sealed exit and triggered a small section of the nearby wall to fold up. In it were two sleek looking enviro-suits. They were completely black, with coated tubes extending from the back that had a combination of a filtration system connected to a personal oxygen store able to allow him to breathe outside safely for a short period. The respirator helmets hanging at the side had an oblong shape and were mostly translucent along the fronts.

"What... what are you doing?" She scrambled backwards, but the androids moved behind her to make sure she had nowhere to go.

Cassius stepped into one of the suits and sealed it over his body. Then he pulled the helmet down over his face and latched it into the metal collar, which released a soft hiss once sealed. When he was done he grabbed the other suit and approached Nora.

"You're going to need this," he offered it to her, his voice muffled by the helmet. "I learned a few things while serving as a Tribune. Careful planning was one of them."

She sneered at him, refusing to take the suit. Cassius shrugged before he activated the HOLO-Screen on his bracer and keyed in a few commands. Then he held on to the wall. When the sealed panel began to open he watched with a smile as Nora frantically put on the suit. She barely finished before a gust of icy, Titan air rushed in. The androids grabbed onto her arms to keep her from moving and when the change in pressure was complete Cassius stormed forward and took hold of her from them. He dragged her squirming body out onto the terrace where they would be visible.

It was incredibly noisy, the winds of Titan whistling through the shattered glass and pelting their visors with sand and dust. Once the panel was all the way up he saw a swarm of more transports approaching. Beyond them the *Calypso* was turning to face his compound so that they could see down the long barrel of its tremendous railgun.

"Tell them to pull back," Cassius demanded.

Nora shook her head defiantly, trying her best to ignore the lethal androids standing just behind her.

Cassius pulled out his pistol and held it against her temple. "Tell them," he snarled.

She didn't have much of a choice. Reluctantly she reached up to her ear and held down the button on her com-link. "Don't engage... I repeat, hold back!"

The closest of the incoming ships sailed overhead and wheeled back in the opposite direction.

"There we go. Easy." Cassius patted her on the shoulder. With his free arm he glanced at his HOLO-Screen and saw the countdown at 1:53 in the corner.

"What do you want now? How do you possibly see this ending?" She tried to summon her most intrepid voice, but he could see how frightened she really was. Her eyes were peeled open as wide as they could go, and the entirety of her person seemed to be seized by a relentless tremble. It had been a long time since she was a soldier.

"I don't see it ending. Not yet," he responded as he continued to stare impatiently at the counter. *1:31.* It couldn't come fast enough.

"I will not be some bargaining chip! I am a Tribune!"

"You are nothing!" He struck her in the back of the head with his pistol, knocking her onto her face. When he went to pull her back up two other androids entered the room.

"Creator. The other Units have boarded the *White Hand,*" the robots announced at the same time. They passed over the dozens of corpses without even a downward glance.

"Good. Seal the door," Cassius commanded them, not forgetting that Sage remained unconscious outside and in need of breathable air. Then he turned back to Nora.

"Is this what you've been doing here... building an army?" Nora wheezed as she got onto her hands and knees.

"Not an army. That comes later."

"What happened to you?" Nora released a grueling cough, and Cassius realized that the tube attached to the back of her helmet had been ruptured at the base from his blow. "Is this all for your son? Nobody could have stopped what happened that day on Earth."

As Cassius leaned over to try and fix it, her words made him stop. He grabbed her by the throat and growled. "Don't you dare talk about him! My son gave his life for your Earth. He didn't just wait for change, he made it, and now you wear the plant he grew there like a badge of honor!" He roared, his dark eyes smoldering with rage. He lifted her up by her neck with one hand and squeezed.

She groped at his arm, squirming and thrashing for her life until Cassius' limb suddenly gave out. His muscles didn't have the same endurance as they used to be.

"Fire the rail! Kill him now with me!" Nora took the unexpected opportunity to scream into her com-link. In a hurry, one of the androids seized her, but not before getting the orders got out successfully.

"Bitch!" Cassius barked. He wheeled around quickly with his gun drawn and fired a shot into the center of her chest. Blood dripped down from her mouth beneath the mask as she looked down, fingering the wound with both hands. Then her eyes froze, a haunting stare aimed in his direction as her body was held upright by the android.

Cassius stormed forward with a grumble and grabbed her by the collar. He yanked her out of the robot's grasp and heaved her with all his might. Her body sailed over the railing and off the top of the Ksa Crater's rim, tumbling through the frigid air until she vanished beneath the hanging smog.

When he looked up, a dull, white glow augmented over the center of the *Calypso.* It was too late. It had already begun charging its main gun. His heart skipped a beat, but that was before his wrist beeped. He looked down anxiously to see that the countdown had reached zero. *Just in time,* he thought, relieved.

The laboratory buried deep beneath his feet exploded, causing the room he was in to shudder. He stumbled back into the arms of an android that somehow managed to keep its balance. But despite all that was going on below, Cassius wasn't looking down. His eyes were fixed on the sky where the murky silhouette of the Conduit Station was being approached by a rapidly moving black shadow. When the two shapes met, the atmosphere was painted with a conflagration of blue and orange. He couldn't feel the blast, he couldn't even hear it, but the whole sky lit up momentarily as if a second sun was rising.

The *Calypso's* railgun slid back along the surface of the ship and was ready to fire when suddenly a massive, fiery chunk of debris rained down from the sky and crashed into the bow. The Cruiser pitched forward from the impact, throwing off its aim just as a blinding beam of whitish light shot out from it in a wide arc that blasted through the tops of at least three of Edeoria's Shafts. The initial shockwave was so strong that it blew Cassius, and even the androids this time, back onto their rears.

Flames and smoke coiled up from smoldering gash in Titan's surface. Chunks of metal and rocks were spewed all over, as more fragments from the damaged Conduit continued to shower the colony. Cassius watched in awe, hardly even noticing as the androids lifted him back to his feet.

Then, as if called down from the heavens, the pearly stern of the *White Hand* banked around the complex and blocked his view. It began hovering just at the edge of the terrace and the androids hurried over to the ledge.

"Creator, you are in danger. You must come," they said in unison as one of the androids extended its hand. The others leaped into the open hangar of the *White Hand*.

Cassius ignored his creation, instead stepping to the side to capture another view of the destruction. All of the smaller ships were scrambling out of the way of flying wreckage. The *Calypso* was attempting to pull up from its crash course so that it would miss the heart of the colony and instead slam into the rim of the Ksa crater.

"Creator. You must come," the android implored him.

"Give me a moment," Cassius responded calmly.

He took a moment to gather his senses and take everything in. Then he hurried to his bed and tore off the sheets. While carrying them, he reopened the entrance to the hallway and stepped through to see Sage still lying peacefully on her back. Taking his time, he wrapped the blanket around her entire body and lifted her so that she was cradled between both of his arms.

Cassius glanced down the hall, seeing all of the Holographic faces staring forward as if he wasn't there. *More than a face of stone,* he thought as he used the stand of his son's effigy to get a better grip on Sage's limp body.

"We're survivors, you and I," he whispered in her ear, looking over her brow at the face of his son. He nodded at the hologram before wheeling around to head toward the terrace where the *White Hand* was waiting.

"Are you ready, Creator?" the waiting android asked.

He drank in one last gulp of the devastation he wrought. They were the people he was charged with, but they were his father's people. *There is no other way*, he assured himself as he began to walk toward the edge, each stride growing longer and more confident. Once he was there, the android grabbed hold of him and Sage and they jumped, the three of them landing safely in the ship before it took off toward the scorched sky.

The cargo bay ramp sealed shut and Cassius took a seat against the wall, Sage's body lying over his tired lap. As he did the familiar voice of ADIM spoke into his ear, "Creator, the gravitum bomb performed as anticipated."

"What perfect timing." He took a deep breath and got a better grip on her body. Then his eyes shut and his lips curled into a scant grin. "It is good to hear your voice."

Chapter Forty-One
The Desecration of Kalliope

The Shadow Chariot was sitting silently on the surface of a Kalliope's smaller satellite asteroid. ADIM lay inside in a dormant state, awaiting commands. A violently seething orb of blue protruded from the top of the ship's hull, appearing unstable enough to explode at any moment.

ADIM, Cassius' cool voice spoke directly into him. *Proceed as planned. Use any means necessary.*

ADIM wasted no time. His bright red eyes flashed on and his radiant core began to smolder.

This unit is primed, Creator. Will move to penetrate Kalliope defenses now. The *Shadow Chariot* began to hum as the engines flipped on and it slowly lifted off of the rocky surface.

Good, Cassius said and then there came a lengthy pause. The *Shadow Chariot* was already racing out across the stars toward the somewhat elongated body of Kalliope before Cassius continued speaking. *Good luck, ADIM.*

This unit does not require luck. With the will of the Creator guiding it, the odds of failure are minimal.

Noted, Cassius replied softly and took an audible breath. *ADIM you may not be a human, but I care for you all the same. You understand that I hope?*

This unit understands. A man can feel love for whomever he chooses. One day, when we're done, there will be other humans worthy of your will.

Perhaps. But until then I have you. Goodbye ADIM.

Goodbye, Creator.

ADIM banked hard around the asteroid. The strange emptiness, which always took him after those words returned, but it was easier to deal with when he was on a mission. As he headed for the entrance port into the mining colony, all he was looking forward to was completing his task so that he could speak with Cassius again. It was a sense of longing he was beginning to understand, or rather, accept. It made failure an impossible contemplation.

When he was close enough, two mounted turrets above the hexagonal gate imbedded into the side of the asteroid unleashed a hail of anti-air rounds. He took complete control, the *Shadow Chariot* becoming like an extended part of his being. It shot upward, getting higher so that the Gravitum Weapon bomb was in no danger of being hit. Then he spiraled out of the way of incoming fire and shifted downward, his ship's forward guns tearing through one of the turrets. A missile sped under his wing as he corkscrewed up and around, coming at the second turret from the flank and ripping it from the wall with precise fire.

With the surprising lack of outer defenses swiftly dispelled, he guided the ship's landing gear to touch down against a scabrous surface just above the vertical gate. It was a densely plated entryway, and ADIM had no doubt that those inside had been alerted of an assault. He disconnected the circuits binding him to the ship as the cockpit opened with a snap-hiss quickly muted by the vacuum of space. Then he climbed over the edge and pushed off so that he drifted across the vacuum. When he slammed against the gate he switched on his magnetic limbs to keep him steady.

With one arm he began to concentrate his wrist-laser into the metal. Clambering around on all fours he slowly traced a circle until both molten ends met. Then he moved a small distance down and repeated the same steps but in a much smaller ring. Leaving the second incision three-quarters finished, he fired a missile at the first circle. The disk exploded inward at first before the intense change in pressure sucked it back into the void along with everything else inside that was loose.

ADIM waited until all of the scraps of metal, pieces of equipment, and a few human beings were pulled out before smashing through the second hole with both feet. He wielded the circular plate like a shield as he landed in a large, open hangar that was flashing red with wailing alarms. The guards and miners inside had taken up arms, but they had been heaved off of their feet by the release of pressure. Having already donned their helmets they were able to breathe despite the breach, and so ADIM bolted horizontally, firing accurate shots with one arm as he shielded from a rampant spray of bullets with the other. He ducked behind a pile of crates.

Six adversaries on the floor. Five more up top. ADIM quickly assessed the situation and planned his moves.

He poked his arm over the rim and sent a missile into the engines of a parked transport vessel the defenders were using for cover. Plumes of smoke and flame shot out from it in every direction and he leaped over the crates, now using both arms to unleash a barrage of carefully aimed shots. He ran forward, his eyes and body revolving rapidly as he continued firing up onto the catwalks. Bullets whizzed by his frame, but he had calculated the route, and when he reached the remaining slag from the transport, there was nobody left to kill.

After making sure there were no enemies hiding, ADIM turned around and entered into the engineering room on the broad side of the space. The translucency facing the hangar was shattered, the men inside filled with bloody holes. He pulled one of the corpses off of a chair and placed his palm against a console, tapping into the security systems. The hexagonal gate began to open and he ran outside to climb up the rim. The corpses and fragments of the transport were languidly being dragged across the floor toward the opening as ADIM climbed back into the *Shadow Chariot.*

It lifted off and he maneuvered it slowly through the hangar. Its small size was to his advantage now. The sealed entrance on the other side of the space, which led deeper into the mine, had to be tall and wide enough to fit a mining Mech. He fired two under-wing missiles into it and coaxed his ship forward through the smoke and splayed metal. The tips of the wings barely scraped against the sides as he emerged through into the spacious, residential cavity of the colony. The ship's bow crushed a few guards standing just inside before a line of gunfire rained down on him from a bridge.

Tilting the ship up, he fired a missile into it and the shooters soared up into the air, slamming against the tall ceiling, or the dish-like metal structures cropping out from the craggy walls. Then he rose up the cavity. More pulse rifles flashed in front of the structure across the bridge illuminated by a sign that read, *The Elder Muse.*

The *Shadow Chariot's* forward guns slashed across its length, cutting a wide gash in the serrated walls stained by eviscerated bodies.

ADIM's sensors picked up almost a hundred more heat signatures hiding throughout the space and inside the disk structures, but no more guards showed themselves to slow him. Satisfied, he coaxed his ship forward where he was presented with three different tunnels leading into the depths of Kalliope. He remembered from his preparations with Cassius that he should take the left one.

It was dark as he delved in, black as the night on earth. He switched his sight to night-vision. Then down through winding channels he plunged, until the birth into his final destination was too slender for the ship to fit.

ADIM set the *Shadow Chariot* down in front of it, detached himself from the circuits and hopped up onto the hull. The churning, blue orb released an aura that illuminated the entire cavern, which was beneficial since being so near to it was scrambling his sensors. He unlatched the four restraints around its circumference and cautiously lifted it out. The Gravitum inside was heavy and so he hoisted it up on top of his back and made his way through the narrow passage.

It was a low cave filled in densely by gnarled pillars and dripping stalactites. He went to the center and carefully placed the Gravitum Weapon in the smoothest niche he could fine. Then, as he took a step back, his sensors picked up a presence. He quickly wheeled round to see a Mining Mech bounding toward him. A colossal arm smashed across his chassis, knocking him against the wall of the cavern where he was pinned down by a giant clamper. A drill powered toward his head, and he quickly fired a missile into the legs of the Mech, knocking it back through a pillar of rock.

The cavern began to rumble as cracks formed along its roof. ADIM dove forward, rolling around the Mech as it scrambled to its feet. He jumped onto its back and shoved his fist through the plated exterior, ripping apart the proper circuitry without needing to see it in order to render it useless. Then he flipped off of it, landing nimbly between the Mech and the Gravitum Weapon as the immense suit fell backward and its chest cavity opened up. ADIM hurried around the front to see a bulky, dark skinned human sitting in the cockpit with his strong arms wrapped around a small child. ADIM aimed at the man's head as he stepped up onto the Mech's frame and pulled the chamber all the way open.

"Please," the man groaned. He was shaking uncontrollably, a look of dread dawning over him as ADIM's red eyes grew nearer. "She's strong….Spare her… I promised…" His quivering fingers ran through the little girl's hair as her limp head rested on his forearm. She was knocked unconscious from the fall.

"This unit must execute the will of the Creator." Without hesitating he shot the man in the head, but as his arms gave out and the girl fell forward ADIM caught her before she tumbled over the edge of the Mech. He lifted her by the back of her neck, turning her from side to side as his curiosity kicked in. He had never seen a human child before, so ready to be shaped and molded.

She's strong, ADIM repeated to himself what the man had said. *She has yet to reach her potential.* He lifted her eyelid, but she was unconscious. He then remembered back to all the times Cassius would bring up his son and how his expression would darken and the rate of his pulse would hasten. *If she is strong, then the Creator and this unit can make her a human worthy of his will.* Arriving at this verdict, he got a better grip on the girl and dodged a few shards of falling rock. The roof was beginning to cave in.

ADIM began to approach the Gravitum Weapon, but as he did he recalled how hazardous it was to Cassius. He turned his body and held the girl out in front of him so that his chassis was firmly between her and the weapon. Then he hurriedly reached behind himself to grab the handle on the top of the sphere without looking, and pulled it up until a cylindrical console appeared. When it came to a lock he turned the handle and the Gravitum Weapon began to emit strange whining noises as if it were in pain. Once it was triggered he tossed the girl over his shoulder, ran to the *Shadow Chariot* and vaulted over the side.

With the girl positioned on his lap he powered on the engines and guided the ship forward into the tunnel. Having already memorized the route he rushed around corners and through tight openings until he debouched into the residential cavity. People had gathered on all of the balconies and precipices to see what was going on but he rushed past them, shooting through the hangar and out into space.

His ship's ion-engines traced a line across the stars as he drove the ship forward at full speed. When he reached the satellite asteroid he swung the ship around and hovered above it, facing Kalliope with the girl lying silently on top of him.

It didn't take long before bluish waves of energy sliced out of the asteroid every which way, like crescent shaped blades. After expanding more than a mile the particles were sucked back inward and there was a moment of calm before the entire rock split into three enormous chunks. They appeared to be tumbling in slow motion apart from each other, leaving a darkened void in the center with coruscating beams of blue distortion dancing throughout it.

Creator. The Gravitum bomb performed as anticipated, ADIM informed Cassius as he watched the fragments diverge.

What perfect timing. Despite his prompt response Cassius sounded weary. *It is good to hear your voice.*

ADIM took quick note of the change in his tone. *Creator, are you harmed?* he questioned.

Never better. Cassius assured him by putting a little extra vigor into his words. *Safely aboard the White Hand. The first strike against the Tribune has been cast.*

The girl on ADIM's lap began to wheeze and he remembered that she needed more oxygen then whatever the ship might have trapped while still in Kalliope. He switched on the life support systems Cassius had installed in case of an emergency and felt her lungs to ensure that she was breathing properly. She was.

This unit shall return to Ennomos with a gift from Kalliope.

A gift? What could that desecrated piece of rock possibly have to offer? Cassius responded in a surprised tone.

The Creator shall see. Another extension of your will.

I look forward to it. I too will soon bear a gift, one that has helped keep humanity alive for hundreds of years.

The Solar-Ark is under your command?

I'm on my way to seize it now. Prepare Ennomos for its arrival. He paused, his excited breaths audible. *We have waited too long for this. Today the Circuit has been forever changed. I shall see you soon, ADIM.*

This unit... ADIM's eyes began to spin as a human phrase jumped to the forefront of his consciousness...*Is looking forward to it.*

The unwelcome silence returned as he turned the *Shadow Chariot* around and rocketed away from the shattered mining colony toward the endless black of space. But it did not come with the usual sense of vacancy that he detested. In fact, as he looked down at the placid face of the young girl, his gift, if ADIM could've smiled he would have.

CHAPTER FORTY-TWO
TRACE THE STARS WITH BLOOD

Talon jolted awake. He had been trapped in the long, dreamless slumber induced by his Cryo-Chamber aboard the Solar-Ark *Amerigo*. As his eyes adjusted, the tubes and needles piercing his body all over began to slide out from beneath his skin. leaving in their wake a feeling like liquid ice running through his veins. Then the frosted glass in front of him peeled away and he fell forward onto his hands in a pool of chilled liquid.

It was hard to hear anything clearly, but alarms were wailing and blobs of frantic figures sprinted in both directions. He looked to his side as others fell forward from their chambers. Most of them seemed accustomed to waking from Cryo-Sleep, but all the newcomers, like him, were crawling as if they'd just emerged from the womb. It had only been a week or two, but to him it felt like learning how to walk all over again. His teeth chattered as his whole body was seized by relentless shiver. He was freezing to his core. He felt like was walking on the bare outer surface of the dark side of Ceres.

"On your feet!" the voice of Keeper Tarsis shouted out.

Talon was suddenly hoisted up to his feet. He half expected to topple over once he was there, but his muscles adjusted almost instantaneously until he wasn't even wobbling. Then his limbs began to tingle from his toes and fingers inward, slowly awakening until even the coldness began to dissipate. It was an unpleasant experience at first to be sure, but when all the effects of Cryo-Sleep wore off Talon felt fresher than he had in years. The soreness of the Blue Death was gone. Every one of his muscles felt as youthful and alive as they would have been if he was healthy.

Not having to focus on ignoring the symptoms of his disease

provided him with the awareness which once made him a fearsome mercenary. He noticed something different about his surroundings. All of the Keepers were running around fully armed, but they didn't look angry or eager to fight. They all looked terrified.

He reached out and grabbed Tarsis by his metal suit, turning him around so hard that he almost knocked him over. He wasn't used to feeling so strong. "What the hell's going on?" he demanded. "Why isn't the ship moving?"

"It was badly damaged over Titan." Tarsis hardly bothered to stop as he continued helping the other new recruits to their feet all the while making sure to keep his rifle aimed straight ahead. "The sail was damaged and we had to shut off all auxiliary engines to repair it."

"By who?" Talon shouted as he followed after him.

"No idea! Intruders came upon us after we stopped. Now, get your suit on! We need all the guns we can get!" Tarsis pointed to a sealed container at the base of Talon's Cryo-Chamber before bending down to aid another recruit.

A few loud gun shots resonated from the far reaches of the ship, causing Talon to jump as he reached into the container. He quickly pulled out his own suit of Nano-armor and began to dress himself. It had a snug fit despite being older than he cared to imagine. The black color was faded and the armored, blue-outlined portions over his joints were dented and scratched. Once it was on he grasped the pulse rifle lying inside the container and turned to catch up to Tarsis.

Just as he began to run more shots rang out, this time from much nearer. The ship's main lighting system flickered off and the man getting ready beside him toppled over. Blood squirted out of the man's neck onto Talon's cheek. He hastily dove behind the fallen body and began firing blindly at its waist. Screams of horror filled his ears. Glass shattered and circuits spit out steam and sparks. All he could see through the shadows were the barrels of rifles flashing and the glowing blue of other Keeper's armor as they collapsed one after the other.

Talon held his hands over his ears as he remained in cover, completely disoriented and unsure where to go. He peered over the body, trying to catch a glimpse of what was attacking through all the commotion. All he could make out were a few glowing spheres of deep red skittering around from the floors to the walls at inhumane speeds.

Bullets tore into his cover, dousing him in more blood as he scrambled to lie back down flat. It wasn't like any skirmish he'd ever experienced. The lines of bright gunfire only served to make it more disorienting as bodies piled up all around him. Muddled voices cried out, but there were less and less of them with each passing second. And the more sporadic they grew, the more intense the feeling of inescapable doom began to take hold.

Talon looked behind his position where he was able to see the edges of the staircase leading up into the Solar-Arks corridors. Whatever the attackers were, he stood little chance of survival out in the open.

This is my chance to escape! he realized suddenly. He pictured Elisha's smile and grit his teeth before positioning himself against the corpse. After a few quick breathes to prepare, he put his renewed vigor to the test and hauled the body over his back. Then he sprung to his feet and began to run as fast as he could. Bullets whizzed around him and into the corpse as he sprinted. Keepers fell all around him as they tried to stand their ground—blood falling like crimson rain.

Everything became a blur of fear, darkness and blinding flashes until Talon reached the stairs and let the body tumble off of his back. He scrambled up to the top and fell against the wall panting, his shoulder searing from the weight. His heart felt like it was going to beat out of his chest, but he made it. There was little time for rest, however. He raised his rifle and slowly pressed forward through the black corridor.

There was no reason to switch on the flashlight along the barrel of his gun and risk exposure. The bluish glow of his armor was enough to at least see if he was going to bump into anything. He took it one step at a time, trying to keep his nerve as his feet brushed against what were obviously the limbs of dead bodies. He struggled to keep his breathing down, which was all he could hear except for the occasional scream and gunshot. He was getting further away from them. At the far end of whatever corridor he was moving down he could see a viewport with a glimmer of starlight peeking through.

Even though he didn't know where he was going, Talon knew he'd be safer in the light where he could see his enemies. His eyes were trained down the sight of the rifle, snapping around every time the ship's ancient circuitry groaned. When he arrived at the T- intersection where the translucency spanned across, he poked his rifle around the corner. As soon as he did the barrel of a gun pressed against the back of his head. He was ready to wheel around and fight one last battle when a familiar voice spoke up.

"By the Ancients, it's you!" Tarsis glanced over Talon's shoulder and pulled him around the corner.

"Holy…" Talon wheezed, holding his chest in shock. "You almost gave me a heart attack."

"Did you see what hit us?" Tarsis grabbed him by the shouldered and asked anxiously. "How could this happen?"

"No… I … I don't know…" Talon gathered his breath. "They're all dead, I think."

"We have to save the ship," Tarsis commanded. "Come on, the command deck is this way!" He charged around the corner when all of a sudden a hand emerged from a dark hallway to seize him by the neck.

Talon followed him, ready to fire, but what he saw froze him in his tracks. A pair of red eyes turned to face him. Tarsis was tossed against the translucency, and before Talon could get a shot off he was tackled onto his back and the gun ripped from his fingers. A mouthless face stared down at him, void of all manner of emotion. There was no hate or regret; no resolve or hint of purpose. As Talon's trachea was being crushed beneath its powerful grip all he saw was death—a being of dark metal with nightmare eyes as hot and as bright as magma.

Just as Talon was about to lose consciousness there was a loud blast. Both he and his mysterious assailant were hurled across the corridor toward the translucency, which was shattered.. The metal being was able to catch itself against the opening as Talon was yanked into space by the rapid change in pressure. Just before he tumbled into the void, Tarsis snatched him and pressed a button on the collar of his armor, causing a helmet to form around his head.

The visor snapped down and Talon gasped for air. His lungs

were in unimaginable pain from that half-second exposed to the vacuum of space. His vision blurred. When he finally was able to regain his composure he looked down. Tarsis was holding onto the ship with one hand and clutching Talon's forearm with the other. There was almost no gravity, but it felt like a gust of wind was gushing through the opening in the ship. The metal exoskeleton Tarsis wore began to split along the joints as his limbs were pulled as wide as possible.

Talon knew that the amount of oxygen in their suits was enough to only last for a few minutes. They didn't have long. He did his best to throw his body in the other direction and reached out with all of his might. After a few futile lunges he was able to grab hold of Tarsis and pull himself closer.

There they embraced at the edge of silent oblivion. The stars sat idly watching, unmoving as the Solar-Ark itself hovered in place. They could see the ravaged Solar Sail scraping along the bow, glinting as its fractured remnants clung on. The ship itself was dark, a mile long bar of metal powered down and lifeless as if it were no more than a hunk of asteroid drifting through space.

Talon turned to Tarsis. The man appeared in pain, but he shouted something inaudible through the visor of his helmet before looking toward the shattered translucency. Talon didn't need to hear him to understand. The rush of pressure was almost gone and together they clambered along the plated exterior of the ship. Helping each other all the way down, they twisted through the opening and into the ship where their feet began to hold weight again. Once they were inside, Tarsis fell against the opposite wall.

They were both in shock, with Tarsis breathing so hard that his visor began to fog over. The arms of his metal exoskeleton were sparking, the wires and circuits keeping it in tact, exposed, and ready to snap. He attempted to stand but the suit hissed and he collapsed.

Talon looked down at the man who had saved him. There was such sorrow in his pale blue eyes that all of the pain shooting through Talon's body was suddenly wiped away. He couldn't leave him. They had to get deeper into the ship where they would be able to breathe again.

Without hesitating any further, Talon reached around Tarsis' back and helped him to his feet. Using each other's weight to counterbalance, they began moving down the corridor back toward the Cryo-Chamber hall, hoping that the unnatural attackers had already moved on.

Once they were far enough from the breach, Talon pressed the button to make his helmet recede and helped Tarsis to do the same. They stopped there for a moment to take a few deep gulps of air. It was quiet. There were no screams or gunfire, only the loud crackling of Tarsis' exoskeletal-suit as it struggled to keep him upright.

"What was that thing?" Talon voiced what they were both thinking.

Tarsis moaned in evident pain. "I don't know," he replied. "We must get to the command deck. The Solar-Ark cannot fall." He began to try and make a move in the opposite direction before Talon pinned him against the wall.

"It has fallen!" he whispered fervently. "We have to get off of here before those things come back."

"'We will serve on this ship, and we will die here,'" Tarsis recited solemnly. "I am a Keeper of the Circuit. I will not watch these abominations defile it!"

"Then don't waste your life here like the others! We're doomed in here, but if we escape we can find help!"

"I will not abandon my post!" Tarsis declared, his face flush with swelling anger.

"Then help me get out!" Talon didn't mean to raise his voice, but he couldn't help it. He didn't care if he was being selfish, not when Elisha was involved. He let go of Tarsis' shoulders and took a heavy step back. "I don't know the layout of the Ark, but there must be escape pods on a ship this big."

"To help a Keeper escape is betrayal in itself." A conflicted Tarsis looked down the long, dark passage with a frown.

"To betray what? You didn't choose this." Talon leaned in, his eyes fiery and desperate.

"Fuck fate. Fuck service to this place. Fuck this disease! You saved my life, now let me save yours. You can go home, Tarsis. To wherever that was before you were damned to serve here. You can die free."

"Home…" Tarsis laughed weakly and began to cough. "I have forgotten the worlds beyond these walls."

"Then let's see them together! See what you're willing to guard with your life. We can find out what happened here so it never happens again!" Talon's brow furrowed as he struggled to think of more ways to try and persuade him. Then the sound of footsteps echoed from down the hall, followed by a faint, reddish glow.

"It's coming!" Tarsis stepped forward into Talon's arms so he could help him walk again and they urgently began moving through the corridor. "There's no time to argue. I'll take you on a quicker route to the escape pods, but let's hope we reach them first!"

Talon didn't bother to waste time or breath on a response as Tarsis led them through the shadowy corridors. They passed over countless fallen bodies, through smoke and drizzling sparks, the sound of the footsteps growing nearer and nearer. Random shouts and gun shots would echo out occasionally, but they didn't break pace until they reached a small hatch nestled against a wall. It couldn't fit more than one at a time.

"This leads straight down into the emergency bay," Tarsis said.

Talon nodded and made Tarsis go first, knowing that it would take him longer with his damaged suit. Just before he was ready to follow, a brooding, red aura entered around the corner. He held his breath, climbing into the hatch as quietly as possible. It didn't matter. Whatever the thing was it noticed him instantly, even through the stifling darkness. Two red orbs snapped toward him and bullets began peppering the wall behind his head. He pulled the hatch shut and slid down the ladder, knocking Tarsis over as they tumbled through the bottom.

"One of them is coming!" Talon shouted as he picked Tarsis up and began to rush forward. "Where do we go?"

"In there!" Tarsis pointed to one of the rounded openings lining the hall and pushed Talon in. He then began keying commands on the HOLO-Screen located just outside.

"Get in!" Talon shouted as he strapped himself into one of the four seats.

"Just a few more seconds!" Tarsis finished at the console, but as he began to move he froze in the entrance of the pod. He bit his lip nervously.

"Tarsis, don't give your life away!" Talon struggled to pull off the restraints, cursing at himself for strapping in so prematurely.

He could see it in Tarsis' face…a man torn in two. That was when Talon saw what would have become of him. It was not only fear of betrayal that stopped Tarsis, but fear of leaving the one place that he had called home for the final years of his cursed life. It was the one place that made the suffering tolerable, where he could share the pain of the Blue Death with the similarly afflicted.

"We'll find out who did this!" Talon urged him. The restraints were prepared for the pod's launch and there was no way to get them off. There was a loud crash at the base of the ladder and the whole room filled with terrifying red light. "Get on!"

A bullet nicked the metal back of Tarsis' leg seconds before he grit his teeth and made his decision. He leapt into the pod and the entrance slammed shut just behind him. A powerful blow dented the metal door, but before a second one could land the ship was shot out into space.

Talon grabbed onto Tarsis and held on as tightly as he could. Through the rear viewport he could see a pair of unsettling red eyes receding into the distance as the pod accelerated, until they were too far to make out. Only then did he feel safe enough to gather his breath and help Tarsis into one of the other seats.

"I didn't think you were going to come," Talon exhaled and leaned back, relieved.

Tarsis was staring at the dark mass of the Solar-Ark, which eclipsed a cluster of stars even though they were already miles away. "Neither did I," he said softly.

"Thank you," Talon whispered. Images of Elisha flashed through his mind. He wasn't sure what had just happened aboard the *Amerigo,* but all that mattered to him in that moment was that he had a chance to see her again. No matter what the cost. "Thank you."

Chapter Forty-Three
Gravitum

Cassius Vale sat in the command deck of the *White Hand* and looked out through the translucency. His ship hovered above the Solar-Ark known as *Amerigo*. A gash in its plated, metal exterior ran like brightly lit scars along the lower side of it, as if some giant creature had dragged its claws along the hull. The rest of the ship, by contrast, appeared only as a deeper blackness within the blackness of space.

The androids had already been dispatched and so all he could do was wait. Too anxious to stay still he got up and headed into corridors of his ship. He strolled through them leisurely until he reached the medical bay. Sage was lying on a table in the center of the white room. HOLO-screens along the wall were monitoring her as she remained unconscious, her chest slowly expanding and retracting as air flowed into her.

"Captain. The Executor has experienced no setbacks in her recovery," Gaia announced through the ship's speakers.

The white blanket was draped over her to conceal most of her body, but he could see where her artificial arm latched onto her shoulder. He was careful not to move the blanket and reveal anything as he ran his fingers over the dark-metal of the limb he created. It wasn't the first time he had seen her in that position, her fragile life preserved within the confines of his ship. It was where he brought her after the fateful day when his son turned up dead.

Cassius looked down and ran his hand through Sage's somewhat trimmed, strangely red hair. She looked so peaceful lying there, as if none of the Executor training had tainted her mind and turned her into a ruthless weapon. She was the only connection to Caleb he had left beyond the message within a small metal sphere. He reached into his pocket, just to make sure it was still there, but as he did he was interrupted by the voices in his one unsuspecting ear.

Creator, the group of androids aboard the Solar Ark addressed him. *These units have eliminated all resistance. As directed, the captain is with the other survivors in the command deck awaiting you.*

"I will be there shortly," Cassius responded a little too loudly, as if he was stirred from a dream. "Gaia."

"Yes, Captain?"

"Break open one of the viewports so that we can dock. No reason to waste this suit after I took the time to put it on." He walked over to a counter, picked up the oblong helmet and placed it over his head. Then he headed down the adjacent corridor, having to use the walls for support as the *White Hand* banked hard to the right.

When he reached the Cargo Bay, a sudden jolt almost knocked him off of his feet. It was followed by the muted sound of two explosions in quick succession.

"The Ark has been sufficiently breached, captain. Shall I deploy the bridge?" Gaia asked.

"Go ahead."

"Please step back from the Cargo bay."

Cassius obliged, and once he was out of the space the entrance slammed shut to seal him out. He could hear a loud, whining sound on the other side as the pressure changed.

"Process complete." Gaia announced, the door re-opening simultaneously. The area of the cargo bay exit ramp had extended a latticed structure out through the void that bridged the gap between the *White Hand* and the Solar Ark. After a few steps, his feet were lifted off the ground by zero gravity, forcing him to slowly pull himself across the link until the artificial gravity floors of the Solar Ark pulled him back down.

One of the androids was there to greet him, almost invisible inside the dark hall but for his glowing red eyes. "Creator." It stated. "Two humans were able to reach an escape pod. Shall this unit pursue them?"

"No. You have your orders. They are no threat to us now." Cassius responded.

"This unit will lead you to the command deck."

Cassius nodded. He followed android down the shadowy, silent corridors of the Solar Ark *Amerigo*. Blood began to lap at the soles of his boots, leaking out of the countless dead bodies in his path. He paused for a moment to look at them, and the ghastly, lifeless eyes gazed back at him from almost every direction. He welcomed their frozen judgment. Each body was a member of the foundation for the future he could begin to taste on the tip of his tongue. He stepped over the bodies, wearing the look of a man who was neither proud nor regretful the entire time.

"This way, Creator."

The android led him up an airy staircase with a mound twisted limbs piled up along the base. At the top there was a massive door, the center of which had visibly been pried open. Cassius ducked through the low opening of bent metal and into the *Amerigo's* command deck.

It was a tall space ripe with HOLO-screens, exposed metal structures, and technology both old and new that served to keep the ship running. Out of a semi-circular translucency at the far end, the glistening, golden solar sail was visible. It was lightly damaged, but remained impressive…a technology honed by the ancients, and one he was eager to study firsthand when he got the chance.

"Who are you?" A defiant voice addressed him.

Cassius had hardly even noticed any other presence as he continued marveling at the sail. He looked down to see the captain of the Ark bound and kneeling in the center of at least two dozen similarly captive Keepers. Webs of unnaturally blue veins spread across their temples, a mark of the Blue Death ready to claim its prey.

Poor bastards, Cassius thought as he let his eyes wander down the paths of their infected veins. *It would almost be a service to end their suffering.*

The well-dressed captain had no such symptoms. He was pale from spending a lifetime aboard the ship, but that was all. Standing in front of them with weapons drawn, silent and still as specters, and with spine-chilling red eyes, were the other four of Cassius' newest creations. The imposing sight of them had all of the Keepers, captain included, trying to hide the fact that they were trembling in fear.

"I could ask the same of you?" Cassius replied courteously. "The people of the Circuit rarely get a chance to thank those who keep it running." He positioned himself in front of them and bowed his head. "I thank you all."

"This is how you thank us?" The captain gestured to the many dead bodies strewn throughout the room. "Do you command these monsters?" He groused while he attempted to get back on his knees without the use of his hands.

"I do indeed... Stunning aren't they?"

"Wait a minute," One of the older Keepers spoke up. He was bearded, grimy looking and undoubtedly Ceresian. "I recognize you. You're Cassius Vale aren't you?"

"I am." Cassius bowed his head.

"I knew it." The man's face flushed with anger. "I was one of the few survivors at Vesta after you slaughtered our entire colony!" He shuffled forward angrily on his knees, but was swiftly kicked onto his back by one of the androids. "Seems you haven't changed a bit." He spat in Cassius' direction.

The captain placed a consoling hand on the rowdy Keeper's shoulder to calm him, and then gazed back up at Cassius with daggers in his eyes. "Since these ships were built by the ancients more than five hundred years ago nobody has been so bold as to claim one for himself. You're a fool, Cassius Vale, to think you'll get away with this!"

"The Tribune buys your loyalty with labor and promises of peace. Do not look me in the eyes and claim neutrality." Cassius countered calmly. Much of his energy had been expended in his confrontation with Nora so he had no desire to argue any more. "It is no matter. This ship belongs to me now."

The captain sneered. "Yet only we know how to run it."

Cassius turned around patted the chest of one of the androids. "That is why you will help teach my creations how."

"Teach them?" The captain looked at Cassius as though he had just heard a joke he didn't quite understand. "You think we'd help a man who thinks he can own the Circuit? 'We will serve here, and we will die here.'"

"I suspected as much, but I grow tired of words. I only need one of you." He made eye contact with an android. "Disable any tracking systems that may be built into the Ark, then do whatever is necessary to get one of the Keepers to talk. If the extent of their valor lives up to reputation then tear apart these old computers apart until you find what you need to get this ship moving."

"Yes, Creator." The androids responded in unison before they slowly began to approach the Keepers.

"I'll be looking over the cargo." Cassius said as he headed out of the command deck.

"Ancient's damn you, Vale!" The captain shouted after him.

Cassius didn't bother to look back. He never expected praise for doing what he knew had to be done, not until the end. War had made him the veteran of countless battles, but he knew there would be none harder than opening the eyes of an entire people. Voices cursed his name from behind as he made his way down the stairs. By the time he reached the bottom the shouting was drowned out by hair-raising screams.

He did his best to ignore them as he tried to decide which way the storage lift was. It was his first time aboard the main body of a Solar-Ark so he only had the vaguest clue. He decided to follow the path littered with the most bodies, and as expected it led him to the comforting silence of Cryo-Chamber hall. The glass vessels lining the walls were all dim and empty, most of them still sparking from the firefight that had clearly taken place there. Bullet holes littered the metal floor, filled to the brim by freshly drawn blood. The harsh smell of death lingered on the stale air, but he was far too used to it to notice.

Cassius traversed the stifling darkness until he found a wide lift set into the floor at the far end. He stepped onto it and pressed a button built into the rail. It began to sink down through the floor, plunging into a vast, open space below.

Colossal mechanical arms and claws extended from the walls and ceiling, each of them holding massive storage containers and crates, some big enough to hold the *White Hand*. All of the room's machinery was still, but one group of containers stood out through the dim light. They were all around him, piled high, dwarfing him as he spread his arms out wide. The glow of a blue element shone through the ventilation rifts cut into their side—Gravitum. More than he had ever seen in a single place. Enough to get started on half a dozen more bombs.

END BOOK ONE

About the Author

Rhett Bruno grew up in Hauppauge, New York, and studied at the Syracuse University School of Architecture where he graduated cum laude

He has been writing since he can remember, scribbling down what he thought were epic short stories when he was young to show to his parents. When he reached high school he decided to take that a step further and write the "Isinda Trilogy". After the encouragement of his favorite English teacher he decided to self-publish the "Isinda Trilogy" so that the people closest to him could enjoy his early work

While studying architecture Rhett continued to write as much as he could, but finding the time during the brutal curriculum proved difficult. It wasn't until he was a senior that he decided to finally pursue his passion for Science Fiction. After rededicating himself to reading works of the Science Fiction author's he always loved, (Frank Herbert, Timothy Zahn, Heinlein, etc.) he began writing "The Circuit: Executor Rising", The first part of what he hopes will be a successful Adult Science Fiction Series.

Since then Rhett has been hired by an Architecture firm in Mount Kisco, NY. But that hasn't stopped him from continuing to work on "The Circuit" and all of the other stories bouncing around in his head. He is also currently studying at the New School to earn a Certificate in Screenwriting in the hopes of one day writing for TV or Video Games.

CPSIA information can be obtained at www.ICGtesting.com
Printed in the USA
LVOW13s0029270614

391888LV00001B/53/P